A Novel by
Richard Rudomanski

Dedication

To my wife, Patricia, and the real muse, our Labrador, Scout, your belief, your support, and your love is in every page of The Note!

CHAPTER 1

Something was gnawing at Robert, but he didn't know what it was. The feeling had started as he stood at the bar with Hank Steffnek, discussing the abundance of blue crabs that summer, and continued to hang over him throughout the evening. When they left the party, the uneasiness felt more pronounced. It had followed him into the house, churned in his gut as he climbed into bed, and haunted him as he tried to sleep. Now, with the full moon cascading through the bedroom window, Robert wrestled with his pillow, shaded his eyes with the back of his hand, and finally flipped to his other side. He squinted at the clock—one fifteen. He took a silent breath and tried to clear his head.

He laid there a minute more and then eased his body from the bed, snuck into the bathroom, and closed the door. Outside, a barn owl's call echoed across the marsh.

Robert listened as he stood at the bathroom sink. When the owl stopped, he turned his attention to the mirror and studied the image in the glass. His disheveled gray hair, age-lined face, and clouded blue eyes reflected back an image of a tired seventy-two-year-old man. As the owl started up again, Robert turned to the bathroom door and froze. He thought of his wife in the bedroom, in their wicker-framed bed, asleep.

The evening had gone exactly as he had planned. The surprise seventieth birthday party for his wife at Jessup's Inn had all the makings of a memorable night. Their island friends had all turned out. When they sang happy birthday to Nora, her eyes had glossed over, and he watched as she tried to hold back her tears. He knew the evening had been a huge success. But whatever had been hounding him the entire evening had separated him from the crowd. He had felt physically detached and emotionally void. And it irritated him that he had been preoccupied with some intangible sensation at the cost of enjoying his wife's birthday celebration. He shook his head as he turned from the door and gazed back into the mirror.

What's gotten into you, Robert?

He splashed some water on his face and again tried to clear his head. After he dried himself with a towel, Robert returned to the moonlit bedroom. He stopped at the bedroom door, which opened into the hall. He listened, but he heard nothing downstairs. After a moment, he tiptoed back to bed. He started a conversation in his head about closing up the house next week. And as his mind drifted, Robert Williams fell silent and still.

As Robert was deciding what day he'd pull the crab traps out of Woodmans Cove, he felt Nora move in the bed. He half-opened his eyes and looked at his wife. As he watched, she picked up a book and rolled onto her side. He was careful not to move. It was unusual for him to be awake and to witness her insomnia. He knew the routine, but seeing it made it real, adding yet another layer to his angst. He exhaled silently and closed his eyes.

He had been aware for years that Nora went to her daughter's bedroom so as to not disturb him while he slept. So one Christmas, Robert gave her an Ultra Optix EZ reader book light, which changed her life. Nora had read two books a month for the last thirty-three years—all of them consumed in the dead of night. Robert had learned decades ago a full night's sleep for Nora consisted of three to four hours. He had never seen her so excited as when he handed her the box and she discovered the light inside. Then, as he delighted in his purchase and his wife's response, he listened as she described to him how important her novels were and what they meant. "Without the abundance of written works," she told her husband, "I would be a lost soul drifting through the darkness of the night."

Robert had taken the practical side of her sleeping disorder and explained it away with a mathematical equation. "Your books," he said last year when he did the math, "add up to seven hundred ninety-two novels in all. Thank goodness Benjamin Franklin created the library because after running the numbers, those books add up to almost twenty thousand dollars." Then with his dry sense of New England humor, he added, "Without that institution, Nora, I would have had to find a second job."

Robert had an accountant's mentality. He had owned a clothing store in Kruger Falls, New York for thirty-eight years. His job had been to order the inventory, balance the books, calculate the quarterlies, and figure the payroll. He controlled the entire operation of the shop, and he only believed in that which he could see, smell or touch— Empirical Knowledge 101. He had a working man's ethics and solved problems with an analytical mind. But tonight when that strange feeling had surfaced at Jessup's Inn, it defied explanation. Whatever it was, intuition, premonition, or sixth sense, it didn't belong in Robert's world. Yet, its existence persisted throughout the night.

Now, his circuits were on sensory overload and he was ready to crawl out of his skin. His eyes popped wide open, and he looked to his wife.

"What was that?" he asked.

"What, Robert?"

"I thought I heard something."

"I didn't hear anything. You must have been dreaming."

Robert listened as a gust of air wisped under the open window sash and shook the wooden frame against the jamb. He slid out of bed and stumbled to the bedroom window.

"Robert?"

He scanned the landscape to the north. The dunes appeared deserted except for a swamp rat that dashed across the sand toward the salt marsh. Robert backed up to the bed, sat on the edge, and rubbed his forehead with his hands.

"Robert?"

He flipped his head upright and turned it to the side. He listened as he gazed at the clock—two forty-five. The copper weather vane on the cupola above his head squeaked. He glanced toward the ceiling and then to the bedroom door. He stared at the opening for a moment. Then he stood up, slipped into his wool bathrobe, and slid into his slippers.

"Robert, what in the name of God are you doing?"

"Nora, stay quiet."

"Robert?"

"What?"

"What is it?"

"Shhhh…stay put, keep quiet."

The top stair creaked as his weight bore down, and his hand crept down the wooden hand rail. He felt his heart thump in his chest, and he drew a breath to steady himself. When the stairway came to a ledge, he stopped, peered around the corner, and combed the moonlit living room—nothing. He advanced to the last step and examined the front porch from the stairwell window. His eyes swept to each end of the porch—again nothing. He flicked the switch to his left, and the lantern hanging from the porch ceiling illuminated the first floor landing. Then he moved down the step and on to the front door.

What the hell?

He swung the door open, hustled to the porch rail, and scanned the sandy access road beyond his parked car. He searched the dunes and the sides of the house as a cool breeze flicked his thin, grey hair. He leaned his backend against the wooden rail and rubbed his eyes with his hands. Then his gaze scoured the ten-foot span of the porch, reached the front door, and locked onto the envelope taped to the glass. On the front, in thick dark letters, was the name Robert Williams.

Jesus Christ!

He staggered to the door, pulled the envelope loose, folded it in half, and shoved it into his bathrobe pocket.

"Robert?"

He looked up the stairs at his wife.

"Robert, is everything all right?"

"Yes, Nora."

"For goodness sakes, you scared me near to death. What did you put in your pocket?"

"It was the receipt from Jessup's Inn. I must have dropped it when we got home."

CHAPTER 2

After the breakfast dishes were done, Nora went to town. Robert sat at the kitchen table with the envelope in his right hand angled toward his face. As his mind's eye drifted into the past, he gazed out to Woodmans Cove. He tried to keep the memory down, but the thoughts of Central Park were rising to the surface, and his throat began to close. He flipped the envelope over and slipped his gold commemorative letter opener into the corner of the flap. After the paper was cut, he slid the letter out. His head fell back. He closed his eyes and tried to calm the chaos churning in his gut.

After a few seconds, he unfolded the sheet, and the black words pounded onto the linen paper took only three lines to spread their terror. He read them in silence with his right hand attached to his wrinkled forehead and his left hand attached to the note.

"Mr. Williams," it started, "1960...do I have your attention? Let's get you more focused, shall we? New York City, Central Park West, August 9, 1960—enough said. Instructions will follow, Mr. Williams, how are you feeling....now?"

His fist banged the table top so hard the vase holding the wild red roses tumbled over and broke. He jumped up and grabbed the dish rag hanging under the sink. After he finished cleaning up, he sat in the chair with both elbows resting on the table and propped his head up with his hands. What would this do to his wife and his family, he thought, if the truth became public back in Kruger Falls? His mind drifted back to seven years earlier.

After operating a successful business for thirty-eight years, Robert had just sold his clothing store. The community had honored him at a retirement dinner at the luxurious Holden Mill Inn. It was attended by some of the most prominent families in Kruger Falls. Mayor Tomlin, as he addressed the crowd, described Robert Williams as a kind and caring man whose generosity was hidden behind a long-kept secret. One, he said, that needed to be told.

Then Tomlin looked to Robert as he spoke. "You all know the Robert Williams who has given back to the community by his continued support of our little league baseball program, his commitment to the commerce of Kruger Falls, and his years on the rectory of St. Luke's Episcopal Church. What you don't know is the Robert Williams that silently brought hope and the spirit of humanity to those less fortunate than he. For the last twenty-two years on the evening of December 24th, Robert opened his store to one poverty-stricken family of Staggler County. He then proceeded to outfit the entire family with a new set of clothes. That's the man I am proud to say we honor here tonight. Robert Williams understands the true meaning of Christmas. And, he understands that the true spirit of giving lies not in the recognition of his deeds but rather abounds in the unspoken silence of the night."

That evening encapsulated everything Robert had worked for and tried to represent. It was the essence of his being for forty-seven years, and he was proud of his impeccable reputation. It made him sick to think one incident decades ago could erase his life's work and threaten what he had worked so hard to accomplish.

His attention drifted back to the kitchen table. Robert's head slipped from his hands, and he looked down at the note. Both ends of the folded paper stood upright forming a channel as it lay across the envelope. Horrific memories flashed through his brain. His face felt hot and flush, and he took several breaths, afraid he was having a heart attack or a stroke. He grabbed the envelope and the paper off the table top and crumbled them in his hand as if in defiance of the recollection it summoned and whatever its message meant.

He stood up and marched to the stone fireplace in the living room. With the cleaning shovel, he made a nest in the spent ashes and knelt with the crumbled note in his left hand. He placed the ball of paper in the carved out ashes, along with the envelope, and lit the corner with a match. It started slowly, but as the paper took the flames, it exploded into a ball of fire and turned orange and blue. Soon, it imploded and fell to ashes. He poked it, making sure the entire pile had incinerated and broke it apart into tiny pieces. Then he mixed the new ashes with the old and placed two shovels of spent ashes on top.

Still dazed, he strolled to the dock with his baskets and crabbing equipment. The wooden structure extended ten feet into the brine of the cove. Tied to the wooden handrail were twelve sets of rope. At the end of the rope, underneath the water, were twelve metal crab traps. He stopped at the right side rail, at the first tied off trap, and pulled on the line. The first trap broke the surface of the cove, and he elevated the metal cage up to the hand rail and lifted it over and onto the deck. Then he opened the trap door, and as he did, Robert's mind raced back to 1960.

At twenty-three, Robert had been working in the garment district for almost two years hoping to fulfill his dream of designing his own line of clothing. He had met a woman named Tristan McCobb through a mutual friend. It was a fate that would soon find him fleeing the streets of Manhattan for the isolation of Kruger Falls.

On their fourth date, Robert sat across from McCobb in a charming little restaurant on 82nd Street near The Met. He watched her as she sipped her wine in little tea-toddling spurts with her brilliant blue eyes combing the room. He examined her as she looked away, her soft blonde hair, the incredible features of her Bardot-like face, and he thought back to the previous night. They had made love at his little SoHo apartment and afterward he found himself riddled with insecurity. He had never been with a woman so beautiful. He knew with her stunning looks she could have anything or anyone she wanted. He had nothing to offer a woman like this. And as he smiled at

McCobb from across the table, he wondered how long he'd last.

His head turned at the sound of a voice.

"Tristan?" the man asked.

Robert studied McCobb as the two interacted. He felt uncomfortable. He detected a connection between them, perhaps something from the past. When she invited him to sit down, he squirmed in his chair. He stared at his wine glass as the two conversed. With each chorus of laughter, Robert felt a fire rage up inside. He twitched his glass and sipped the liquid as she touched the man on the arm. And in his aloneness, he began to talk inside his head. Until finally, he exploded. "I think you should leave," he said to the man.

"Robert?" Tristan asked, looking confused.

"You heard me!"

Robert studied the man as he got up, kissed McCobb, and shook his head as he walked away. The even-tempered Williams had experienced his first bout of jealousy and paranoid mistrust, but he believed Tristan McCobb was worth it.

The memory of McCobb hadn't been on the forefront of his mind for decades, but her image had now taken center stage. He gazed out over the marsh and then opened the parlor to the crab trap. A large crab clawed the metal as he pulled it from the trap. On a normal day, he knew "a keeper" by sight, but not now, not after the arrival of the note. Robert shook his head and used the culling stick to measure the crab's length—six inches; the legal limit was five. He placed it in the bushel basket and lowered the trap into the water without re-baiting; the bull lip was still good.

As the second trap rose from the water, his worry had turned to panic. Time was ticking, and the next event could get Nora involved. The third trap broke the surface, and he heard a voice. On one knee, he turned and spotted his wife at the end of the pier waving her arms and yelling.

"Robert, phone!"

With the trap hanging just below the deck, spilling water out its bottom, Robert stood. He held the line over the rail and looked to the end of the dock. "I'll call back, take a message."

He watched as Nora took a few more steps toward him and yelled again.

"He says it's important. He needs to talk to you, now, Robert."

"Hold on."

Robert pulled one crab from the trap and tied off the line. He traversed the ten feet of dock, grabbed the phone, and hustled back to the traps. He watched his wife as she headed back to the house. "Hello," Robert said.

A deep, low disguised voice responded. "I trust you received my note?"

He crept further out toward the end of the dock and looked back to check on Nora. "Who is this?" he whispered, as if the marsh had ears.

"Good, I have your attention."

"What is it you want?"

"You'll find out soon enough."

"Who is this, damn it? What do you want?"

Silence.

"Damn it, I asked you a question. What do you want?"

The caller had hung up. Robert's throat closed as he tried to swallow, and he felt a sickening sensation in his stomach again. He strolled back to the end of the pier and pulled the fourth and fifth traps up, collecting three more crabs. He dropped the last trap into the cove, pulled the phone from his back pants pocket, and looked at the caller ID. It said unknown. Robert placed the phone on the handrail. As he turned, the basket hit the phone. It slid off the rail and splashed into the water. He exhaled as his chin fell against his chest.

The screen door banged behind him. The crabs scratched at the wooden basket. He placed the basket next to the wash sink, on the wooden cutting board, and opened the old refrigerator door. The small back room off the kitchen had been his personal haven for years, but its familiar comfort was gone. His hand shook as he reached into the basket to grab a crab and place it into the bottom drawer. As he put the last of the blue crabs into the refrigerator, he froze at the sound of Nora's voice. He listened. She was talking on the phone in the kitchen. Out of instinct, he reached for the handset in his back pocket then remembered it was at the bottom of Woodmans Cove.

Christ! Who's she talking to?

His wife went silent. He maneuvered his body just inside the door jamb and turned his head. "Ah huh," she said and then nothing. A long pause and his mouth went dry. He felt like a fool, a seventy-two-year-old man married for forty-four years eavesdropping on his wife.

Say something!

Then he heard her voice.

"I'll tell him," she said and then silence fell.

He rinsed his hands and collected himself the best he could. Then he walked into the kitchen like the floor was lined with land mines. He spotted Nora at the breakfast table staring out to the marsh. She hadn't noticed Robert walk in.

"What is it, dear?" Robert asked. He waited, but she didn't answer. He tried again. "Nora, is everything all right?"

She looked up at her husband. "Not really, Robert."

He tried to sound calm. "What's wrong?"

Nora took a deep breath, and as she exhaled, she let out a long and painful sigh.

"What is it?"

"That was Deborah," she said.

Robert exhaled.

"She's upset about her brother. She wanted John to come for Thanksgiving as a surprise, but he doesn't return her calls."

"Nora, he hasn't returned one of our phone calls for the last ten years."

"Well, our daughter's upset, Robert, and she asked if you would try to call him."

"What's the point?"

"John's very busy. Please just call for your daughter?"

"All right, Nora, I'll try calling John."

She looked back up to Robert.

"Who called, Robert? What was so important?"

"An old school mate."

"What did he want?"

"Our fifty-year anniversary is next year. He's trying to get his old classmates to attend."

Robert turned away. He hadn't lied to his wife in forty-four years and that was the second time in one day.

"I'm going to clean the crabs," he said.

"Robert."

"What?"

"What happened to the rose vase?"

"I hit it, and it broke."

Robert strolled to the back room, off the kitchen, and spent the afternoon steaming and cleaning the crabs. When he finished, he announced he was going up stairs to take a shower. He started up the stairs with his hand on the rail, and he climbed in a slow and shaky motion. He recalled the year he had moved to Kruger Falls, in '62, fleeing the city of Manhattan in an attempt to erase his past. Nora had lived her entire life in the small town of Kruger Falls. At twenty-six, she was working as a secretary for the building department in the seventy-five-year-old neo-classical town hall. Robert had stopped by code enforcement to check on a building he wanted to purchase for his clothing store. He had met Nora as she tended the front desk.

Robert found her simplistic lifestyle as intriguing as Nora found his big city past. Within nine months, not only were they married, but Robert had opened his shop. The town took to Robert as he and Nora settled in, and his clothing store made for a comfortable life. The memory of Manhattan and the incident in Central Park drifted far away from that quaint little town. So far, Robert had almost forgotten it existed at all.

But now, forty-six years of denial had just landed in his lap and had hit him like a falling brick. The reality that he had never confided his secret to his wife made the numbing blow exponentially worse. It was an omission, he thought as his left foot descended onto the second-floor landing, that after forty-four years of marriage felt tantamount to betrayal. He staggered through the master bedroom and into the bath trapped in his own deceit.

After a hot shower and a change of clothes, Robert examined his options. *What are the chances Nora will find out? Think Robert, someone must have stumbled upon an archived newspaper article. They've taken the trouble to find you. Wait to see what they want, use your head, Robert! What's the difference if you tell Nora now or two days from now? It's been forty-six years. A few more days won't matter.*

He placed the brush on the shelf in the medicine cabinet, slipped his hands into the pockets of his cardigan sweater, and went down the stairs.

Robert lit a fire in the fieldstone fireplace and then poured Nora a glass of wine. He liked beer before dinner—only two a night—one before and one with, but Robert gulped the first like he had a blazing fire burning in the back of his throat. It relieved the tension.

He turned on the light next to his sitting chair that faced the fire and the one next to the couch which faced the hearth. He settled in the chair with his copy of Einstein's *The World as I See It*. A short time later, Nora came in and sat on the couch. He felt her stare for a moment and then she spoke. "Robert," she said.

Robert looked up from his book. "Yes?"

"I saw Sara Jessup in town today. She said Sheriff Taylor passed away last night. He went to bed and never woke up."

"I'm sorry to hear that."

"He was seventy-four. He was a good man, Robert, wasn't he?"

"Yes, he was. Ben was a good man."

"He kept his word, Robert, didn't he?"

"He did," he said and took another swallow of his Pabst Blue Ribbon beer.

"Indeed, he did," Nora said.

"I'm having an extra beer tonight. Would you mind fetching one from the kitchen while I throw another log on the fire?"

"No, dear."

"And will you bring in the can of nuts?"

"Yes, dear."

"Sheriff Taylor understood the meaning of justice, Nora, and we can be very thankful for that!"

CHAPTER 3

Robert spent three days closing up the outside of the house. After all the outside décor had been placed in the shed, he stacked the crab traps in a square pattern on the shelves and wondered why he hadn't heard a word from the author of the note. It had been four days since the phone call, and it unnerved him knowing someone was out there playing games with his head. And it was becoming more difficult with each passing day to keep his secret from Nora. As he put the last trap on top of the others, he tried to assess if his anxiousness had been obvious to his wife. He turned and looked toward the house as he closed the shed door and clicked the master lock shut. *She doesn't have a clue, Robert, relax.*

With the inside of their summer home prepared for winter, Robert closed the wooden shutters on the front porch windows. He heard the car door close behind him, and he looked at the packed Volvo station wagon in the sand parking spur. He spotted Nora inside. The passenger side window slid down, and Nora stuck her head out.

"Let's go. We'll miss the boat."

Robert nodded his head. "All right, Nora, we have plenty of time. Relax."

He walked toward the car and scanned the outside of the house. He climbed into the car, put the stick in reverse, and pulled away from their brown clapboard cape. As he drove down the sandy access road, past the huckleberry bush and scattered scrub oak, he looked into the rear-view mirror. He studied the plywood panel over the glass of the front door and thought about the night he had discovered the note. The sensation he had felt that evening, which had started at Jessups Inn, still haunted him. It told him something was up, but where had it come from? How had he known? He rolled his eyes from the mirror to the upcoming street, turned left onto Bennett Farm Road, and headed to the Schaums Head ferry.

The ferry to the mainland took fifty-five minutes, and the drive to their house in Kruger Falls took another three hours. Robert parked in the driveway and then walked through the house. When he finished unpacking the car, he pulled the Volvo into the garage and stopped at the hanging tennis ball. He shut off the engine and pulled the keys from the ignition. As he did, something caught his vision to his left. He turned toward the entrance to the house. *What the....!*

He jumped from the car and yanked the envelope from the wood frame of the door. His heart raced at the sight of his name. His arms felt weak and his hands shook. *How the hell did he get in?* He scanned the garage with his eyes. The window appeared locked and undamaged. Suddenly, Robert felt dizzy and confused, and his vision became blurry.

He folded the envelope in half and shoved it into his right coat pocket. The veins in his neck thumped harder than before. His chest felt tight, his face flush, and the heat and pain in his head seared his brain. He reached for the door handle, but his right arm was numb and his vision blurry. His balance failed. He called for Nora, but the words made no sense. He attempted to call out again. The right side of his body lost function, and he fell hard against the door. He slid against the wood panels and fell onto the garage wall. He tried screaming for Nora again— hhhhhhuu…hhaau. The pain burned like hot knives piercing his scalp. He tumbled back toward the car and hit the concrete with such force, his head bounced off the floor. The impact knocked him out.

The curtains were closed. The bed was surrounded by all sorts of medical devices. The monitor showed his heart was beating—albeit erratically. Nora sat in a chair by the bed crying. Outside the curtain, their daughter, Deborah, and her husband, Ramone, were talking to a doctor. Nurses scurried in and out checking the vital signs and pumping some type of fluids into the lines. It was a flurry of fast-paced emergency procedures to stabilize Robert. When he opened his eyes, he was scared and confused. Nora stood and tried to console him.

"You've had a stroke, Robert," she said, holding his hand.

Robert rolled his eyes to his wife. He tried to move, but his body was disconnected from his brain. A doctor slid through the curtain followed by Deborah and Ramone.

"Hello, Mr. Williams," the doctor said. "My name is Dr. Stockard. You've had a stroke and we're going to take you upstairs and run some tests." The doctor turned his attention to Nora. "I know this is difficult, Mrs. Williams, but please go to the waiting room and as soon as we have the results, I'll go over them with you."

A nurse pulled back the curtain and two men prepared the bed for transport. Nora, Deborah, and Ramone watched as Robert was rolled away. Ramone took Nora's arm and led her to a waiting room down the hall.

In the small room with a couch and four cushioned chairs, Deborah lifted up her pocket book and placed it on her lap. The air was thick with a mixture of tension and despair. Deborah turned to her mother.

"Mom," she said, "I need to call John."

Nora didn't move.

"Mom, did you hear what I said? I need to call John."

"Oh, yes, dear," she said with a blank stare on her face. "Call John."

"Ramone, why don't you and Mom go get a cup of coffee. It's going to be a while before we get any results."

Ramone nodded his head to Nora. She got up, and they walked to the cafeteria together. Deborah separated from Ramone and her mother and continued to the main entrance. She stepped outside.

Her cell phone sat in her pocketbook, right next to a pack of Marlboro lights. She took out the lighter and fired up her sixth one of the day. She drew in a couple of deep draws and looked around for a place to sit. There was a bus stop located in the middle of the parking lot. It had an unoccupied bench under a plastic roof. She walked over and sat down, worked on her smoke, and dialed the phone.

"Williams Investment Bank, how may I direct your call?"

"Hello, this is Deborah Sanchez, John Williams's sister. May I speak with my brother, please?"

"Just a minute, I'll connect you to his secretary."

"Mr. Williams's office."

"Hello, this is Deborah Sanchez, John Williams's sister. May I speak with my brother, please?"

"I'm sorry, Ms. Sanchez, he is in a meeting. I'll have him return your call when he gets out."

"This is an emergency; his father's had a stroke. Please, I need to speak with John."

"I am sorry, Mrs. Sanchez, Mr. Williams is not to be disturbed."

"Jesus Christ, his father could be dying. Put John on the God damn phone!"

"I will take your number, Mrs. Sanchez, and relay the message to Mr. Williams."

She dropped the cigarette on the ground and smashed it with her sneaker. *What an asshole.* Another Marlboro, another flick of the Bic, and she inhaled a long draw.

The last time she spoke with her brother was on their mom's sixtieth birthday—ten years before. John was a no-show: no call, no card, no help with the expenses. He was on his way to Europe, his secretary had said, some big deal he had brewing that couldn't wait. When she finally spoke to John, Deborah was irate. She told him he was an arrogant, selfish son of a bitch. She called him a self-absorbed egomaniac whose only interest in life was chasing the almighty buck...so much for call backs. Deborah earned the number one spot on the no-call list. Her parents soon followed.

She dropped the cigarette on the ground, crushed it with her foot, and re-entered the hospital. When she arrived at the waiting room, Nora and Ramone looked distant and detached. They were both staring into the empty air.

Nora turned to Deborah. "Is John on his way, dear?"

"His secretary refused to put me through," Deborah said.

"I'm sure he'll call when he gets a chance," she said.

"Right, Mom, I haven't talked to John in a decade."

Nora's head dropped toward the floor. She whispered in a despondent tone, "He'll call. I'm sure he'll call back."

"Right."

The room fell back into silence. It seemed like hours, but after forty-five minutes the doctor opened the waiting room door. He came in and took a seat. "The stroke was caused by a cerebral hemorrhage. A CAT scan has verified the bleeding has stopped, but the extent of the trauma to his brain will not be known for several days."

"What happens now?" Deborah asked.

"We wait. We will keep Mr. Williams in a medically induced coma. It's important to let his brain recover without movement or activity. This is a critical time for Mr. Williams. The swelling of the brain must recede before we allow your husband to regain consciousness. I've ordered another scan for tomorrow afternoon. When I get the results, I will contact you. Until then, we will closely monitor him in the ICU."

Nora looked horrified. "How bad is it?" she asked.

"Mrs. Williams, we won't know the extent of the damage until we bring him out of the coma. I can't predict the severity of the damage. We are doing everything we can to give your husband the best chance of a recovery. All we can do is wait."

Nora was not about to leave her husband alone. She sat in the chair next to his bed and dozed in and out all night. Trish, his night nurse, helped make her comfortable with a pillow and blanket. She tried not to disturb Nora when she came in to check on Robert's vital signs and pump medications into his line. Toward morning, Nora awoke to the horror of the ICU, and her sleepy face showed it. Trish recognized the look.

"I'm sorry; I didn't mean to wake you," Trish said.

"What time is it?"

"Three-thirty."

"May I talk to you for a minute?" Nora asked.

The nurse nodded and pulled a chair beside her.

"What are my husband's chances of coming out of this?" she asked.

"When the doctor makes his rounds tomorrow, he'll take you and your family into the conference room and explain Robert's condition and what you can expect over the next few days. His vital signs, at the moment, are stable."

CHAPTER 4

At seven-thirty in the morning, Deborah stepped outside the kitchen door. She walked over to the flagstone patio and sat on the bench under the big red oak. With her elbow resting on her knee and her forehead in the palm of her hand, she massaged her temple and tried to relax.

The phone call she had made to her brother's office the afternoon before had brought on an onslaught of repressed memories. A recall she had worked hard to block out. But last night, in her sleep, the horrific nightmares had returned. Vivid images of the cruelty her brother, John, had perpetrated upon her in their youth. And now, she closed her eyes and rubbed her hand down the length of her face. She pushed hard against her skin and tried to erase the demons that had haunted her during the night.

By the age of thirteen, Deborah had developed into an attractive, yet provocative, young woman. Physically advanced for her age, she enjoyed the looks and attention her body invoked from the teenage boys. Her brother, when home from prep school, made crude remarks about her short skirts and skimpy tops. One day he caught Deborah in the basement with a boy from down the street. Deborah was kissing the boy as they leaned against the wall. Even though it was the normal behavior of two pubescent teens, John lost all control. He called her a sleazy little whore and threw the Jackson boy across the room. Jackson fell over a chair and onto the floor. He stood over the stunned boy with both his fist clenched.

"You touch her again, Jackson, and I'll break your legs," John said and then slowly backed away. He stopped and shook his head at his sister.

"What a little tramp!" he said. "Everyone will know you as the neighborhood whore."

Deborah raised her eyes from the flagstone walk. She had forgotten how malicious her brother had been. And she was relieved, as time went on, that he returned less and less. She took a draw on her smoke, slid out her cell phone, and stared at the touch pad. Then she raised her head up toward the sky, took a long breath, exhaled, dropped her chin to her chest, and punched in the numbers with her thumb.

"Williams Investment bank, how may I direct your call?"

"I'd like John Williams's secretary please."

"Who's calling?"

"This is Deborah Sanchez, John's sister."

"One moment please."

"Mr. Williams's office."

"Yes, this is John's sister calling—again—I'd like to speak to my brother."

"I'm sorry, Ms. Sanchez, he's not in the office this morning. Is there something I can help you with?"

"Yes, stop telling me he's unavailable and put John on the line!"

"I'm sorry, Ms. Sanchez, but Mr. Williams is not in the office."

"Bullshit, he's probably sitting at his desk fifteen feet away. Why don't you get up off your lazy ass and go knock on his door. This is his sister for Christ's sake!"

"Yes, Ms. Sanchez, I know who you are, and if Mr. Williams was available, I'd put him on the line. Is there something I can help you with?"

"Tell my brother to start acting like a human being and call his sister back. His father could die for Christ's sake. Is there anyone human in that office?"

"I'll give him the message, Ms. Sanchez."

She flipped the phone closed. Her eyes stared at the ground. *Jesus Christ!* She reached around the back of the bench and pulled out a hidden bag from under the azalea bush. The cap turned twice and popped off. The bottle rose to her mouth. The clunk of liquid passed the neck as it ran into her mouth from the bottle.

"That's the last time," she muttered. "I'm done with that son of a bitch—forever!" She stomped down the flagstone walkway and slammed the door behind her as she entered the house.

A short time later she arrived at the Kruger Falls Memorial Hospital.

Deborah entered the conference room off the ICU. She took a seat and watched as Dr. Stockard stood at the white board, with a magic marker, diagramming the inside of her father's head. He circled the left side of the brain, made a pointed arrow at the location of the bleeding, and subsequent swelling, then popped the top back on the blue marker and proceeded into stroke and brain function 101.

"Mr. Williams suffered a stroke of the left hemisphere," he said. "A left hemispheric stroke causes paralysis to the right side of the body. This is known as right hemiplegia. This area also controls speech and language. Robert's paralysis, however, is on both sides of his body.

"We believe Mr. Williams experienced dizziness, lost his balance, and had additional trauma to his head that caused him to black out. We don't believe this second incident will affect Mr. Williams's recovery, other than a small welt on the back of his head, but we will continue to monitor the wound.

"What happens next? It is possible Mr. Williams's paralysis could be reversed with the help of physical therapy. His brain function will depend upon the damage from the swelling. A condition we call aphasia may occur. This is a condition which affects speech and language function. The problems range in severity. It can be specific such as his ability to move his speech-related muscles, or a combination of problems affecting writing, speech recognition, and reading. We are keeping him sedated until we are sure the swelling has dissipated. By tomorrow afternoon, he should regain consciences, and we will make further assessments at that time."

As Dr. Stockard left the room, Nora sat speechless in her chair. Still shocked by her husband's stroke and traumatized by the doctor's briefing, she appeared overwhelmed and unable to cope. Deborah recognized this and convinced her mother to go home for the night. In forty-four years of marriage, Nora and Robert had been apart only twice: for John's birth, and then again for Deborah's birth. Nora had never been alone in the house. Given her present state of mind, Deborah agreed to stay the night.

After lunch, Nora decided to take a nap so Deborah visited the garden to have a smoke. As she sat on the bench, her cell phone rang and she pulled it out of her side coat pocket. She looked at the caller ID—Ramone. He was interested in the meeting with Dr. Stockard and wanted to know what he had said. After she explained to Ramone her father's condition, she hung up.

She marched inside the house and poured herself three fingers of Jack Daniels straight up. Her two phone calls to Williams Investment Bank had left her a mess. She returned to the garden bench, sipped the colored liquid, and tried to stop her hands from shaking. She lit up a smoke, and as she exhaled, a voice snapped her head around.

"I thought you quit?" Nora asked.

"I tried to talk to John again!"

Nora had no response; she looked stunned. Her face was stone cold white, and she was staring out to the stone wall that demarcated the neighbor's lot.

"What is it, Mom?"

Still nothing.

"Mom, what is it, is it Dad?"

Still nothing and Deborah swung her legs around and put her feet on the flagstone patio.

"Mom?"

"Yes, dear."

"What is it?"

"I found this in your father's pocket," she said and showed Deborah the envelope with her father's name printed on the front.

"What is it?"

"Read it."

Deborah turned it over and pulled open the ripped flap, slid out a piece of beige linen paper, and as she unfolded it, she studied her mother's face. She read it aloud.

"Mr. Williams, you have been found guilty for your crime of 1960 in Central Park. You will be sentenced on the tenth day of October, 2006. Signed, the honorable Justin Blanchard, August 9, 1960."

"What the hell is this mom?"

"A letter of some kind."

"But what is it?"

"I don't know."

"Who is Justin Blanchard?"

"I don't know."

"What happened in 1960?"

"I met your father in '62. He never mentioned anything about this to me."

Nora shook her head. She was confused and upset. She sat down next to her daughter, put her head in her hands, and sighed.

"Our last week at Crab Point, your father acted kind of strange. Do you think this had something to do with it?"

Deborah picked up her glass and consumed what was left of the Jack. She swallowed and looked at her mother.

"Where did you get this?" she asked.

"I told you, in his coat pocket. Your father has no idea what it says. It was still unopened when I found it."

"And you have no idea what this means?"

"No."

"Is Dad keeping something from you?"

"Oh, no, dear, your father would never do that. He never got the chance to read it."

Deborah studied her mom's face. The life had drained from her mother's eyes. Her small mouth and thin lips were curled downward. She grabbed the note from her mom's hand and read it again, this time to herself.

"What do we do now?" Nora asked.

"We wait."

"For what?"

"Tomorrow, for when Dad regains consciousness, and hope he can talk."

CHAPTER 5

His eyelids opened slowly. For a minute he stared at the ceiling. Without any movement of his head, or his body, he blinked. In his groggy and confused state, he surveyed his small cubical, straining the boundaries that his eyes could reach. After a moment they fell upon Nora, to the right of his bed holding his hand, but he had no awareness of her touch. He made a grunt as Nora stood over him, but his lips did not move with the sound. He connected with Nora's eyes; the communication was simple and brief. Robert Williams was frightened to near panic. He closed his eyes as if to go back to sleep.

Deborah stepped around her mother and stood to her father's left. She wanted to wait, but she couldn't. She pulled the note out of her purse and held it in her hand.

"Dad, we found this in your pocket."

His eyes went ballistic. They shot from Nora to Deborah and then closed. Deborah persisted.

"Dad, who is this from? Who is Justin Blanchard? What happened in 1960?"

"Deborah, that's enough!" Nora said. "Your father needs rest."

She grabbed at the note in her daughter's hand, but Deborah pulled it away.

"Deborah, leave your father alone, for God's sake, he just woke up."

"Dad, should I go to the police?"

Robert closed his eyes. They slowly re-opened rising up to Nora.

"It's ok, Robert," she said, "get some rest."

She nodded her head to Deborah giving her the signal to step outside the curtain. Outside, Nora pulled her close to her side.

"Deborah," she whispered, "leave it alone. He's had enough. Let him rest."

Deborah grabbed her purse and bolted for the first floor exit. Nora slipped inside the curtain and sat beside the bed.

Two days passed without any answers. Robert was stronger and out of ICU. Deborah consulted with her husband, Ramone, and together they set up a simple system to communicate with her dad. One blink meant yes, two blinks meant no. She waited until her mother went to the cafeteria for a cup of coffee. She explained the rules to Robert and began her interrogation of the note.

"Dad, do you know who sent this letter?"

It was followed by two blinks.

"Do you know who Justin Blanchard is?"

One blink.

"Did something happen on August 9, 1960?"

 One blink.

"Is Justin Blanchard alive?"

No blink.

"You don't know, is that it?"

One blink.

"Do you know where he last lived?"

One blink.

She explained the next set of rules. She would go through the alphabet, and when she reached the proper letter of the state, he'd blink once. She arrived on the letter "N."

One blink.

"The state begins with 'N?'"

One blink.

"Nevada?" she asked.

Two blinks.

She ran through the names in her head: Nebraska, New Mexico, New Orleans, New York, New Jersey.

"Is the first word, 'New?'" she asked.

One blink.

"New York?"

One blink.

"New York State?"

Two blinks.

"New York City?"

One blink.

"Justin Blanchard lives in New York City?"

One blink.

"What are you doing?" asked an annoyed voice.

Deborah was startled by the question and turned.

"Nothing, Mom."

"Deborah, leave your father alone! Can't you see he needs rest?"

"Mom, we need to find out what's going on."

Robert's eyes rolled to Nora as she spoke. He blinked once.

"What is he doing?" she asked.

"He said 'yes,' Mom, he said 'yes' with his eyes."

"How do you know that?"

"When he blinks once, that means yes, twice means no."

"What?"

"Once means…never mind."

"I want you to stop pushing your father, Deborah. He can't handle this stress."

Deborah smiled, said goodbye, and zipped out of the room. Nora positioned herself next to Robert, in the chair, and sat guard the rest of the night.

CHAPTER 6

Jack Fatner was a thirty-two-year veteran of the Kruger Falls police department in upstate New York. Sergeant Jack Fatner, as the other detectives knew him, but just Jack to Deborah and Ramone. He lived across the street from them on Summit Ave.

He was a gruff man, married twice, lived alone, and had one month left on the force. That wasn't his idea. The newly elected police chief wanted younger blood, so Fatner was pushed out. He bought a place in the Palm Coast, in Florida, and planned to move there in three weeks—just after the retirement party Chief Sticket was throwing in his honor. The rules were the rules, Fatner would always say, but Sticket had changed all that. So when Deborah turned to him for help, he was more than happy to bend a few. He treated it like a homicide, one last opportunity to show his seasoned investigative prowess, leave the neighborhood an investigative legend. Sadly, it was about all Fatner had left.

Sergeant Fatner worked the case, or so he called it, for about three days when he agreed to meet with Deborah and Ramone. Thursday night he was off duty, he said, and everything he had to say was off the record. Fatner had all but patented the expression "off the record." It made even little cases seem big, especially when he talked to Stram Borden, the reporter from the *Kruger Falls Gazette*.

After five minutes in the Sanchez's house, Fatner reminded them he was off duty as he popped his first beer and gulped a slug. "This is off the record. You didn't get this from me." He lifted his Coors and began his briefing.

"Been a tough one to crack," he said. "I had to pull some strings on this one."

He downed two more mouthfuls before continuing.

"I worked a case in '88 on a fella named Stick McCord. A dick out of Brooklyn was tracking him down and traced him to Kruger Falls."

He polished off the rest of the can.

"Wouldn't mind another," he said.

Deborah went to the kitchen and got one for Jack and one for her nerves as well. Jack popped the top and continued.

"I found him. McCord was slippery, took a day and a half, but I traced him to a cousin's house down on Market Street—nothing but trash if you know what I mean. If you're looking for trash you head straight to the dump. That's what I did. I figured he owed me a favor. You know, the dick in New York, especially after working the case on McCord. What's your interest in this guy Blanchard?"

"Just an acquaintance of my father," she said.

"Yeah, sorry to hear about your pop, never met anyone in Kruger Falls who didn't like Robert. He—"

"Jack, what did you find out about Blanchard?" Ramone asked.

"Yeah…well…slippery guy, this Blanchard. He had three addresses in four years. His last address was Barnes Avenue in the Bronx."

"What do you mean his last address?" she asked.

"He's dead, ma' am."

"Dead?" Ramone asked.

"Dead," he said, "been in the ground five years."

Deborah looked to Ramone.

"I'm listening," Ramone said.

"He did some time at Sing Sing: two years for fraud. He's got a kid living in New Jersey."

He handed Deborah a piece of paper with one hand and took a swallow of his beer with the other. "Here's his address. His name's Buck Blanchard, but I wouldn't be too inclined to visit Big Bad Buck. Remember what I said about the dump."

"We owe you, Jack," she said.

"Just hand me another one of those cold ones and we'll call it square."

Fatner made his way to the door with his Coors. Deborah followed him out. She told Ramone she was taking out the trash. She needed one of those smokes hidden next to the garbage can in the garage, and the bottle of vodka right next to the pack.

Standing at the side door of the detached garage, she leaned against the door jamb looking out toward the neighbor's backyard and thought about what Fatner had said. *Buck Blanchard?* She said to herself. She read the handwritten address out loud. "1216 Baker Street, Brooksdale, New Jersey."

Deborah looked up toward the sky in thought. Then she snapped her attention back to the address. She said it out loud. "Brooksdale, New Jersey—hmm—I guess we'll have to pay Big Bad Buck a visit."

CHAPTER 7

The phone conversation, although brief, had assured Deborah she could handle a man like Buck. After all, she had learned in high school how to manipulate even the toughest of studs using her flirtatious dialogue and eye-popping curves. It taught her the rough edges and crude talk was nothing more than a theatrical façade—a barrier built on testosterone waiting for her heat to melt its shield. There wasn't a high-octane teenage boy in Kruger Falls that she couldn't break, and Buck Blanchard, although tougher and cruder, was nothing more than that.

She hit her husband with the news at the dinner table.

"I want to pay big Buck a visit."

"I have a friend from high school named Hans Janssen," Ramone said. "He's a private investigator. I think we should hire Hans Janssen instead."

Deborah looked up from her dinner with a half-bent grin.

"I'm not paying an investigator to do what we can do," she said. "What's the matter, Ramone, you scared?"

Even with Ramone's dark complexion, a reddish tone seeped onto his face. His black brows curled as he scrunched his eyes and stared at his wife from across the table. Ramone had grown up in a tough New York City neighborhood. And even though he escaped the *barrio* by continually advancing his education, he never lost his hard edge. It was an intrinsic tool that played a major role in his success as the principle of an inner city high school. Deborah knew it and used it to her advantage when Ramone needed a nudge.

He rubbed his short black hair with his hand and spoke. "All right, Deborah, we'll go, but I think you're making a big mistake."

Deborah cracked a smile as she looked down to her plate. "I made the appointment for tomorrow," she said, "ten o'clock in the morning."

They left for New Jersey at eight Saturday morning expecting to arrive by ten. The exit for Brooksdale came up about twenty minutes over the George Washington Bridge. At the bottom of the ramp, Ramone made sure the doors were locked. A car behind them rumbled and thumped, and both of them felt the concussion from the bass. Ramone checked the rear-view mirror. A young kid with a cocked baseball cap, gold chains, rings, and tattoos bounced his head back and forth. The small car was painted metallic purple.

Ramone brought his vision back onto the street and made a right turn. A group of kids with their pants hanging below their back ends stood around a black Monte Carlo. The car's body was jacked up a foot above the tires that were encased in shiny Donk-style rims. The car door was open and rap music pounded out onto the street. They were drinking something out of a bag and passing it around as they danced. The car bounced to the thuds of the bass.

Ramone looked in the rear-view mirror again. The thumper behind him turned his car into the group. When he stopped, the gang jumped around the car making weird hand gestures, passing around the drink bag with cigarette butts hanging from their lips. Deborah and Ramone still heard the pounding a block away. That's when Ramone turned toward his wife and made a rather obvious observation.

"This may have been a mistake, Deb."

She had no response.

Ramone drove past a long row of individual shops closed up with armored curtains. Papers blew around the deserted street, strewn with crumpled beer cans and empty liquor bottles standing upright, left exactly where they had been drained. One store had its protective plates pulled up, and a punk stood out front. He followed their car with his eyes. Ramone looked straight ahead. They passed a small gas station on the right, deserted, and one of its pumps was ripped from its mooring. They cruised past a four-story brick building on the left, abandoned, with most of the windows broken or torn out. That signaled the center of the war zone.

"What do you think, Deb, it looks pretty bad?"

Still not a word.

His eyes scanned the streets, sliding side to side, half expecting a bunch of punks to jump out, guns drawn, and shoot them if they didn't stop. At the next light, Ramone took a left. That's what Buck had said, the first light take a left, then take the second right, and it's the third house on the right. As he approached Buck's house, he slowed and pulled to the curb.

At the house next door to Buck, on the front porch, two kids were smoking cigarettes. One sat on a 2" x 6" sill, attached to a solid wall, which ran the length of the porch. The other leaned against a column that supported the roof overhead and looked at one time to be painted white but now looked dirt brown. They both turned their attention to the car as Ramone stopped in the street. One of the punks made a gesture and pounded his chest and then made another gesture. Ramone shut off the engine, thinking it was all a big mistake.

Deborah reached into her pocket book and pulled out a cigarette and lit it up.

"What the hell are you doing, Deb?"

"I'm having a smoke, Ramone."

"I thought you quit?"

One of the punks bounced down the steps toward the car, and his upper body slid side to side as he moved. Ramone got out.

"Yo, what's up?" the kid asked, his head tilted sideways. Deborah, amused, watched from the car.

"Yo, what's up?" the kid asked again.

"Is this where Buck Blanchard lives?" Ramone asked.

"Yo, dude," he said as he looked Ramone up and down, then looked up toward Buck's house, and then back to Ramone. "You his bro?"

"I have an appointment with Buck."

"Yo, Chandell, the spic says he got an appointment with Mr. Blanchard. What kind of business you talking? Yo, Chandell, maybe good lookin' here's brought some batu. Is that what the bitch is smoking in the ride man?"

"Yo," came down from Buck's porch.

The kid looked up. The man on Buck's porch, despite the cold, had just a wifebeater on. One arm had a big cross tattoo. Each hand had some colored tattoo on the backs. His arms were big and the t-shirt fit tight, exposing the muscles in his gut. Even though he was white, he had long dreadlocks that fell from under a twisted leather cap. Ramone studied the punk who had approached his car and saw a look of terror on his face. The punk turned and started back to the porch. He didn't look back, and he didn't look at Buck.

"Yo, what's your name?" Buck asked.

"My name's Ramone."

"Come on up, dude. I'm Buck."

Deborah had exited their Acura and gazed over the roof to her husband Ramone.

"Let's go," she said.

Ramone had a troubled look on his face, and he stood half dazed, examining his wife. Her lack of apprehension concerned him, but he had seen it before. She seemed carefree when she should be scared to death. It was almost as if she had no sense about her safety, and the oddity of such an inappropriate response in the face of what could be a dangerous situation deeply disturbed him.

"Come on," she said again and started to walk toward the house. Then stopped and turned, "Let's go, Ramone!"

Ramone shook his head and caught up to his wife. When they reached the porch deck, Buck waddled over to the rail like he had a load in his pants. He glared at the punks on the porch next door. He made some type of hand move, stared for a moment, then signaled Deborah and Ramone to follow. Ramone figured his car was safe.

Buck sat at the kitchen table, slouched back, smoking a cigarette. It hung from his lips as he studied the two. The kitchen stank of garbage, like on trash day when the garbage truck goes by and the air hangs long after the truck is gone. Dishes were piled in the sink and spilled out onto the counter. The table, stacked with beer cans, dirty plates, and a freezer bag full of pot in the middle, completed the crack house look. Buck sucked a draw on the butt in his mouth and then leaned in toward the table.

"Ramone," he said, "you a spic?"

"My grandfather came from Mexico."

He took another draw and leaned back in his chair rubbing what was supposed to be a mustache and chin beard. It was so straggly it looked more like leg hair. He blew some air from his lips, like a "so what" kind of noise. With the cigarette still hanging from his mouth, he reached over and grabbed the freezer bag. He opened it and began rolling a joint. When he finished, he put his cigarette on the edge of the table, lit up the joint, made a sucking sound, and then tried to talk holding his breath.

"You two cops?"

"No, of course not," Deborah answered.

With that he took another hit and reached over to Deborah with the lit joint.

"No, thanks," she said.

He nodded and took some more.

"What's, sssssshp, sssssshp, what's your interest in my old man?"

"Have you ever heard the name Robert Williams?" Ramone asked.

"Should I?"

"He knew your father," Deborah said.

Buck turned his attention to Deborah. His eyes checked her up and down. Her auburn hair and brown eyes accented the sharp clean features of her face, and Buck shook his head in approval. He rolled his eyes down to her chest and didn't hide his examination of her breasts. Her tight sweater accentuated the eye-catching curves, and she seemed to enjoy Buck's attention. He smiled and looked down at the bag of pot.

"Big fucking deal," he said, "a lot of bros hung out with the old man."

Ramone noticed Buck's examination of his wife had started again. He jumped in to interrupt it.

"Look, someone left a note that had your father's name on it and the date 1960. Something happened then and someone's after my father-in-law. We're just trying to find out the truth," Ramone said.

Buck turned to Ramone. "Why the fuck should I care?" he asked as he lit another smoke.

"You're right. I'm sorry we wasted your time," Ramone said.

"Don't know what I don't know."

"Is your mom still alive?" Deborah asked.

Ramone looked to his wife, irritated.

"Nosy bitch, eh?" he said as he fondled his chin again and turned to Deborah.

"She won't know shit. The old man was a motherfucker. He hit the street when I was five. I had a few times with the son of a bitch, but he stayed away from her."

"Do you mind if we talk to her?" Ramone asked.

Buck turned toward Ramone and his eyes rose up to his. Ramone locked on.

"Have at it," Buck said. He wrote the address down on a napkin. He walked them to the porch. Ramone held Deborah close as their feet landed on the first step.

"Hey, spic," Buck said.

Ramone turned.

"That's a fine-looking bitch you got. There's some bad mother fuckers who'd slice you up for her."

The message was loud and clear. Buck looked next door and stared the two punks down and then his eyes swept back to the car. As they started to drive away, Buck flicked his butt over the rail and turned toward the door. Ramone locked the doors and drove away fast. The speed limit was twenty five; he pushed forty. He ran traffic lights, stop signs, and zipped along at forty-five.

The car turned left onto the main road that led to the entrance to I-95. The engine hummed louder. They were well over the George Washington Bridge before either one said a word. Ramone was angry that his wife had enjoyed being involved in such a dangerous situation. Deborah knew it and was letting him stew. When she finally spoke, Ramone turned his head in her direction.

"See, Ramone, that wasn't so bad."

"I'm calling Hans Janssen in the morning."

"What?"

"I said I'm calling Hans Janssen in the morning. That's it...end of discussion!"

CHAPTER 8

After one week in physical therapy, unable to take one step with a walker, Robert Williams was discharged. The prognosis was not good. Dr. Stockard had said he might, with the assistance of a walker, regain some mobility, but he would need to continue his therapy as an outpatient. His speech, though, was another story. Robert had not spoken one syllable since the stroke. His voice was likely lost forever. The prospect seemed improbable to Nora. She believed Robert would regain not only his ability to converse, but the rest of his faculties as well. And, she refused assistance at home dealing with Robert's care. After two days, she looked tired, worn, and aged, but yet she was still resolute in her determination to be Robert's sole provider.

Robert and Nora had always been intensely private people. They took care of each other and rarely reached out for help. Early in their relationship, when Robert opened up the store, Nora was there every day. They were young, without kids, and the two of them were determined to succeed. As their clientele increased, and the store expanded, they stretched their hours and worked every day of the week. Even when Nora became pregnant with John, she didn't back off. And though Robert eventually hired help, they tackled the issues that arose in the store together. They kept it to themselves and rectified it by themselves. That principle was written in stone and woven into the fabric of their marriage.

So to Nora, Robert's condition was only an extension of exactly that. It was how they lived their lives together for forty-four years. Nora believed in it, breathed it, and would have it no other way. No stranger would attend to the personal needs of her husband Robert—not as long as she was alive. And even though she knew her daughter would try to convince her otherwise, Nora's mind was already made up.

Deborah arrived mid-afternoon to discuss the Blanchard meeting and found her mother sitting at the kitchen table, exhausted. She realized immediately her mother was overwhelmed. Frustrated at her stubbornness, and her unrealistic attitude toward her father's care, she spoke out.

"Mom, he's not capable of feeding himself, washing himself, God…even going to the bathroom himself. You need to either put him in a facility, or get extra help."

"I see improvement every day."

"Jesus, Mom…"

"Hush now, your father will hear you."

Nora left Deborah in the kitchen and went to check on Robert in the bedroom. He was in his wheelchair watching the news.

"Are you warm enough, Robert?" Nora asked. "Yes, that's right, Robert. Deborah is here. She said she had something to discuss."

"Mother…"

Startled, Nora turned her head.

"Deborah, you scared me half to death. What is it?"

"We need to talk."

"In the living room, so we don't disturb your father."

In the living room, Nora sat on the couch. Deborah sat on the other side of the coffee table in a cushioned chair. She described the meeting in New Jersey: the two punks on the porch, Buck Blanchard and his colorful use of the English language, the oversized bag of illegal drugs, and his still surviving mother. Nora looked miles away in a self-induced trance.

"Mother…Mother, did you hear a word I said?"

Nora brought herself back. She had a confused look on her face and turned her head toward her daughter.

"Mother, do you understand how serious this is?"

"Yes, dear."

"Ramone called his friend from high school this morning, Hans Janssen. He's a private investigator."

"We don't need a private investigator, Deborah."

"Right, Mom, just bury your head in the sand and it will all go away."

"Deborah…"

"Look, Mother, someone knows something about Dad's past. We need to find out who's behind this and whether Dad was involved in anything illegal and if so, could he still be held accountable. Until then, we keep this to ourselves—understood?"

"What about John?"

"What about John?"

"Shouldn't we call him?"

"He's a self-centered son of a bitch!"

"Deborah!"

"It's the truth and you know it."

"That's your brother, Deborah."

"Go ahead…call him. See if he'll talk to you, or better yet, even call you back."

"Deborah…"

"I need a smoke."

Nora sat in the kitchen staring at the birds feeding on sunflower seeds outside the window. Robert was in the bedroom hunched over in his wheelchair, asleep. Deborah hung out in the garden and smoked a Marlboro, played with the cigarette pack, and thought about what to do. The clock was ticking and she knew it. She leaned her head against her finger tips and pulled out her phone and flipped it open. *I'll be damned if I call John again—ever!*

The Bombardier Challenger 605's maiden flight from Los Angeles to New York hung somewhere over the United States at forty thousand feet screaming through the air at Mach 0.80. Williams Investment Bank had just taken delivery of the twenty-eight million dollar gem, and John Williams was on board at his desk.

"God damn it," he said into the phone. "You tell Stooser to get his ass on board or there's no deal— understood?"

He looked to his secretary.

"Martha, where the hell's my drink? Look, Calhoun, I'm sick of your pussy footing around. You get this deal done or you're toast!" He slapped the phone closed. "Martha?"

"Yes, sir?"

"Get me Fred Atkins on the line."

John lifted his Crown Royal and surveyed the sun glimmering off the wings of his latest acquisition. He slurped a sip of the colored liquid and then inhaled the smell of twenty-eight million dollar leather. He let the aroma dance in his head before pulling another sip from the crystal glass. *It's a beauty*, he thought, *the damn finest machine I've bought yet.* He looked at the proposal sitting in front of him, on the bird's eye maple desk, and without looking up he yelled, "Martha, where the hell is Atkins?"

"I'm getting him now, Mr. Williams."

He took another sip and pulled his lips together.

"I've got him, Mr. Williams."

"Hi, Fred, John here. I've been going over the deal with Sanddeck Inc. Fred, I think two and a half bills is fair…What's that…No, Fred, that's the best we're going to get…Fred, Conicur Air went for one point five billion last year; I think this is a solid proposal…All right, I'll let them know."

"Mr. Williams, your sister's on the line; she said it's important."

"Damn it, Martha, I told you not to bother me with that!"

"She said it's urgent."

"Is the old man dead?"

"She didn't say."

"I'm not here!"

Rubbing her forehead with her fingers, Deborah stared at the old dogwood tree. *Asshole!* She flipped the phone closed and walked back to the house.

CHAPTER 9

HANS JANSSEN
Private Investigator

The name was painted in black capital letters on the frosted glass of a door on a side street building in White Plains, New York. Behind the name, there was one room with an old maple desk, a wooden chair, faded gray linoleum floor, a red wool upholstered wing back chair, and one framed print of a wind mill in a sea of tulips hanging on the wall. Janssen was Dutch two generations back. He had spent ten years as a homicide cop working the streets of Manhattan. It was ten years cracking drug deals gone wrong, hookers floating in the Hudson, and street gangs with a beef. He had seen it all.

In '93, he cracked the five-year-old murder of Blaine Driest, a wealthy diamond merchant living on Park Ave. His signature arrest hit the front page of every major New

York newspaper, and he was a star on the six o'clock news. His career, however, went down as fast as it went up. Three months after becoming a legend, internal affairs accused Janssen of taking sixty thousand dollars from a botched drug deal on 42nd Street. A four-week investigation resulted in a stalemate, and he was re-instated. But he had enough of politics and left the force to pursue the exotic life of a PI. One problem, the stigma hung with him, and he was considered a double-edged sword. Janssen was tops at what he did, but when he did it could he be trusted? Internal affairs said with Hans Janssen you rolled the dice.

He wasn't cheap, though. A hundred and twenty-five bucks an hour, plus expenses; Deborah Sanchez choked on the sum when he said it. Janssen took a fifteen hundred dollar retainer, the name and address of Buck's mother, a photo copy of the note, and Robert's social security number. And he was anxious to get to work.

Hans had worked the case for three days, and the interview with Buck Blanchard's mother proved useless. She smoked, drank, and barely remembered the man she divorced when Buck was three. The background checks on Justin Blanchard revealed an unemployed street hood. He mostly had a number of arrests for small-time nickel and dime crimes. His biggest rap was embezzling twenty thousand dollars from an eighty-year-old woman. The crime landed him four and half years in the Arthur Hill Correctional Facility in Staten Island, New York., followed by two years of probation.

Blanchard had unconfirmed ties to the mob, lived at Belmont Park betting on the long shots, and died in a car crash labeled suspicious but tagged accidental. Janssen was about to dig into Robert Williams's life when the phone rang. He was informed by Nora Williams a new piece of the puzzle had just arrived. He held off on the background check on Robert Williams and headed to Kruger Falls.

He was told by Nora that she had gone to the front door to get the Kruger Falls Gazette. The envelope was taped to the glass of the front door. Her voice trembled as she described how she had sat on the bench next to the front entrance, held the envelope in her hand, and looked down at her name printed on the front. And now as Janssen drove, he thought about the contents of the note. In his head, he recited what Nora had read to him over the phone.

So you understand, Mrs. Williams, your husband is not the man you think he is. Central Park, August 9, 1960. Have Mr. Janssen look it up. You will get instructions at precisely 11 a.m. on October 19th by phone.

As Janssen changed lanes to pass a truck, he smirked at the mention of his name.

When Janssen arrived he checked the video surveillance from the cameras he had set up. It showed a hooded person in a dark coat walk up to the Williams's house from the street at 2:36 in the morning. The person approached the front steps, stopped, looked to the left, looked to the right, and then looked behind him before he stuck the note to the front door. He turned once and looked in the direction of the house as he walked back toward the street, presumably to check that the note was still attached, and then disappeared to the left. The person's gender and physical appearance were impossible to discern.

Janssen shared the contents of the surveillance tapes with Nora and Deborah as the two sat in the living room on the couch. It was the second time Nora had met the man his daughter had employed, and she felt safe around Hans Janssen. At six foot three, he towered over her small frame. His eyes worked constantly, taking in data, processing the facts. His mouth always tilted downward, never up. The deep strong tone in his voice kept an offensive edge to those around him. Two decibels stronger, he'd clear the room.

He finished examining the correspondence, folded it back up, and slid it in the side pocket of his Brandon car coat. He rubbed his nose between his thumb and first finger. Deborah and Nora sat quietly, waiting.

Finally, he spoke. "This one's addressed to you, Mrs. Williams. They obviously know of your husband's stroke. They have eyes and ears not far off. That's clear by the reference to my name. These people are professional. They make it their business to know every detail, every fact."

"Why are they doing this?" Nora asked.

"I suspect we'll find that out on the 19th," Janssen said. Then he fell silent.

Deep in thought, his eyes turned upward and then down to Nora sitting on the couch. "Mrs. Williams, I need you to bring Mr. Williams into the room."

"Please, Mr. Janssen, I don't want Robert upset. He needs to rest."

"Mrs. Williams, I have some information to share, and I want to see your husband's reaction when I say it."

"What is it, Mr. Janssen?" Deborah asked.

"I want you all to hear it together, please, Mrs. Williams."

"Mom, bring Dad in!"

Nora stood up and walked toward the kitchen. Her face was pale when she left the room. When she returned pushing the wheelchair, Robert was visibly disturbed. His eyes shot around the room, and they settled on Hans Janssen sitting in the chair parked in front of the couch. Nora pushed Robert next to the wing back chair and sat next to him.

Deborah looked to her father. "Dad, this is Hans Janssen. He is a private investigator."

Robert's eyes whipped from Hans to his wife, and she put her hand on his.

"What is it, Mr. Janssen?" Deborah asked.

Janssen pulled out the envelope from his pocket and slid out the note. He unfolded the sheet of paper, scanned the lines with his eyes, and then raised his head.

"The reference to August 9, 1960 is a reference to an unsolved murder committed on that date in Central Park."

"Oh God!" Nora said. "There is no way my Robert would be involved in that."

Hans studied Robert's eyes, but he didn't have to look very hard. They looked up, down, side to side, and then closed. Deborah had her forehead in the palm of her hand.

"I need a cigarette," she said.

"Please, just a minute," Janssen said.

"Jesus Christ," Deborah said, "there's more?"

"A young twenty-four-year-old woman named Tristan McCobb was murdered on that date. From Mr. Williams's reaction, I believe he knows something about it."

"Do you think my father had something to do with it?"

"Stop this, stop this now!" Nora said. "You've upset Robert enough."

"No, Mom, we need to find out the truth."

"No, I don't want him disturbed."

Deborah ignored her mother.

"Dad, we need to ask you some questions. Just like before, you blink once for yes and twice for no."

"Stop it, Deborah."

"Dad, were you in Central Park on August 9th, 1960?"

"Deborah!"

"Quiet, Mom. Dad, were you in Central Park?" One blink.

His eyes darted around the room and landed on Nora.

"Stop this. Please stop this."

"Mr. Williams, did you know a woman named Tristan McCobb?" Janssen asked.   Robert's eyes didn't answer. They shot side to side and then dropped down.

"Dad, answer the question," Deborah said.

Robert looked to Nora.

"Robert, you don't have to answer."

"Yes, you do, Dad. You need to answer the question. Did you know Tristan McCobb?"

His eyes suddenly went still. The fight had drained from them, and they looked empty and dead. He slowly raised them to his daughter and blinked once.

"No, Robert!"

"Mother, quiet!"

Robert's eyes blinked wildly. He looked at Janssen, and then Deborah, and then back to Janssen. Nora was hysterical and crying with her head buried in her hands. Robert looked again at Janssen and Deborah and finally Janssen responded.

"Did you harm the girl, Mr. Williams?" Two blinks.

"You did nothing to the girl, Dad, you had nothing to do with it?"

Two blinks.

Exhausted, he closed his eyes.

"Thank God," Nora said, as she jumped up and shot to the back of the wheelchair and pushed him to the bedroom and sat next to him. The tears streamed down her cheeks. No one could disturb them now; she had locked the door on the way in.

Deborah and Janssen retreated to the front porch so she could finally have her smoke.

"What's going on here?" Deborah asked.

"You've hired me to find that out."

"What do we do?"

"Wait until they tell us what they want."

"In the meantime?"

"I am afraid, Mrs. Sanchez, I'll need another retainer."

"How much?"

"Twenty-five hundred."

"My God!"

"It's getting complicated. I'm working on getting the police file. In the meantime, this could get expensive. Are you sure you don't want to go to the police?"

"Yes!"

"Well then, I'll need a check."

"I'll have my mom write you a check. Just find out what's going on, and fast. My parents aren't made of money."

"What about your brother?"

"What about my brother?"

"He's very big."

"No, and don't ask about him again!"

CHAPTER 10

Hans Janssen pulled some strings. Working homicide for ten years, you pulled favors, and you gave them out, and it was Janssen's turn to cash one in. Dick Callahan worked the Central Park Precinct as lead Detective in '92. He made a name for himself busting one of the biggest drug dealers in New York: Carlos Lumbino, aka The Slippery Lump.

A detective that worked homicide had brought in a suspect for questioning on the murder of a politician's son. The suspect had made a deal, and it included information on Carlos Lumbino. The detective told Callahan and Callahan nailed The Lump. That detective with the information was Hans Janssen. Dick Callahan owed him big time and handed him the file to the forty-six-year-old murder on the ninth day of August 1960 in Central Park. Hans had the file for two days, no more, and Callahan's debt had been paid. Callahan made that clear before he'd let it go.

Janssen lived in a small cape on Saddle Brook Road in White Plains, New York—twelve hundred square feet of loneliness. After three divorces, he was lucky to have that. In need of paint on the outside and cleaning on the inside, Janssen spent his time in a ten by ten room with computers, high tech gadgets, recording devices, and a small area to sit. The three-inch thick murder file was on his desk, with a Budweiser to its right, and a ham and cheese deli sandwich wrapped in paper to the left. Hans fired up the computer, opened up dinner, popped the top on the bud, and went to work.

Janssen worked the file. As he did, he ripped bites of the ham and cheese sandwich, gulped down cold suds, and scribbled notes on a yellow legal pad resting on his lap. Periodically, he checked the computer to back up the facts on the internet. He conducted traces on various names and accessed death records to determine if individuals were deceased. The lists of suspects, as might be expected for an unsolved homicide, could have filled the seats on a Greyhound Bus. Justin Blanchard's storied career had just begun, and he was a prime suspect. Local thugs, sexual predators, purse snatchers, homeless bums, all with their little biographies short and sweet, made the cut. And the star attraction was Robert Williams, whose name adorned the pages that comprised twenty-five percent of the unsolved murder file.

Robert Williams, it said, was twenty-six and worked in the garment district. He had a close association with the deceased. He was intimately involved with the victim for six months. They were last seen in Central Park engaged in a heated argument. Their voices were so pronounced that a couple who sat on a bench turned and watched. The suspect stormed away leaving the victim alone near the skating rink. Shortly thereafter, the police found the deceased in a small wooded area in the direction Robert was last seen storming off. Her throat had been cut.

Robert was holding the victim in his arms, his clothes soaked in blood, his left hand bleeding, and he repeated over and over how sorry he was. Williams claimed he walked back to apologize and spotted a man running from the scene. A man he could not identify. He claimed he couldn't remember his height, how old he was, or the clothes he wore. The cops released Williams for lack of evidence; the weapon had vanished. The lead homicide detective kept tabs on him for two years until Robert moved to Kruger Falls. By the third year, the case went cold.

Janssen took a swallow from the cold can of Bud. He thumbed through the papers and pulled out the transcripts of Robert's interrogation. It was the typical good cop, bad cop M.O. It didn't work.

Robert had stated the argument started over a co-worker's of McCobb. She had gone out the night before with a group from work. The man, who had personal interest in McCobb, was present. It wasn't the first time, though. Early on in their relationship, this man had repeatedly made advances toward McCobb. One night, when Robert and Tristan were out to dinner, he showed up, sat down, and Robert finally asked him to leave. McCobb enjoyed his attention and that drove Robert to the edge of rage. So when Robert heard about the gathering, and that the man was present, he snapped.

He admitted to the outrageous fight, but not to any involvement in the crime. The cops insisted he had lured her into the park for the specific purpose of murder. That meant it was a first-degree premeditated homicide, but if he copped a plea they'd reduce it to second degree. An act perpetrated in a jealous rage, the good cop had said, and he totally understood how Robert could have lost it, particularly when it had happened over and over again. That's when he decided he'd said enough and asked to speak to an attorney. He was released an hour after that.

Janssen ripped off a piece of the hard roll and stuffed it into his mouth followed by a wash of beer. He ran back through the other suspects and looked for clues the cops might have missed. Justin Blanchard's name, used in the note Robert received, stuck out like a donkey at a horse race. He pulled the workup on Blanchard.

Ex combat vet from Vietnam, it said, sent as one of the so-called military advisors in '58. A Green Beret, Blanchard finished his tour in '59 and was dishonorably discharged in '60 for attacking his commanding officer. It took three seasoned Berets to restrain him.

That same year, on a mob stake-out in New York, Blanchard appeared in a photograph talking to Joe Bonanno, then New York City's crime boss. Next to him stood two goons—one on each side. The two goons, Giuseppe "The Hammer" Piglatelli and Mario "Bones" Barcelone, were both suspected hit men. Two weeks later, McCobb's throat was slashed in Central Park. On a tip, Justin Blanchard was brought in for questioning. Street smart with Green Beret training, Blanchard kept his mouth shut and was released. The lead detective hauled him in days later on another tip, kept him forty-eight hours, but released him once again for lack of evidence. Blanchard stunk like a five-day-old dead fish, but there was nothing the cops could do.

Janssen spent the next two hours scanning in all the documents from the police file onto his computer. Dick Callahan had been clear about the folder being back in his hands in two days. Janssen had to work fast.

He pulled out the pictures of the crime scene. The girl, Tristan McCobb, was twenty-four years old. The autopsy said she had been grabbed from behind: her mouth secured with the assailant's left hand, her throat slit with the assailant's right. One well-placed slice meant to be thorough and quick. Janssen took a swallow of his Bud and picked up his pen.

He examined the photos a second time and started jotting notes. Tristan McCobb's purse lay next to her, unopened. There were no visible cuts on her hands, arms, or face. The ground around her was matted. It was probably disturbed by Robert. The kill was quick, perhaps a matter of seconds. Janssen scribbled down *"professional hit?"*

The murder happened in broad daylight, which made it hard to explain the possibility of a potential get away. It was hard to run in the light of day with blood splattered all over one's clothes, at least without being noticed. Janssen stopped, lifted his beer, and thought about the question jumping up and down in his head. *If Robert committed the crime, why would he be sitting on the ground holding the bloodied corpse?* He took the last gulp from the Bud and tossed it in the basket underneath the desk. He crumbled up what was left of the ham and cheese sandwich, and it banged the side of the can as it went in. It was time to look at motive.

Detective Stump, the lead detective working the case back in 1960, believed it came down to two possible theories. The pocket book had not been opened, her wallet, credit cards, and cash were all in place, so robbery was out. Tristan McCobb had not been sexually assaulted, nor was there any attempt to sexually attack her. Rape was out. The severity of the crime led Stump to believe either it was a random act of violence—the type done by a serial killer—or Ms. McCobb had been taken out.

As nothing ritualistic, no sexual elements, or apparent psychological gratification appeared to be involved, Stump went with the second. Tristan McCobb had been the victim of a hit. Hans Janssen agreed. If true, however, Janssen needed to find out why. The other question that banged against Janssen's brain was how come Robert Williams kept this a secret for forty-six years? Was Williams capable of taking the life of another human being? He thought about that all the way to the kitchen as he popped the top and took a pass on his second Bud.

CHAPTER 11

Involved in a one-way conversation, Nora sat next to Robert at the breakfast table. She lifted the spoon of pea soup to his mouth and never missed a beat.

"Robert, I think we should call John. We need his help now. I know, dear," she said as she scraped the bottom of the spoon on the side of the soup bowl, "John is very busy, but he is our son." She patted the corner of his mouth with the cloth napkin and scooped another spoon of the soup. "Yes, Robert, I think it's time we call our son."

John Williams sat in the board room of Sanddeck Industries with Fred Sanddeck to his left. To his right was the law firm of Trake and Trake, eight members of the current board, and waiting on conference phone in a separate Manhattan office downtown was Stephan Douglas III. Douglas was the third-generation CEO and chairman of the board of Tritant International, a multi-conglomerate with offices in Japan, Germany, the United Kingdom, and the United States. Sanddeck was another piece of the Douglas puzzle in fulfilling the vision of becoming the communication czar of the Northern hemisphere. A compulsion his father had entertained the last ten years of his life.

The price offered by Tritant was two and a half billion dollars. Mr. Sanddeck was about to pocket seven hundred and fifty million. John Williams, as adviser, and investment banker, was about to pocket a paltry twenty-five. Fred Sanddeck had worked thirty-two years building the company into what it was today. John Williams had spent the last three months bringing Sanddeck and Tritant to the table. He believed he was being grossly underpaid.

Meanwhile, Williams's Challenger 605 sat on the tarmac at Teterboro Airport, gassed, re-stocked, with the full crew on board ready to fly. John Williams had a dinner date in Los Angeles at seven-thirty that night. He was anxious to wrap things up, so he pushed ahead.

"This is a fair price," he said, "and Fred has agreed, any questions?"

"Yes," a board member said. "I think Sanddeck is being taken out cheap."

"Well, Mr. Valdez, even though the votes are already in place, I'll indulge you, sir. The two and a half billion represents fifteen times cash flow. Conicur Air went for twelve. I'm sure you missed that in the prospectus. Tritant is willing to pay a premium for Sanddeck, Mr. Valdez, and you'd have to be daft to pass this up. Are there any more questions? Good all in favor? It's unanimous then—Fred."

"Yes, thank you, John."

Sanddeck pushed the button on the speaker phone. "Congratulations, Mr. Douglas, you've bought yourself a company."

"Thanks, Fred, let my attorneys in and they'll take care of the paper. Good day!"

"Well, gentlemen, I believe you can take it from here," John said. "Fred, let me know when you want to play Westchester."

The Bell-429 screamed over the Manhattan skyline with John Williams buckled in after a tough day at work. Teterboro was a ten-minute jaunt from Manhattan, and as his helicopter raced toward New Jersey, John worked the phones. Another deal was on the fire—even though the ink hadn't dried yet on the twenty-five million dollar check—and time was money and this one had a lot more zeros attached.

The Bombardier Challenger 605 sparkled in the late afternoon sun as the Bell hovered over the hangar. The four hour fifty-three minute flight to LA, at Mach 0.8, was just a short commute. At the other end, Janis Wells, Hollywood's newest box office queen had waited days for the 605 to land. The deal maker had big plans with Ms. Wells: oysters from Maryland, lobsters from Maine, champagne from France, and for desert, Janis Wells from Hollywood. The big shot in the Bombardier was never denied. He always saw to that.

John Williams heard yes when people said no, saw a door open, when it was closed, and made a mega-marriage of companies when others saw divorce. The only thing larger than his private mansion was his personal ego, which had the capacity to steam roll you so fast it was considered hit and run.

Unannounced to Janis Wells, this was her one big night, her one shining moment with the young handsome tycoon. Tomorrow, the Challenger 605 would be headed to its next big paycheck, and Janis Wells would be headed to her shrink.

The 605 received clearance and was in the air ten minutes after John arrived. He sat at his desk with CNBC on the flat screen. He wanted to admire his work. Stephan Douglas III was blazing a trail, and when he bought, it was international news. John didn't have to wait long. Douglas must have taken the direct express to Wall Street and was already standing on the trading floor. He was being interviewed by Maria Bartiromo about his latest deal. His ticker symbol, TRI, sat at the bottom of the screen flashing green, 72.13 up 2.5.

"Mr. Williams."

"What is it, Martha?"

"Your mother's on the line."

"Jesus Christ."

"She asked to talk to you."

He stared at Douglas on the flat screen.

"Mr. Williams."

"What is it, Martha?"

"Would you like me to put her through?"

"No, I'm busy. Get me a Crown Royal, no ice."

"That's just like John, dear, flying off somewhere exotic. California, I think she said. Here, Robert, one more spoon left, dear."

Robert looked to his wife. On the outside, his body was paralyzed and his voice had been taken away. On the inside he felt the emptiness of being cut off from the rest of the world. He had so much he wanted to say.

Robert had always believed that his family came first. He had purchased Crab Point with his children in mind as a place to enjoy their summers on an island that was isolated and safe. And it became exactly that. Each year from June to August they loved living on the island of Schaums Head: the Fourth of July fireworks over Saggart's Harbor, the fishing in Woodmans Cove, the evenings looking out over the marsh as the family sat on the back porch. But then, things changed.

By the age of nine, John had become defiant, angry, and aloof. His cruelty toward his sister often brought her to tears. Their arguing became constant and fierce. Robert intervened, but the harder he pushed John, the farther he pulled away. That June, John refused to go out to Schaums Head. In response, Robert put his son in a sleep-away camp for the summer. As John's outrageous behavior escalated, he enrolled him in a full-time boarding school that fall. His decision had broken Nora's heart.

As he looked to Nora, Robert tried to speak with his eyes. He wished he could talk to her now. He thought he was doing the right thing with John, but in hindsight he realized he should have reached out for help. He took a breath—pride seemed such a shallow thing to him now. He turned his eyes away from Nora, slowly closed them, and fell back into his voiceless world, alone.

CHAPTER 12

On October 19th, the morning of the scheduled call, they all gathered in the living room. Hans Janssen sat in a kitchen chair that faced the living room couch. The cordless phone from Robert's office sat in his right hand. Deborah sat next to her mom on the couch, and Robert was slouched in the wheelchair to the right. Nora had been instructed by Janssen to pick up the phone on the count of two and remain calm. She was a nervous wreck. Her hands were folded and on her lap next to the cordless phone from the kitchen. As they waited, she stared out the bay window and studied the empty street. At exactly 11 a.m. the phone rang. Nora picked it up. She looked to Jansen.

He whispered, "One...two..."

She pushed the button and answered the call.

"Hello," she said.

There was only silence.

"Hello," she said again.

"Listen carefully," an electronic voice said. "I am in possession of the knife that killed Tristan McCobb. Both Robert's blood and Tristan McCobb's blood are present on the weapon. It has been sealed in an air-tight plastic bag for forty-six years. You have two weeks to deliver five million American dollars into a numbered Swiss account. If you fail, your husband will spend the rest of his life institutionalized for her murder. A word of caution, Mrs. Williams, do not test my resolve or the validity of the evidence. That would be a grave mistake."

The call went dead.

"Hello…hello…" Nora said. She dropped the phone to her lap.

"What did he say?" Deborah asked.

"Oh sweet mother of God."

"What did he say?"

"It's what I figured," Janssen said.

"What?"

Janssen's head swept upward and he stared at the ceiling in thought.

Deborah exasperated asked one more time. "What?"

"It's blackmail. The murder weapon in exchange for the cash," Janssen said.

"I don't understand. My father said he was innocent."

"He claims your father's blood is on the knife, along with the woman's blood," Janssen said.

"We can go to the police."

"No," Nora said.

"Dad, did you kill that girl? Dad… look at me…did you kill that girl?"

Robert's head was down, and his eyes were hidden from view.

"Dad, answer me. Did you murder Tristan McCobb?"

Robert looked up and blinked twice.

"They're bluffing."

"Maybe, maybe not," Janssen answered.

"That happened forty six years ago," Deborah said. "They can't go after him now."

"There's no statute of limitations on first-degree murder," Janssen said. "They sure can. If Mr. William's blood is on that knife, they could try him for murder."

"My father can't stand trial, look at him."

"They could find Robert incompetent to stand trial, which means they could still institutionalize him. There's also McCobb's family. They could file a civil lawsuit and take everything you've got."

Deborah looked at her father sitting in his chair, with his head hung down to his chest. She glanced over to her mother then to Janssen and shook her head.

"What do they want?" she asked.

"Five million," Janssen said.

"What?"

"That's a lot of money," Janssen said.

"My parents don't have that kind of money. These people must know that."

"It seems they know quite a lot. It stands to reason they'd know that," Janssen said.

"Then why ask for such a ridiculous amount?"

"Perhaps they know more than you think."

"What does that mean?"

"These people are smart. They've done their homework. They'll extort John using your father's past."

Nora looked shocked. "You think they're really after John?" she asked.

"Makes sense. Why else ask for that kind of money?"

"I need a smoke," Deborah said and started to walk out. About halfway to the kitchen, she turned. "That son of a bitch is heartless," she said. "You think he's going to part with five million bucks?"

"Maybe not," Janssen said.

"So if these people are so informed, how do they not know that?"

"Doesn't matter."

"What do you mean?"

"They have nothing to lose. They are betting your mother will go to John, and they are betting in the end he'll pay up. From what I understand, that's nickels and dimes to your wealthy brother."

"Right," she said and stormed outside to the garden where she lit up a Marlboro and took a drink from the flask.

Meanwhile, Janssen had gone to his van to work the electronic side of the call. When he returned he told Nora the results. "Bad news," he said, "the call was routed through slave computers and then dialed from the office of Zintrex. This guy not only knows how to embezzle, he can hack too."

Deborah had come back from the patio and heard the tail end of Janssen's briefing. She approached him and stopped.

"Do you think he did it?" she asked.

"Your father claims he's innocent," Janssen replied.

"I understand that. I'm asking you if you think he killed Tristan McCobb."

"My job is not to speculate but instead to uncover the facts."

Deborah shook her head.

"Can you get to the truth?"

Janssen looked to Nora sitting at the kitchen table, staring out the window with her hands on her lap.

"How do you want to proceed, Mrs. Williams?"

"What do you mean?" Nora asked. "I won't take the chance with Robert. We give them what they want."

"And how, Mrs. Williams, do you propose to do that?"

"My John will come through, Mr. Janssen."

"I think they're bluffing," Deborah said. "I don't think there is any knife."

Janssen turned to Deborah. "What makes you so sure?"

"Because if the knife existed, why wait forty-six years?"

"Do you want to call their bluff?"

"No!" Nora said. "We go to John. I want you to find out who is doing this. I want you to find them, Mr. Janssen."

"I'll need another retainer."

"Of course you will, how much?" Deborah asked.

"Five thousand."

"Jesus Christ," she said. "Five thousand?"

"Maybe more."

"I'll write you a check," Nora said.

"Mom, no, this is ridiculous…five thousand dollars, where does it end?"

The heated conversation had stirred Robert. His eyes shot around the table. They froze on his wife. She knew what he wanted to say, but she wouldn't budge.

"I don't care, Robert," she said. "I'm paying Mr. Janssen."

"What if you can't get the money from John?" Deborah asked. "What will you do then?"

"He's our son, Deborah. He'll help."

She gazed at her mother with her eyebrows scrunched and her mouth puckered.

"I think we should go to the police."

"No!"

"Mom?'

"No!"

CHAPTER 13

Nora watched a male cardinal peck at the sunflower seeds in the birdfeeder hanging from the red oak tree. Her right hand rose up to her forehead, and she massaged her temple with the tips of her fingers. She had defended John for almost a decade, made excuses for his unconscionable behavior and total disregard of his family. Yet with all of her deflection, she had never tried once to contact her son. She prodded her husband or her daughter to call. The pain wasn't so intense insulated through Robert or Deborah, but now she had no choice. She exhaled as her hand slid down to the pocket of her blue and white apron, pulled out the phone, and looked down to the keypad. Within seconds, the call was ringing through.

"Williams Investment Bank, how may I direct your call?"

John's office was located high above Broad Street, overlooking the financial district on the left and the harbor on the right. Straight ahead, the Statue of Liberty stood on an island with her torch raised, and her symbolic image reflected off the glass of John's office window. The placement of Williams Investment Bank on the twenty-eighth floor, high above Wall Street, was no mistake. His field of vision always looked down, never up, and mediocrity remained below him as he traveled to his home.

Williams's Bell-429 was parked on a helicopter pad, high above Manhattan, three stories above his office. When John gave the word, his pilot cranked up the rotors, secured his boss inside and shuttled him off to Greenwich, Connecticut. The working Manhattan herds squeezed onto trains, fought the stop and go traffic on the Merritt Parkway and I-95, or rode the subway underground. John Williams flew the exclusive highway reserved only for the powerful and the rich—twenty-five hundred feet off the ground. It was a quick fifteen minute commute, and it ended in a place that few could imagine or ever afford.

Rolling Hills Estate was fifteen acres of manicured landscape hidden within the affluence of the Manhattan suburbs. It boasted a three-thousand square-foot horse barn built of granite and slate. Its twelve-thousand square foot mansion sat on a ridge and was securely enclosed in miles of stone and mortar with two massive two-inch thick iron gates. From the air, its presence cut through the night sky like an island in the middle of the Pacific. The grounds were lit up by an array of lighting, which shot up sixty feet into the heart of the mighty red oaks, outlined the rhododendron bushes, and illuminated the front façade of the mansion—a statement to the rest of the world John Williams lived here. When the Bell-429 landed on its concrete pad, a servant would open the door, and the short walk to the side entrance took all of twenty-five steps. It was one of the few pieces of hallowed ground that was worthy of John Williams's feet.

It was not a surprise, though, the Williams family had never walked the pristine grounds of Rolling Hills Estate, or had an invitation into the sprawling mansion—not even once. Only the little people who worked the estate were allowed inside. It was a sanctuary, John had explained to his secretary, isolated from the vile touch of the useless masses and the repulsive world in which they lived.

His private life, which only a few reticent servants had exposure to, commenced the moment he landed inside its walls. Upon his arrival, a hush fell over the estate. Those who worked inside disappeared. His desires were fulfilled to the extreme. The wine cellar was carved out of the massive granite ledge the manor was built upon. It was complete with eighteen thousand bottles of the finest wines and champagnes money could buy. Inside the wine cellar lay an authentic French bistro façade, with a café table in front. It had been dismantled from an eighteenth-century café in a little town called La Moutonne in the south of France. It was his own private restaurant where he dined each night.

As he passed through the attended side door, the servant neither spoke nor looked in his direction. It was as if a ghost had entered the manor, and he couldn't be seen or heard.

He climbed the massive stone staircase to his second floor bedroom and changed into his evening attire: black silk shirt, black silk pants, and black leather slippers (custom made of course). He rode the elevator, which was located in his second floor bedroom, to the east room, as he called it. The servant served him his Crown Royal on the rocks in front of the medieval fireplace that already had been stoked into a small flaming bonfire. He sat in the large black leather arm chair, pulled open his book, and read.

A short time later he rode the elevator, again, and descended down into his multi-million dollar playground—the underground French bistro with a table for one.

The round table parked in front of the wood-paneled café façade had a goblet half filled with '55 Lafite. A dim street lantern, hanging from a wrought iron arm above the store front window, spilled a soft yellow glow onto the marble table top. John read as he sat with his book in his right hand which was held out to capture the light. His left arm rose in the air, as he mimicked the words in the book. "Alas, Peter, go!"

His open hand swirled in the air and cast a dancing shadow onto the planked wooden floor. A candle flickered, as his eyes consumed each word like a starving child's first meal after two hungry days on the street. Each phrase rolled from his lips with an ease and comfort, as if the character stood beside him and spoke. When the wine glass rose to his mouth, his eyes never turned from the page. He was alone in his dimly lit cavern, sitting in front of a pretend French bistro, and all else around him had ceased to exist.

When the servant brought the rack of lamb, garlic mashed potatoes, and gorgonzola salad, John slid the book to one side. He held it off the table in his right hand and remained undisturbed by the man in the tailcoat and white gloves. The man knew not to speak. The servant arranged the silver, straightened the plate, poured the Lafite, and then walked toward the stairs. "I'm with you, Peter, by God I'm with you!" echoed up the stairwell as the servant climbed the curved stone steps. John let out a hardy yelp, and the heavy oak planked door to the cavern closed with a solid thud. John Williams was not to be disturbed.

Nora's head fell into her hands and she began to cry. Softly at first, but then the tears came with such force a river formed under her eyes and ran down her cheek. "Why won't he speak to me?" She asked. "What am I going to do?"

CHAPTER 14

Nora was working with Robert on his morning therapy when Sheriff Porter of the Schaums Head Police called. He was the only cop left on the island after the summer season ended. He didn't waste any time.

"Mrs. Williams?"

"Yes?"

"This is Sheriff Porter out at Schaums Head."

"Yes, Sheriff?"

"I was out to Crab Point early this morning, and I'm afraid there's been a break in."

"Oh dear."

"I'll need you to come out and file a report. We need to do an inventory of what was taken. Sorry for the inconvenience, Mrs. Williams, but I'll need that done sooner than later."

"Oh, I can't come out...my husband...ah."

"Yes, I'm sorry to hear about Mr. Williams, ma' am, but we need someone that knows the place."

"Perhaps my daughter, I'll give her a call."

"That would be fine, Mrs. Williams."

"I'll call her and see if she can go out today."

"Thank you, ma' am. She'll need to call me when she arrives; I'll need to meet her out at the house."

"Yes, of course."

She took down Sheriff Porter's number and hung up the phone. She saw the questions in Robert's eyes and explained what had happened. Nora slid the phone out of the pocket of her flowered apron and dialed her daughter's number. She looked out toward the bird feeder as she listened to it ring. On the third chime, Deborah cut in.

"Hello," she said. "What is it, Mother...I can't...because I'm supposed to pick up Ramone's dry cleaning and...no...I said...look, Mother you know how I feel about Crab Point. I...all right...I said all right. Mother, back off!" Deborah hung up the phone.

She caught the two-thirty ferry out to Schaums Head. She wrapped the long wool coat around her body as she leaned on the rail and searched the wake beginning to swell behind the boat. The house hadn't seen a visitor after September in eight years. It was not built to support winter. The walls had no insulation, the windows were single pane, the doors lacked weather stripping and only the downstairs had heat. But she planned on staying in town at Jessup's Inn, not out to the secluded cape—not alone.

The summer John refused to spend his vacation on Schaums Head, everything changed for Deborah. The small cape didn't feel the same to her when she arrived. She couldn't explain why, but she didn't like being out there anymore. It scared her. It started back in Kruger Falls. She detested the arguments between John and her father. The closer it got to their summer vacation the more intense the fighting became. Sometimes she'd go to her room and put her head under her pillow just so she couldn't hear the yelling. She was only seven years old and the turmoil tore her apart. When John went off to sleep-away camp kicking and screaming, it made her sick and empty inside. After that, Crab Point never seemed the same.

When they arrived at the house that summer, without John, she was afraid to leave her parents' side. Deborah slept in their bedroom the entire two and a half months. Her parents understood and they didn't try to force her back to her bedroom.

"After all," her mother would say to her father, "she's only seven years old. She's probably afraid the family is breaking up, Robert. She doesn't understand about John not being here, and I think she's scared and misses him too."

Those memories hadn't surfaced for Deborah since that summer of '74. She had repressed them and now having those thoughts fresh in her mind made her shiver. She pulled the lapels of her coat upward until they blanketed her cheeks and gazed up to the squawking sea gull above the bow. Her long, auburn hair brushed her face in the breeze, and she held it back with her hand, threw the smoke over the rail, and stepped back inside the cabin.

The ticket window, unlike summer, was empty. The ferry line pulled back to one run a day after Labor Day.

Only two hundred sixty-five braved the winter on Schaums Head. That group included one Episcopalian minister and the retired Dr. Bruss. Not many of the hard-core islanders ventured to the main land much. So the ferry was empty except for the two deck hands, the lady at the ticket counter, and a local she didn't recognize. She paid the fare and walked to the front of the boat.

Deborah settled at the bar in the bow of the boat and watched the empty landscape as it rolled by. The bar tender doubled as a deck hand, so she wasn't bothered with talk. The first beer slid down easy so she ordered a second. Halfway into the second the landscape of Schaums Head appeared. She felt her body tense up accompanied by a small bout of panic.

The realization had sank in that the ferry she was on was the only ferry of the day. The boat was docked for the night in Saggart's Harbor and the next run wasn't until tomorrow morning. She squeezed the mug, raised it to her lips, and drank half the beer in the glass. She placed the mug back onto the wooden bar top and watched as the island approached. The warm glow of the buzz had taken hold of her brain. It had numbed part of her panic. She looked away from the horizon and took another swallow.

She lit a smoke and scanned the locked glass door behind the bar. The bottle of tequila looked inviting, but she decided against a shot. She had to meet with Sheriff Porter. About five minutes from the dock, she went to her car and waited for the bow door to rise. When it did her body stiffened and her throat tightened. She started the car and rolled it forward. The tires thumped as they cleared the ramp, and she stopped in the empty paved parking lot. Her gaze swept over the deserted town.

It had been taken over by a few screeching sea gulls, some papers scampering across the pavement, and a steady northeast breeze twitching the barren tree branches. She looked across the street. Jessup's Inn looked dark and shut down. *Shit!*

Deborah pulled up to the front porch. She got out and read the note attached to the front door. "Gone to the mainland for two weeks," it said, "be back the second week of November."

She stumbled back to the car with her hands in her coat pocket and a look of terror in her clouded brown eyes.

The Inn disappeared as she took a left on Sea Breeze, drove two blocks, and turned left into Granger's Market. She parked in one of the vacant spots in front. As she stood outside the car, she buttoned her coat and lifted the lapels on the collar. Deborah pressed the button on the fob to lock the doors and slipped her hands in her pockets. The left double door slid open, and she went inside.

The store had a skeleton crew, and Stewart Granger, who sat in his raised office to the right of the registers, waved. Helen Granger, behind the deli counter, put together a chicken salad sandwich. They chatted as she did, but Deborah didn't feel much like talking. She pulled a jug of Chardonnay from the wine shelf, half turned toward the isle to the register, reversed her direction, and grabbed a second jug. She tucked it under her arm and ambled over to check out. The old man smiled as she approached. "Let me have two packs of Marlboros," she said. Then she swiped her card and left.

When she arrived at the house, she sat in the car and stared at the brown clapboard cape. The red shutters her dad had clamped shut covered the glass windows. The house looked like it belonged in a ghost town, in the desert, and the abandoned look made her insides quiver. She snapped the Bic, and the flame torched the end of the cigarette hanging from her mouth. Soon enough the sun would fade and Woodmans Cove would fall into night. That was the thought in Deborah's head as she opened the car door and got out.

The sound of car tires crunched and slapped the packed sand. It brought her back from her Stephen King moment, and she swiveled her head toward the noise. Sheriff Porter pulled up behind her and stopped the car. He stepped out, put on his black campaign hat that said Schaums Head Police on the front and nodded.

"I'm Sheriff Porter," he said. "You must be Deborah."

She acknowledged that she was, shook his hand, and they stepped onto the porch. Deborah freed two of the window blinds from their hold backs and left the rest of them locked. The security appealed to her. Sheriff Porter informed her that the back door had been breached, so they walked around to the back of the house and went inside. There wasn't anything to steal except furniture, lamps, inexpensive prints, and a few old family photographs. Her parents left nothing of value in the house.

Deborah and Sheriff Porter climbed the wooden staircase to the second floor and checked the two bedrooms first.

"The dressers in both bedrooms appear to have been rummaged through," Porter said.

Then they stepped out into the hall and the sheriff pointed. "I thought this odd," he said. "The hatch is ajar. It looks as though someone went into the attic."

Deborah got the ladder from the hall closet and Porter climbed to the fifth rung and pushed the hatch aside. He pulled his Maglite flash light from his belt and searched the space.

"All clear," he said and started to close the cover.

"Leave it, please. I want to check something later."

"Suit yourself."

They continued downstairs and checked the living room, kitchen, bathroom, and utility room. As they did, Deborah studied Porter's .45 caliber Smith and Wesson strapped to the side of his hip. She thought about how much safer she'd feel staying in the house with that.

"Ms. Sanchez...ma' am?"

"Yes, sorry."

"Is there anything missing from the house?"

"No, sir."

"Are you sure?"

"Not that I can tell."

They stopped at the front door.

"More than likely a couple of kids looking for something to steal," he said. "It happens this time of year. Are you going to be all right out here alone, Ms. Sanchez?"

"I don't know."

"Well I'd have you to my house, but the dog is none too friendly. Too bad about the Jessup's being gone. Would you like me to call around and see if I can find you a place to stay?"

She thought that over for a moment and then realized staying with a strange family would put a limit on her drinking. "Thanks anyway, Sheriff, I'll do my best out here."

"It's mighty isolated, Ms. Sanchez. Are you sure?"

"Yes, thank you for asking."

"If you need anything call me. It doesn't matter what time of night."

"Thanks, Sheriff, I'll do that."

She stood on the front porch, smoking a cigarette, and watched the sheriff drive away. As the cruiser disappeared behind a cloud of swirling sand, a chill brushed the back of her neck. She turned and looked to the north, toward the dunes, and studied the barren landscape. It looked empty and cold as daylight turned to twilight. The oak scrub at the base of the mounds twitched in the breeze that swept off Woodmans Cove. She took another draw on the smoke, tossed it over the porch rail and her body froze on the spot in fear. She was out at Crab Point for the night—alone.

CHAPTER 15

Darkness engulfed the isolated cape as Deborah scrambled about the house. She slid the dead bolts closed, checked the sash locks on the windows, and barricaded the doors with the kitchen chairs. She stopped at the kitchen counter and opened the jug of wine. When she tipped the jug and tried to pour the wine into the glass, her hand trembled. The first of the liquid jumped out of the neck and formed a puddle on the brown Formica top. She tipped the jug again. This time the chardonnay made it into the glass. She picked it up and drank the liquid in three continuous swallows. As the empty glass hung in the air, her eyes shot from the door to the windows.

It was the blackness behind the panes of glass that shot terror through her soul. It had been that way most of her life. She snapped her gaze away from the night and moved swiftly into the living room with the jug of wine pressed to her side. The front-door glass was still enclosed by the plywood, and the room felt safer and more secure. She downed two glasses of wine before she summoned the courage to inspect the rest of the house. She intended to make one last pass before she hunkered down in a cordoned off living room for the night.

She climbed to the fourth step of the ladder and stuck her head into the dark hole of the attic. Just inside the opening, to the right, a string hung tied to a nail. She reached in and yanked it, but the string broke. She scanned the darkness and pulled her right leg up into the opening. It landed on the wooden floor. Her right hand reached for the broken string, but it wasn't there. The cord had broken at the first eye hook attached to the rafters about six feet down from where she sat.

She slid on her knees, one in front of the other. The smell of musty dust clung in her nose as her body tingled in fear. She reached up toward the ridge and the rough surface of the unsanded ridge board scraped her skin. Her finger located the eye hook. It was empty, and her body froze.

She turned toward the light behind her and reasoned she had moved too far. If she needed to escape—bolt down the ladder—she'd be caught before she reached the hatch. A sudden noise on the wood in front of her made her heart thump so hard she thought it would blow out of her chest. Her fingers rubbed the surface of the floor in search of the broken cord. The severed string hit her first finger of her left hand. She pulled on it. Then there was a click and the old storage space filled with light.

Her eyes shot from corner to corner until she was sure it was clear, but then a field mouse scrambled for cover and she screamed. She rolled off her knees and onto her back end and sat huddled with her arms around her legs. Her body trembled, and she started to cry.

She crawled until she reached the opening, and she slung her legs around and down through the open hatch. As she turned her body, and placed her feet on the ladder, she noticed a box to the right. She detected a path in the dust behind the carton where the box had slid toward the hatch. It was clear from the track that the trail was recent. The top flaps had been ripped open. Printed on the side in blue magic maker were the names John and Deborah. She dragged the box down the ladder and placed it on the floor to the right. Then she looked down the hall both ways before ascending back up and reattaching the string and turning out the light. She slid the cover closed, carried the box down to the living room, and fell backward onto the couch.

She drank another glass of wine before she could finish her work. Then Deborah went back upstairs, checked the bedrooms, and bolted back down the stairs. She checked the front and back door one last time, brought the last of the supplies from the kitchen to the living room, rechecked the sash locks and pushed the tall hutch in the kitchen across the opening. No one could get to her without making a tremendous noise, waking her if she dozed off.

The fire in the fieldstone fireplace set a warm and comfortable tone, but it didn't matter to Deborah. She watched as the light from the flames struck shadows that moved throughout the room. The box from the attic sat on the coffee table in front of her. She drank her wine, stared at the box, and thought back to what the sheriff had said. Sheriff Porter had pointed out it appeared someone had gone into the attic—but why? She looked back down at the box and for the moment curiosity had trumped her fear.

When the flaps of the cardboard box flipped open, it revealed a hand-written note that sat on top of objects wrapped in newspaper. Without pulling the paper out, she read the words.

John age nine, Deborah age seven
The sun will shine once more

The handwriting was her mother's. She recognized the neatness of the lines and sharp penmanship of the printed letters. She reached into the box and pulled out the paper and laid it on the table before extracting one of the objects wrapped in newspaper. Her unwrapping revealed a blue plastic sand shovel. She put it on the table. The next item was a pail. Inside the pail were plastic molds to make imprints in the sand. She had no recollection of the objects. The container held a number of beach toys that she placed on the table. She opened the last two items in the box: two squirt guns; one blue, one pink. Her eyes began to water as she held them in her hand.

The toy guns had jolted her memory. She thought back to the warm summer nights on the back porch. Her mom and dad sipped coffee as she looked over the railing for John. He hid in the dune grasses as she searched him out. Her mom and dad gave clues as she moved from rail to rail.

"Warmer," her mother would say.

"Colder," her father whispered.

Suddenly, when she had located the hottest of hot and turned her head to search the Indian grass, a cool stream of water bounced off the back of her neck. Then another soaked her shirt from behind.

She pictured John as he rose proudly from his cover, slipped the gun inside the waist band of his bathing suit, and strutted up the porch stairs. He dropped into a chair without saying a word as he sat smiling next to his parents.

An ember in the fireplace popped, and Deborah jumped. The wine from the glass spilled onto her lap. The glowing ember sat on the stone hearth. The loud sound had snapped her back into her looming nightmare. She stood up and with her cigarette pack brushed the red hot piece of oak back into the fire box. Then Deborah sat at the fireplace and lit a smoke. Her body felt like it was on fire. She looked at her watch, half past nine.

By ten-thirty, the second bottle had lost its cork. The breeze had picked up. Sand powdered the front porch, sounding like little animals scratching at the wood. With each gust of wind, one of the unsecured shutters banged against the side of the house. When another loud pop sounded from the fire, she thought she had peed in her pants. As she sat on the hearth, she heard the weather vane with the copper crab atop the cupola creak as it moved in the breeze. She took a long draw on her smoke and huddled closer to the warmth of the fire.

Her bladder needed relief, but she was not leaving the safety of the fortified room. God knows, she thought, what hid in the bath tub behind the sea shell shower curtain waiting for her to sit on the throne. She eyed the old plastic bait bucket she had brought from the utility room and a roll of toilet paper next to it. It was crude, but it would work.

The shutter slammed again, and her bladder almost broke. She eyed the bucket as she squirmed on the couch. *Enough!* As the sound of water collected in the bucket, she looked at her watch—twelve-fifteen. Her chin fell down to her chest.

She flopped back onto the couch and huddled in a ball next to the arm under the drift wood lamp. Visibly shaking, smoking a Marlboro, she held her legs tight to her chest. The weather vane creaked, the shutter slammed, and the wind blew like the howl of a ghost. She felt herself tremble. *Stop it God damn it, stop it.* A big gust of wind blasted the front door.

"Shut the fuck up," she yelled. The shutter slammed the house and she collapsed on the couch. She guzzled the wine in her glass. It was time to get help; she knew that now. She was out of control. She sat huddled in a tight ball, rocking back and forth as she spoke out loud.

"I'll get help. I swear as soon as I get back; I'll get help. Let me get through this night, and I swear I'll get help. If there is a God, please let me get through this night!"

At the first sign of light, Deborah sat on the porch with a cup of coffee and a heavy wool blanket wrapped around her back. Black encircled her eyes, red bloodshot veins around her pupils, and her arms and neck were cramped from the tension. Her body was limp and washed out. She slouched against the wall of the cottage, lit up a smoke, reached down beside her and picked up her silver flask. She poured the vodka into the coffee and then some into her mouth. She swallowed. *It's a beautiful Crab Point morning and now everything will be all right.*

CHAPTER 16

Hans Janssen got his first break in the case. Detective Stump, the original lead investigator on the McCobb case, had a partner named Herman Steinberger. Steinberger was still alive—eighty-two years alive—and Janssen tracked him down to an address in St. Augustine, Florida. After three attempts to contact him, he finally connected on the fourth. To Janssen's relief, he was still coherent and seemed to have most of his faculties. They talked for almost an hour.

Steinberger had confirmed what it said in the file. There were two lead suspects and Robert Williams was not one of them. Justin Blanchard was the first, and a homeless schizophrenic named Harvey Zinc was the second. He said the killing looked too professional to be Zinc's work, and both he and Stump concentrated on Blanchard. Blanchard had a military record—dishonorable discharge—and none of his alibis stood up. They hauled him in twice for interrogation, but the man had street sense and they got nothing from him. Then Steinberger paused a minute, and when he started back up, Janssen got his first solid lead.

"You might want to look into a loser named Barton La Barge. He and Blanchard had ties. We heard they worked together for a while. When Blanchard did time in New York, the sign-in logs had La Barge clocked in on visiting days once a month. A few years later, La Barge was convicted of kidnapping and got sentenced to life. Attica I think. Last I heard, he was still alive in the big house."

"You think he knows something?" Janssen asked.

"Maybe."

"What makes you think he'll talk?"

"Blanchard's dead. Both of them didn't spare words when bragging about a crime they'd committed. That's how Blanchard got caught. He told some car thief in a holding tank about the fraud he'd committed—called it the easiest catch he ever made. Yeah, I figure if La Barge knows anything he'd be the first to chirp. Sorta like having a notch on a gunfighter's peacemaker, if you know what I mean. Your standing amongst the bad boys goes up with what and who you knew and what you did."

"What was your take on Blanchard?"

"I think he did it."

"Why didn't you nail him?"

"The evidence wouldn't have stood up, too thin, and Blanchard knew it."

"What was the motive?"

"Don't know, but we think it was a hit. Too clean for anything else."

Fifty-five minutes later Janssen said thanks and hung up. He went right to work in his little electronics lab and pulled up an inmate search for the State of New York. "Just as Steinberger had said," he mumbled, "alive and behind bars." He decided to pay Mr. La Barge a visit.

Shuttled to the visiting center from the parking lot, Janssen registered according to his position in line—number four. The guards took the first five visitors to the prison entrance, where they waited while a guard called the corresponding inmate. Then they announced La Barge's name, and Janssen removed his shoes, belt, emptied his pockets, and walked through a metal detector. On the other side, he collected his things, like at the airport, and put his belongings back on. As he crossed the yard to the next set of doors, he thought of Hank Steffler in Attica for life without the possibility of parole. He'd rather not run into Hank. Janssen had busted him and testified against him in court, which led to his present vocation—stamping license plates for the wonderful drivers of the state of New York.

He arrived at the door safely and handed the guard the piece of paper with La Barge's name on it. The guard escorted him to his assigned table—a contact visit, no walls or phones. Janssen sat at the table. A few minutes later La Barge walked through the door. He sat down.

Janssen studied La Barge from across the table. His stocky, short frame was slouched low in the chair. His chest barely even with the table. His mouth cocked downward on the right side. A scar decorated the right side of his neck, and his eyes remained half closed. His straight hair hung over his forehead, ears, and collar of his state-issued prison shirt. When he talked, he stared away from Janssen, and squirmed in his chair, but like Steinberger had said, he went off like a politician on the campaign trail.

"Justin Blanchard?" Janssen asked.

"We did some things, but it never got hung on us."

"What about a woman named Tristan McCobb?"

He scanned the room, and then La Barge pulled out a pack of smokes, slipped one out, and lit it up. He took a long draw and cocked his head up toward the ceiling and exhaled. He played with the cigarette box, twirling it around with his two hands, as the cigarette hung from his lips.

"What about her?"

"Did you ever hear the name?"

"I had nothing to do with that."

"Would you tell me if you did?"

"I'm a lifer…what are you going to do, keep me here after I'm stiff? I could give a rat's ass what anyone knows." He checked out the room again, took a draw on the smoke, blew half the smoke upward and continued. "You go to the cops, I'll deny I ever told you anything, got it?"

"Understood."

He sucked on the cigarette and the tip went red; then he pulled it out of his mouth with his right hand and looked up toward the ceiling again, and exhaled.

"What's it to you?"

"I'm working for some people, and her name came up."

"Robert Williams?"

Janssen's didn't flinch, Cop 101 Homicide School, and without so much as a breath, he said, "Go on."

"After all these years looks like someone pulled a ghost out of a casket. What's it been, forty?"

"Forty-four."

La Barge's head turned toward the lady being escorted to the table next to them. He leaned in still gawking at the woman in tight jeans and skin tight t-shirt.

"Forty-four, shit, we was young then."

"You and Blanchard were buddies, right? You help him on that one?"

La Barge snapped. "Blanchard was a psycho. He didn't have no friends."

"I thought you two did some things together?"

"We did things, but I never turned my back on that prick. Stories were out on the street about things he did in Nam. You didn't fuck with Blanchard. He was trained proper and legal to kill, and from what I heard, he enjoyed it."

"Blanchard's dead you know."

"I heard," La Barge said as he crushed his cigarette in the paper tray.

"Did he ever talk to you about McCobb?"

"He didn't mention any names, but I figured that's who it was. It was everywhere you looked. Young attractive girl gets whacked in the park; the cops wanted that one, bad."

"What'd he tell you?"

La Barge slid another smoke from the pack and lit it up before dropping his hands to the top of the table.

"He told me he had a job."

"And?"

"That he was hired by this goon—twelve hundred, I think he said—and that someone with money wanted her stiff. No one paid twelve hundred in them days, unless it was big, and they wanted it done right. Blanchard was a pro from what I heard. The rumor was McCobb had been involved with the governor. He was up for re-election, and she was gonna talk to the press unless she got paid off. I guess twelve hundred was cheaper than what McCobb was asking. I never heard that part from Blanchard. That was the street talking."

"The governor had her hit?"

"That's what I heard."

"Go on."

La Barge worked on his smoke for a minute and let his brain catch up. He rubbed his nose with his first finger and then took another draw.

"You want something, I want something."

"What's that?"

"Ten cartons of smokes."

"Ok, ten."

"You send them next week."

"Agreed."

"I have your word?"

"You tell me what I want to know, and you have my word."

"Blanchard was a mechanic. He learned it in Special Forces he said. One swipe, bang boom, in and out, the mark never knew what was coming. That's where Williams comes in."

"How's that?"

"I told you Blanchard was good."

"Go on."

"Blanchard stalked her waiting for the right time. She was in the park with this guy arguing. People saw it, witnesses at the right time, right place. The guy yelling stomped off, and when she headed down the path, bang—two seconds—he was in and out, and it was done."

"So how does Williams fit in?"

"Blanchard wasn't just good. He was smart."

The guard came over and said they had five minutes left. La Barge crushed his butt in the tray.

"Blanchard knew the cops were close. Some snitch figured it was Blanchard's work and gave up his name. So Blanchard worked a solution. He offered me a hundred bucks to punch a guy out. He didn't give his name. One right hook for a hundred bucks; I told him he was crazy. The catch was I had to wear a surgical glove on my other hand and after the man was down swipe some of his blood.

"I caught him coming out of Tommy's bar in the Bronx one night so I bumped into him, said you son of a bitch, and cold cocked him right in the nose. I busted it good. When he was down, I put my hand over his mouth like I was trying to stop him from calling for help. The blood from his nose went onto the glove, and I ran away. As I ran, I turned the glove inside out and sealed it in an air tight jar. I gave it to Blanchard and collected my hundred bucks."

"What's that got to do with McCobb?"

"The guy's nose I pancaked was Robert Williams."

"What did Blanchard want with the blood?"

"He put it on the handle of the army issue combat knife that had that lady's blood all over it. If the cops closed in on him, some stranger would have found the murder weapon, and Williams would have been charged."

"The cops wouldn't have bought that."

"That wasn't Blanchard's problem, was it?"

"How'd they explain him sitting there, without the knife, holding the girl?"

"He panicked, ran off, threw the knife down, and then came back. He went back later and put it in a plastic bag and hid it someplace. A stranger finds it and bang, boom, he's convicted of murder."

"What's a guy like Williams doing carrying a combat knife?"

"He'd been mugged in the park before...how the hell should I know? All that matters is Blanchard's off the hook. Why do you think Blanchard was never copped for a hit? That wasn't his first you know. He always covered his tracks."

"So what happened to the knife?"

"Time's up," the guard said, "Let's go, La Barge."

"Got me."

La Barge picked up his pack of smokes, stood up, and started to walk away. He stopped and turned close to the door and mouthed something. Janssen read his lips.

"Don't forget the smokes."

CHAPTER 17

The fingers on Robert's right hand moved more noticeably than before. Sharon Labronski, a physical therapist for eighteen years, had pushed him hard the past two weeks. Her technique proved invaluable to Robert's progress. Her combined efforts of skill and technology (a cutting-edge machine called Nerve Help) resulted in Robert standing independently on his walker and moving forward a few steps. Nora was thrilled.

When the transport van arrived at Robert's house, Deborah came out to help with her father. Nora had stopped at the deli to buy lunch meat and hadn't returned home yet. Deborah grabbed the handles of the wheelchair and pushed her father down the flagstone walk, up the wooden ramp, and into the house. She parked the chair in front of the kitchen table. Robert, exhausted, fell asleep.

Deborah smoked a cigarette outside the kitchen door while she waited for her mother. As she did, she thought about Crab Point. But she wasn't focused on the panic attacks, being scared to death of the dark, or the abundance of alcohol she consumed. Any intentions of getting help evaporated with the first signs of light. In her mind, Deborah had a rationalization or an excuse for every destructive episode that had occurred in her life. With such fervor, she had become blind to her own psychotic conviction.

So as she drew on the smoke, she thought about the box of toys, and two questions popped into her head. Why had her mother saved them and what was the meaning of her hand-written note?

They had lunch at the kitchen table. As Nora fed Robert, she told Deborah that Hans Janssen wanted to meet with them late that afternoon. He had said it was important and that he had new information to share. She got no response from her daughter.

"Deborah, did you hear what I said?"

"Yeah, what time?"

"Mr. Janssen said four-thirty."

Deborah shook her head with a puzzled look on her face. "Mother..."

"Yes?"

"Why did you save that box of toys in the attic?"

"What box is that, dear?"

"The box in the attic out at Crab Point. The one that has John and Deborah written on the side."

"I didn't. Your dad put them away."

"What do you mean put them away?"

"Well, the summer John went away to sleep-away camp, your father was not himself. The first thing he did when he arrived at the house was to gather those toys up and throw them into a box. He put them into the attic and said he didn't want to see them again. He was very upset about John. Crab Point meant the world to your dad. He bought the house so you and John would have a wonderful place to spend your summers. I think it broke his heart when John refused to go back out. So much so, he never even took the crab traps out of the shed that year."

"But you wrote the note inside."

"I did. I wrote the note and your names on the side of the box and then sealed it with tape."

"What did it mean?"

"What's that?"

"John, age nine, Deborah, age seven. The sun will shine once more."

"Well…I guess…I guess it meant if you or John had children they would play with them in the sand, like you and John did. They'd have their day once more."

"Really, Mother?"

"Oh yes, dear, but you haven't a child, and John's not even married."

"Has he called you back?"

"Who's that?"

"Your son…John."

"You dumb shit, Kursman, you screw this up and your life won't be worth spit. I'll financially destroy you. Get your sorry ass on the phone with Cochran, Kursman, and make this happen—now! Martha, get me Hansfetal. Jesus Christ what a lame son of a bitch."

The Bombardier was forty-thousand feet over Nebraska when the deal began to fall apart. The biggest payday of his life was about to slip through his hands, because Kursman had leaked that Hansfetal was going to sell off half the company to some Arabs in Dubai. A twelve-billion dollar takeover of the largest satellite company in the world, and John Williams was not about to let this one get away.

"Martha, where's Hansfetal?"

"He's in a meeting, Mr. Williams."

"I don't give a shit if he's on his way to the space station. You tell Hansfetal I want to talk to him, now! What time is it in Germany?"

"It's 4:44 in the afternoon, Mr. Williams."

"Shit, if he leaves for the day I'll never get a hold of him. Martha, get Hansfetal on the God damn phone."

"He's on, Mr. Williams."

"Karl, sorry to bother you…"

"What the hell's the problem, Williams?" he said in a thick German accent. "I was in an important meeting."

"Karl, we've got a glitch in the Hastings's satellite deal. It appears Cochran's got the idea you're going to bust up the company for parts. He says he built the deal on keeping it whole with McNeal running the American side."

"Williams, you get this deal done. I don't care what you tell Cochran. As for the American side, the only thing left for McNeal to run after I'm through will be the New York City Marathon. Get it done, Williams, and I don't care how."

"Yes, sir. Karl, Karl?—shit—Martha, get me Kursman…Jesus Christ…Martha, Kursman."

"He's on the line, sir."

"Kursman, I just got off the phone with Hansfetal. I don't know where you got your information, Kursman, but you're blowing smoke up the old man's ass. Now you listen to me. I have Hansfetal's personal guarantee he has no intention of breaking apart Hastings's Satellite. So you get off your ass and do whatever it takes to get this deal back on track. Hansfetal is ready to sue your ass six ways to Sunday, and I'm right behind him."

"Mr. Williams."

"What is it, Martha!"

"Fred Atkins is on the line."

"I'm in a meeting."

"Sir, this is the fourth time he's called today. He said he wasn't taking no for an answer."

"Jesus, we're going to be landing in twenty minutes. All right put him through. Hi, Fred, how's your golf game?"

"To hell with my golf game, Williams, you son of a bitch. You gave me your word my son-in-law would remain with the company. They twisted the contract, backpedaled, and threw him out. Douglas said you knew all along."

"Relax, Fred, you're seven hundred and fifty million richer with more time to work on your golf game. Besides, the deal's done. You signed off on it. Between the stock and the contract buyout, your son-in-law is set for life. That's just how it goes, Fred."

"You son of a bitch, I thought I could trust you."

"Just business, Fred."

"Business is an honorable profession, Williams. You do the devil's work."

"Martha, no more calls."

"Mr. Williams, your mother has called twice. She's on the line on hold."

"For Christ's sake, Martha, I have more important things on my plate."

The Bombardier hit the Cheyenne tarmac at 12:05 p.m. The realtor met John at the jet's steps and escorted him to an Eco-Star EC-130, about thirty yards to the left. Pamela Thurston was dressed to kill. She was the most successful seller of prime real estate of a thousand acres or more in the state of Wyoming, and she had John Williams on board. At thirty-six, Thurston was the hottest real estate agent west of Cheyenne. She had blonde hair, blue eyes, a face that would stop traffic, and a body sculpted to snap heads. And she used every asset to assist in her sales.

She reached down to remove the detail sheets of the listed properties from her satchel utilizing her first selling technique, her half-open blouse. She took ample time to locate and remove the necessary papers and shook her head side to side as she did. The rotors took less time to reach full propulsion than Thurston's inaugural sales pitch. And, John Williams, who sat across from her, witnessed a show reserved only for clients with ten-figure bank accounts and a thirst for the open range. As the helicopter lifted off, John Williams buckled in and prepared to buy his first Wyoming spread. And how much he was willing to spend was never discussed.

Deborah sat across from Nora, who was shaking her head.

"I told you, Mother, he's not going to help."

"Nonsense, Deborah, he's our son. He'll help."

"What did his secretary say?"

"She said he had two very important clients on board, and he was not to be disturbed."

"I'll bet."

CHAPTER 18

They waited until five forty-five and decided Janssen was a no show. Deborah had just about finished her second pre-dinner cocktail. Ramone sat next to her on the couch hoping she wouldn't pour a third. Her belligerence had escalated with each pass of her glass. It had been mostly in the form of non-verbal gestures with an occasional puff of air from her lips. As she drained the last sip of Jack Daniels in her glass, she stood, looked to her husband and then to her mother, and let her feelings be known.

"I can't believe Janssen hasn't even called," she said.

No one responded.

"I knew he'd pull something like this after he got a big enough check. That's probably why he got thrown off the force."

"He wasn't thrown off the force, Deborah. He quit," Ramone said.

"Why are you defending him, Ramone, because he's your friend? He's got ten thousand of my mother's money and he didn't even call."

"Calm down, Deborah. I'm sure there's a good explanation for his not showing up."

"Yes, dear, I'm sure Mr. Janssen just got busy working the case and lost track of time. He'll show up," Nora said, "you'll see."

"Well to hell with this. If I'm hostage to Hans Janssen, I sure as hell will have another drink."

"Deborah, we have to go," Ramone said. "We'll lose our reservation."

Ramone watched as his wife stomped off to the kitchen unconcerned about reservations, the restaurant, or Janssen's rude no-show. He knew exactly where she was headed. He pictured it in his head. She'd pour three more fingers of Jack and then go out back for a smoke. He heard the kitchen door slam from the living room, confirming his concern and he now dreaded the idea of going out to dinner. He had seen her like this before and each episode seemed to get worse.

A few years back, Ramone had been invited to a Christmas party at the superintendent of schools house. He knew Deborah had been to her doctors that day for her routine physical, and from the moment she came home, her behavior seemed odd to him. By the middle of the day, he thought he smelled alcohol on her breath. Prior to the party, even though Ramone protested, she had two very strong drinks. One hour into the party, he was horrified as she became a stumbling drunk. Their exit was quite the scene.

Since her return from Schaums Head that morning, Ramone was getting the same vibes, and he was ready to cancel their evening out. A dinner date they had made last week to celebrate their anniversary had now lost its meaning. It was certain to turn into a drunken debacle. Ramone had no doubt. He took a breath and exhaled.

He brought his mind back from his impending disaster and looked to Nora sitting in the chair. "Have you had any luck with John, Nora?" he asked.

Her head was pointed toward the floor. She lifted it up and turned to her son-in-law. "What's that, Ramone?"

"I asked if you'd had any luck with John."

"He hasn't returned my calls."

"I see."

Ramone pulled out his Blackberry from his sports coat pocket. He examined his calendar for the morning. Finally, the kitchen door slammed again.

"Well, Nora, we must be getting on," Ramone said. "I wouldn't be surprised if Hans calls within the hour."

Nora shook her head to acknowledge the comment.

"Well I think it's damn inconsiderate," Deborah said as she entered the room. "When I see him again, I'll tell him just that. All the damn money you're paying him. Let's go Ramone; we've waited long enough."

Ramone hustled his wife into the car. He suggested they cancel, but Deborah was adamant they go. When they arrived at Sarley's Steak House, they were informed they had lost their table because they were thirty minutes late. Deborah headed straight to the bar and ordered a martini. She inhaled the vodka and popped the olive in her mouth. Then she raised her hand.

"Bartender," she said.

But before she could order a second Martini, the maître d' informed them their table was ready. Ramone dragged his wife away and asked for some bread, hoping to get something into her stomach other than alcohol. She became angry and irate.

"What are you staring at, Ramone?"

"Deb, please, keep your voice down."

"Don't tell me what to do—Jesus talking loud—I'll give you loud."

"Ok, ok, let's order."

"You're so uptight, Ramone. Why don't you lighten up, have a drink for Christ's sake?"

Ramone called the waiter over.

"Yes, sir, are you ready to order?" he asked.

"No, I'm not ready. I'd like another martini!"

"Deb…"

"Shut up, Ramone. The martini, if you please."

"Yes, ma' am."

The waiter hurried off. Ramone leaned across the table.

"One more outburst like that and we're leaving," he said.

Her drink landed on the table, but barely hit the wood before it was back in the air. Ramone felt his stomach land at his feet. He tried to ignore her, and he picked up the menu sitting on the table in front of him. Deborah stuck her finger in the clear liquid and twirled it. Then she jumped up from her seat and told Ramone she was going for a smoke. She grabbed her purse and headed toward the door. Ramone sat alone, sipping his wine and reading the menu. In between the listed entrees, he scanned the room, then studied the menu some more and nervously played with his glass. She returned and sat down.

"Are you ready to order?"

"No, I said I'm having my drink!"

"Deborah, please, have a piece of bread."

"Don't tell me what to do, Ramone. I'll eat when I'm ready."

Ramone gestured to the waiter and when he arrived, Ramone leaned into him.

"I'd like to settle up, please bring the check…wait!" He took out his credit card and handed it to the man. "Just ring it up."

"Very good. I'll be just a minute."

"What did you just do?"

"Nothing, Deb. Finish your drink."

Ramone inconspicuously took inventory of the room while Deborah shoved a large chunk of bread into her mouth. She ripped a second piece from the loaf, and he looked to her and let out a muffled sigh. The waiter placed the tray in front of him as Deborah knocked over her drink.

"Shit," she said out loud as the restaurant suddenly went silent. "Get me another drink…Raaa…Ra…whatever your name is."

"Thank you," Ramone said as he handed the waiter the check. "Let's go, Deb. We're going home."

"I'm not going anywhere until I get my drink."

"Deborah, let's…."

"Shut up, WAITER, HEY WAITER!"

"For God's sake, Deborah, everyone's looking at you."

"WAITER."

"Let's go, Deborah, now!"

She ignored Ramone and kept trying to gesture the waiter, but the scene had taken center stage, and the waiter wanted nothing to do with it. Ramone stared at his wife. She was falling off her chair as she waved violently in the air.

"You can either come quietly with me, or take a cab home. I'm leaving."

He stood up, slid around the table, and lifted her by the arm.

"Come on, you can have a drink at home," he said.

She stood up and stomped out the door. As he exited the restaurant, the whispers broke the silence as the performance ended. Disgusted, Ramone drove home and never removed his eyes from the road.

As Ramone stopped at the garage, Deborah opened the car door and jumped out. She marched straight inside poured a jumbo wine in a water glass, grabbed her cigarettes, and headed to her retreat out back. Ramone made a sandwich and went to bed. He attempted to read, but the sound of the kitchen door repeatedly slamming shut was too upsetting. He thought he heard her say something the last time the door slammed, but he wasn't sure. He took several breaths trying to relieve the knot in his stomach, hoping she'd either pass out or that he'd fall asleep before she arrived upstairs. Finally the noise stopped, and he drifted off to sleep.

It was 4:45 a.m. and Ramone had shaved, dressed, and was ready to head off to school. He put on his suit coat and sneaked down the stairs to the kitchen and poured a second cup of coffee. Then he went into the family room, sat in the chair next to the couch, and stared at his passed-out wife. Her clothes were wrinkled and disheveled, and her legs were tucked up to her chest. The TV was on, but there was only a picture, no sound. He stayed silent for a moment—gathering strength—and took a couple of deep gut clearing breaths.

He tried to wake her by calling her name, but she did not move. He called her name a second and third time. Finally, he put his hand on her arm and shook her as he repeated her name. Her eyes opened, and without moving her body, she glanced around until she saw Ramone in the chair. He took one more long breath and began the speech he had prepared in his head as he had lain in the dark last night.

"Deb, I can't do this anymore."

Her eyes opened wider. She slowly pushed herself upright and leaned against the back of the couch. With a blank stare on her beat up face, she listened without saying a word.

"I feel embarrassed, angry, disgusted, and sickened at what you've done to yourself, but most of all, truly sad. For some reason it's become unbearable recently. I believe you're trying to drown something inside you, and I have no idea what it is. What I do know is I can't take it anymore. You don't even try to monitor your drinking, and the abuse has become a public spectacle. Unless you get help, I'm leaving. If you decide to get help, I will be there to support you. If you don't, I will be living someplace other than here. I love you, but I will not stand by and watch as you self-destruct, destroy our marriage, and make life intolerable for me."

Ramone stood up with his mug of coffee in his right hand and walked out of the room. Dumbfounded, Deborah watched him leave and listened as the front door closed. With her legs tucked up under her bottom, staring wide eyed through the empty door, she was as void of feelings as she was of thought. She had no idea what Ramone was talking about because she remembered nothing about last night.

CHAPTER 19

Nora fed Robert his breakfast and encouraged him to put the spoon in the bowl by himself. He lifted his hand off the arm of the chair but was unable to go much farther. His hand dropped down onto the cushioned arm with the spoon clutched in his grip. Nora smiled at the progress, and she spooned more hot cereal into his mouth. Robert finished an entire bowl for the first time since his stroke and drank most of his milk. As she brought the dishes to the sink, the phone rang. She picked up on the second ring. When she recognized the strange sounding voice on the line, her legs went limp. She fell back into the chair as she listened.

"Mrs. Williams, do you have the cash?" the voice asked.

"No, we need more time. We don't have that kind of money. We have to go to our son. We need more time."

"Three weeks from today, Mrs. Williams." The phone went dead.

Robert sat in his wheelchair with his eyes on his wife. The phone dropped to her lap. She sat transfixed on the bird bath outside, but she wasn't aware of its presence. After several minutes, Robert tapped his chair with the spoon and the sound snapped her out of her daze. She picked up the phone and dialed Hans Janssen.

After four rings his voice mail clicked on, and in a weak and shallow voice, she left a message. She hung up and dialed Deborah, and just as the answering machine came on, she heard her daughter's voice.

"Mmghh." Deborah cleared her throat. "Hello," she said.

"Deborah, are you all right? You sound awful."

"I'm...aghh...I'm ok," she said.

"I haven't heard a word from Mr. Janssen, and I just received another one of those calls. What should I do...Deborah...are you there?"

"Yes, Mom. Why don't you call the police?"

"No, I'll call John and wait to hear from Mr. Janssen."

"All right, but I can't help today."

"Deborah, are you sick?"

"Maybe I'm coming down with something," she said and hung up.

Deborah felt on the edge of death and in desperate need of a drink. Her head pounded, and she wanted one of her hidden vodka bottles and a couple of good snorts. As she dragged her body up off the couch, she proceeded to get sick on the family room rug. She fell to her knees and vomited again. Then she crawled to the powder room toilet.

She grabbed a cup of coffee, took her smokes and mug outside, and sat on the concrete bench. As her head throbbed behind her bloodshot eyes, Deborah thought about the little piece of paper tucked in her undergarment drawer. It was the one with the name and phone number of the hospital hidden underneath her pile of slips.

On at least three occasions she had held it in her left hand, with the phone in her right hand, and had gotten as far as the first four digits. It had always been her feeble attempt at redemption, not an ultimatum from her spouse. But now, it was a choice between her bottle of Smirnoff or her loving husband Ramone, and the problem was, the jury was still out.

When Hans Janssen left the hospital, his head pounded like it had been squeezed in a vice, and his arm inside the cast felt like a truck had run over it. His car was totaled, they said, and he was lucky to have only a mild concussion and a broken radius of the left arm. The last twenty-four hours drew a blank, and as he stepped into the taxi, he tried to recall where he had been and exactly what had happened. The police said his car had skidded off the road, bounced off a parked pickup truck, and then slammed into a tree. The truck absorbed most of the impact, they told him, and probably saved his life.

Janssen instructed the cab driver to stop at the pharmacy where he picked up his pain pills and a bottle of cold Coke. He slouched onto the dried-out leather of the back seat and fought with the child-proof top. *Ah shit.* The cab continued down Route 4. The inside smelled of stale cigarettes and cheap sweet cologne. It made his throbbing arm and pounding head worse. Janssen clutched the bottle between his knees and tried to release the cap. The brilliant innovation to keep the young generation safe from prescription drugs seemed more like torture than a safety precaution. The struggle climaxed with half the pills flying onto the seat. He scooped two up, popped them into his mouth, and chased them down with a gulp of Coke.

When he arrived home he listened to his messages and called Nora Williams first. He made two more calls, then struggled to remove his clothes, and went to bed. He slept for nearly two hours, until the pain pounded again. Then Janssen popped another two pills, slept three hours more, and woke up feeling like Joe Frazier after the thriller in Manila.

He stumbled downstairs and poured a bowl of Frosted Flakes. He sat at the kitchen table surrounded by two empty beer cans, an empty spam container, and a stack of newspapers on the floor to his right. The view outside the window was worse. There was a backyard that was once groomed grass, but now looked like a bunch of maple seedlings at varied stages of growth. The now topless pain pill bottle sat to his left. Janssen dumped and tossed two vicodin into his mouth. He sloshed the pills down with a slug of the milk from the cereal bowl using his one good hand.

Groggy, dazed, and tired, Janssen stumbled into his high tech office and sat at his desk. He reconstructed the last forty-eight hours with the help of the computer log. It started to come back: the interview with Barton La Barge, the wonderful ambiance of the New York State prison, the drive home, the transference of the recorded La Barge interview into his electronic files. Still fuzzy about the time, he recalled leaving to meet with the Williamses sometime late afternoon. The drive ended in his memory just outside of Turner Falls. He re-read the police report and studied the photos of the scene, and it all started to come back. A car merged—like it was trying to change lanes. The man at the wheel looked directly at him. He made no attempt to pull back. Janssen swerved to avoid him. The pickup trucked approached rapidly and then everything went blank. *Son of a bitch.* he thought, *someone tried to take me out!* He logged out of the computer with his right hand and closed the lid. He stared at the photos of his totaled car and slowly shook his head.

The next morning, Janssen slid out of bed and went right to work. He brought up the file on Justin Blanchard and checked all the cronies he had worked with, whom he hung out with, and whom he did time with—nothing stuck out. But then something flashed on the screen inside the homicide cop's head. It centered around Buck Blanchard, and their conversation on the phone. Buck had lied straight out. Janssen had the remarkable ability to smell the scent of deception, and, right now, Buck Blanchard stank like the dumpster behind the old Seafood house. It was time to pay Big Bad Buck another visit.

Janssen arrived late afternoon to meet with Nora and Ramone. Deborah, Nora told Janssen, was indisposed. Shocked by the bruises on his forehead and the cast on his arm, Nora looked frighten and scared. She stood speechless at the sight. Ramone, however, jumped right in.

"How close are you to finding who is responsible, Hans?"

"I have some leads."

"Look, Hans, we go back a long way, but the Williamses are not made of money. How much more is this going to cost?"

"I can't answer that."

"What can you answer?"

"There is a knife, and according to my source it has both Tristan McCobb's blood, and Mr. Williams's blood on the weapon. Not a good recipe for beating a rap."

"Right, after forty something years, hardly enough to put Robert on trial."

"Evidence is evidence."

"This is crap. The culprit is a bumbling blackmailer who is trying to make a buck on a bluff. A knife indeed. Enough money has been spent already. Let the cards fall where they may."

"Ramone, I have no doubt you are a first-rate high school principle, and if Mrs. Williams would like it to end here, I have no issues with that. But I'm afraid as a criminal investigator you would have a rather short career. The person behind this is not incompetent. Everything I have witnessed to date indicates this is a well-orchestrated, complex scheme to extort five million dollars. Your brother-in-law is a very wealthy man."

"What's your point, Hans?"

"If Mrs. Williams wishes to terminate my services, I have no problem with that. But understand the facts."

"Ramone, he's right," Nora said, "Mr. Janssen, you continue until you determine who's behind all of this. I will pay whatever it takes."

Ramone eyed Janssen.

"What's next?" he asked.

"I have some leads. I'm working them. That's all I can say right now."

CHAPTER 20

Janssen turned the kitchen chair and slipped down into it with his chest against the backrest. He perched his cast on top of the wooden rail and studied Buck from across the table. Buck was fidgeting with his cigarette box as he sucked on the lit smoke hanging from his lips. His eyes shot side to side as he looked down toward the table. It confirmed to Janssen that his question and the intentional silence that followed had made Buck Blanchard uptight. Blanchard looked up, pulled the cigarette from his lips, and leaned into the table.

"I don't know what you're talking 'bout," he said.

Janssen left it alone—again. Buck slouched back in his chair, raised his feet onto the table, and flicked an ash onto the floor.

"Yo, like I said, Buck Blanchard don't know shit."

Janssen shifted in his chair and pulled a piece of paper out of the side pocket of his LL Bean field coat. He unfolded it and studied the sheet with his cast still resting on the top of the chair. His eyes swept to Blanchard and then back to the sheet.

"What the fuck is that Janssen?"

"Like I said on the phone, Buck, you can talk to me, or talk to the man down town. It's up to you."

"Fuck you!"

"Let me tell you a little story, Buck. A man whacks a young lady forty-six years ago because she's threatening to make life difficult for a politician who's up for re-election. Now fast forward. Forty-six years pass and someone claims they have the knife that slit her throat. Better than that, they say it has the blood of two people tattooed onto the handle—the victim and victim's old boyfriend. Bingo, Buck, blackmail, the murder weapon in exchange for a lot of cash. The old boyfriend has two choices, pay up, or spend the rest of his days playing bitch to some young stud in upstate New York. Sitting here, looking at you, Buck, I'd say your hands are all over it."

"You don't know shit."

"Barton La Barge, Buck, the name ring a bell?"

Blanchard turned white and fumbled with the pack as he tried to rip out another smoke. He cupped the flame and nearly burned his hand. He lit it up and then blew the smoke across the table toward Janssen.

"So what's that mean to me?"

Janssen didn't answer. He let Blanchard talk to himself inside his head. The silence broke when someone pounded on the front door.

Buck stood up with his eyes trained on Janssen, walked around the table, and disappeared down the hall. The muffled sound of a disagreement echoed into the kitchen. Janssen zeroed in on the disagreement as the two voices grew louder. Buck's tone became impatient. He told the man to leave. The door slammed. Buck's boots pounded the wooden floor in the hall. Janssen listened as the pronounced strides grew louder. He arrived back in the kitchen and sat back down. One foot landed on the table as he pushed back and pulled out another smoke. He glared at Janssen as he did.

"Trouble, Buck?"

"What the fuck do you want, Janssen?"

"La Barge talked. He told me the whole story, Buck, blood and all. Here's how I see it. Your old man knew he'd never be caught. He saw to that. One day he confided to his son the entire story, even told him where he hid the knife. Then one day there's a car accident and your old man's a stiff. You do a little research and discover the man whose blood is on the knife has a son, worth big bucks. So in your little pea brain of a criminal mind, you figure the knife's got easy street written all over it. All you have to do is go through the old boyfriend to get to the cash."

"Time for you to leave, Janssen."

"What's the matter Buck, did I just stick a cattle prod up your ass?"

"Get out before I cut ya."

"As sure as I'm standing here, Buck, your ass is going to fry."

Janssen turned and started to walk out.

"Hey, dick," Blanchard said, "hope your other arm don't get broke."

On the ride back to White Plains, the rain pounded the car. Inside, Janssen's instincts were lit up like the 2nd Street Bridge before the Kentucky Derby. He had seen punks like Buck Blanchard a million times on the streets. They always thought they were smarter than they were. Buck hadn't the brains or the finesse to pull off something this big, and Janssen knew it. As the wipers slapped back and forth and cleared the deluge of water running down the glass, Hans Janssen wiggled his stiff fingers which bulged from the white cast. He had Buck Blanchard exactly where he wanted him. Now all he had to do was wait.

The roads were drenched. The rain came down in sheets, and in the darkness the headlights skimmed off the puddles on the side of the road. He reached over the wheel with his right hand and grabbed the turn signal and pushed it down. He turned left onto Parkview and drove about a mile and turned right onto Lampard Street. After another half mile, he pulled into Chubby's Delicatessen. The car came to a halt directly in front of the glass store front, which had the name written on the door in red letters. He didn't try to cover the cast when he climbed out of the car. He hoped it would decompose in the pouring rain. He opened the door with his right hand and went inside. Chubby Hobart looked up from behind the glass display.

"Janssen," he said.

"Chubby."

"The usual?"

"It's Friday, Chubby."

"Right," he said.

Liverwurst on rye, with onions, mayonnaise, pickles and a sixteen-ounce can of Budweiser that washed it all down. Janssen called it a picklewursterwiser, and he had one every Friday night for the last three years. It marked the anniversary of his last divorce—it happened on a

Friday. It had evolved into a romantic dinner under the soft glow of the colored lights of his office equipment. Chubby wrapped up the culinary collage in a sheet of white paper, taped it shut, and shoved it into a brown bag with the Bud.

Janssen parked himself in front of the computer screen, unfolded the paper wrapped sandwich, popped open the can of Bud, and logged onto his laptop. He held the sandwich with his one good hand and wrestled it into his mouth. Onions dropped on his lap. He took a large swallow of the Bud and rolled his chair over to the electronic surveillance station. It looked like something out of a World War II bunker—modernized of course with the latest equipment—stacked four high and six wide.

Janssen slipped the head phones on and began pushing dials and turning knobs until the hard drive was set to begin. Just before lift-off, his feet propelled the rolling chair back to home base. He ripped off a mouthful of the picklewursterwiser, slammed a gulp of Bud, and then sent his body flying backward toward the surveillance station. The beer can glided through the air in his right hand as he soared across the room. He slipped the head phones back on, took another drink of Bud, and began the playback off the hard drive.

The first contact was a drug deal. It was obviously cocaine, as signaled by six separate snorts. After a satisfied buzz from the product, the transaction was completed. Then silence. Janssen took the opportunity to sail back to home base. He kept his eye on the dancing lights. It indicated when vocalizations occurred. He managed to shove down two mouthfuls of food before the horizontal lights fired up. He listened as he washed down a mouthful of sandwich with the cold beer. It was a verbal exchange in the distance: two weak voices barely audible probably at the front door. The conversation grew louder as they approached the room. It was another coke deal, two in less than a ten minute span. *Why didn't he just set up a drive-through?*

He paused the hard drive, took a trip to the bathroom, another stop at home base, then back to the pre-recorded show. About an hour into the recording, a phone rang and Janssen perked up. *Bingo!* He turned up the volume and settled in.

"Buck?" the voice asked.

"Yo, this is Buck."

"I told you not to contact me—ever."

"Yeah…well I did."

"What do you want?" the voice said.

"Cod," Buck said.

"What?"

"Money."

"You've been paid the agreed amount. There's no more."

"Listen, bro, you tell your man one hundred thousand."

"You listen to me you little fucking punk, you contact me again and you'll find yourself swimming in concrete flippers."

"No, you listen. Anything happens to me, my bro takes you down. A pig investigator's on to me. He knows I had the knife. I'm leaving. I need the cash."

"You dumb fuck. He's bluffing and you fell for it."

"A hundred kay."

"You get the cash, you disappear—South America."

"What?"

"You heard me. We'll meet in two days, same location."

"Don't cross me."

"Two days, then you'd better be gone."

Janssen put the headphones on the hook and shut the machine down. His hunch had been right. The device he had planted earlier in the day when Buck answered the front door had just confirmed it.

"What a dumb shit," Janssen mumbled as he lifted the can and gulped the last of his Bud.

CHAPTER 21

Deborah clutched her knees and tucked them into her abdomen. The tears ran down her cheeks and landed on the white cotton blanket below. She squeezed her body together into a tight ball, in an attempt to stop the shaking. Sweat formed above her brow, small beads, and she felt flashes of hot and then cold shoot through her veins. She locked her hands around her knees tighter, and her mouth began to water. She jumped from the bed and bolted the seven feet to the bathroom. She fell to the floor in front of the toilet and hugged it with her arms. In a violent heave, her body contorted, and she vomited until there was nothing left.

Eight hours had passed since her last drink and six since she entered detoxification. After repeated waves of vomiting, Deborah Sanchez was sprawled out on the bathroom floor. She had been locked in an eight by ten room at Shelter Mountain Park, and now she wished she was dead.

It had happened fast: one impulsive split-second decision without time to think or reason it out.

"Act now," Dr. Reed had said.

And before she could take a last splash of booze, she found herself trapped in the car with Ramone driving to the thirty-year-old lock up facility for substance abuse. On the entrance gates were inscribed the words "Shelter the soul until you can trust the heart." The loose translation: we're going to lock you up until you sober up—and decide to quit for good. It was an inmate philosophy, instituted by hardened ex-abusers, and there was only one way out.

Deborah screamed through the night, but they were used to that. Most had experienced it themselves. They understood. Deborah begged to be let out, set free.

"I made a mistake," she yelled as she banged her hands violently against the door. "Let me out of here. God damn it, let me out!" No one came. She tried again, and this time she banged with her hands and kicked with her feet. "You can't keep me here against my will." After two hours, she retreated back to the bed. She ripped off the blanket and sheets and threw them around the room, flipped the mattress onto the floor, and then tried to flip the bed frame. It was bolted to the floor and didn't move.

The second day, she showered twice in the morning. The showers lasted almost an hour. She sat on the stall floor hoping the falling water would either drown her or ease the pain. When they brought her lunch, she attempted an escape, but a second man dressed in blue jeans and a Shelter Mountain Park t-shirt blocked the door. After they left, and locked the door, she hurled the entire food tray toward the door. It bounced off the door and left soup and tuna fish splattered on the wall and floor. By night fall, Deborah lay on the mattress exhausted. She stared at the wall, lying on her side, with both hands tucked in between her legs. Surrender had seeped into her eyes. The fight had drained out hours before. She pulled out a pad and pencil and wrote a letter to her husband, Ramone. When she had finished four handwritten pages lay next to her on the bare mattress on the floor.

When dinner arrived, she consumed it. Afterward, Deborah showered a third time, put on her pajamas, made the bed and climbed in. Sleep was erratic. Her body revolted. She swore bugs had crawled under her night clothes and onto her skin. She slept no more than an hour at a time. Two hours before daylight, Deborah sat on the edge of the bed with her head in her hands, limp, exhausted, and aware any further attempt to rest was futile. She slouched on the floor of the shower, her back against the wall, and sobbed under a cascade of steaming hot water.

On the third day, Deborah attended her first group therapy session. It was followed by a supervised walk around the grounds. In the second session after lunch, she engaged the group for the first time and within moments got clobbered. She claimed she was cured and was ready to go home. A woman named Karla Studnick, the group leader, who lost her husband in 2001 when the World Trade Center collapsed, befriended her. They strolled down the path through the white birch and rhododendron and talked.

"How long have you been drinking full time?" Karla asked.

"I'm not sure I know what you mean."

"I think you do."

Deborah remained silent.

"If you can't admit it, you can't kick it," Karla said.

"I lost my husband, Brian, five years ago. It took only two years after that before I ended up here. My kids where grown up, and Brian had only two years left to retirement. Then one day just like that, he was gone. When that tower collapsed, so did my life. I was devastated at first, then it turned to anger and hate, and then I just didn't care anymore. I gave up because I thought I had nothing left to live for.

"When I arrived here, I experienced the loss of my husband for the first time. I allowed myself the chance to grieve. Before, I was a victim and saw the pain as something someone had done to me. Now, I realize it's my hurt, my reaction to a life I chose to have with Brian. We can either believe that we live life and things happen along the way or that life happens to us and we have no choice. One is a participant, the other a slave. Find the cause, except it as your own, and you'll find the cure. Otherwise you're just another junkie fighting to stay off the sauce."

Deborah walked back to her room and read for a while. In between chapters, Karla's speech played over and over in her head. It was true, she thought, it all made sense. *Stop believing that stopping drinking's the cure. It will only lead to something else—another vice, another drug, another obsession. Find the cause and you find the cure,* she thought over and over. *Find the cause and you find the cure.*

The day of release, Deborah attended three sessions of group work. The last started at four and Ramone picked her up at six. The moment she climbed into the car, she began her confession. It started with the bottle in the garage next to the garbage can, ventured through several rooms in the house, and ended outside with the vodka under the azalea bush. She asked her husband to dispose of them before she went into the house.

Her admission shocked Ramone, not as much, though, as how many bottles had been stowed away in the house. A mile from home, Ramone stopped at the corner gas station. Deborah bought a pack of smokes. She needed them, she had said, to help her get through the first few weeks. At seven-thirty they arrived home, and Ramone claimed the vodka bottle under the azalea bush first. As Ramone cleared the rest of the house, Deborah sat under the big red oak on the bench. Her arms were wrapped around her legs with a smoldering cigarette clipped between her fingers. And as she stared into the darkness, she wondered how she'd cope with life without being a functional drunk.

CHAPTER 22

The alarm went off. Janssen looked down to the laptop sitting on the console. It blinked and beeped, and the red dot started to move. He fired up the engine, slid the gearshift into drive, and drove in the direction of the moving dot. He stayed out of sight: about a block or two from the moving vehicle. The voice of the navigation system, linked to the red dot on the screen, dictated directions. Like ordering a beer in a bar, he thought, not like the old days: sitting in the dark, waiting for the tag to move, trailing two cars behind. He continued to follow as the marked car moved down Maple Street.

The navigation voice sounded again. "Take a right two blocks ahead onto Mulpit Street. One block ahead take a left onto Bean Street."

Janssen slurped his Dunkin' Donuts coffee and looked over the paper cup at the road. As instructed, he turned left. His attention swept from the road to the navigation screen and back to the road as the dot continued to move on the map.

Janssen maneuvered the van through the dilapidated neighborhoods, stripped down frames of burned out cars, and onto the main road leading toward the Jersey Turnpike. Again, the voice called out directions.

"One block ahead make a left and turn onto the entrance ramp to I-95."

The old Chevy van merged with traffic and slowly got up to speed. He looked back down to the console and locked onto the screen. Buck Blanchard was about a hundred yards ahead.

Fifteen miles sped by before the next command was given.

"Exit I-95 two miles on the right at Malcolm Village Drive. Then take a left onto Route 4."

Janssen slipped off the highway and rolled down the exit ramp toward the light at the end. He turned left onto the four-lane road. On the monitor, Buck had stopped about a half mile up on the right. As Janssen approached, he slowed until he spotted Buck's car. He pulled into a small strip mall adjacent to the gas station and snapped the shift into park.

Janssen clicked the short cut key on the laptop and activated the video camera mounted to the dashboard of the van. He zoomed in with the high-powered lens to examine Buck Blanchard's car. Buck unscrewed the gas cap, lifted the hose, hit the octane button, and shoved the nozzle into the tank. Janssen panned the lens back and swept the parking lot.

A green Tahoe, parked in front of the convenience store, idled with a man seated at the wheel. A lady walked out the front door of the 7-11 and climbed into the Tahoe. Janssen rotated the camera back to Blanchard's Toyota Corolla. Buck had stuck the hose back into its sleeve and waited for his receipt to print. Then he climbed back into his car. Janssen reduced the video screen and pulled up the navigation software. Blanchard pulled out of the gas station and turned right. The voice reactivated and gave Hans Janssen a command.

"Turn onto to Route 4, heading south."

About seven miles ahead, Blanchard took a series of turns in a residential neighborhood, and Janssen stayed well behind. Blanchard stopped, turned right, and continued at a slower pace until he came to the end of the road. His vehicle stopped. Janssen approached, minimized the navigation system, and brought up the video screen. At the end of the road, Blanchard's Toyota sat in front of a concrete retaining wall. Beyond the wall, a cliff raced down to the edge of the Hudson River. The engine of the little Toyota, with its jet black paint, thin wheels, and shiny chrome hubcaps, shut down. Janssen pulled to the side of the road, stopped, and zoomed in.

Janssen studied Blanchard's car. The darkened glass and bright sun obscured the view inside. The window slid down, and Janssen aimed the camera at the driver side mirror and honed in. Blanchard was on a cell phone with his elbow on the open window. As he talked, he glanced around the landscape. Suddenly the cell phone snapped shut, the car door opened, and Blanchard jumped out. He stood outside, checked to his left and to his right, and raced around the back of his car.

Janssen felt the rush of adrenaline shoot through his body. He shoved the van into drive and eased the gas pedal halfway to the floor. The van crawled toward Blanchard at a moderate pace. He tried not to give himself up too soon. Blanchard spotted the approaching van and stopped as if pretending to take in the view. He pulled out a smoke and lit it up. The truck, now within thirty feet of his car, sped up. When Buck heard the sound of the engine whine, he turned to look. Janssen slid the van in between Blanchard and his car. He slammed it into park, jumped out, pulled his shouldered holstered .45 Smith and Wesson from its sleeve, and pointed at Buck Blanchard's head only three feet away. Blanchard's arm lowered toward his side. Janssen moved a step closer.

"If your hand moves one more inch, Buck, you'll wish you still had five fingers."

He signaled with his head to Blanchard; nodding it twice toward the van. Blanchard walked to the sliding door.

"Open it and get in."

Blanchard pulled down on the handle and slid the door back. He lifted his left leg onto the running board and grabbed the assist brace with his right hand.

"Hold it, Blanchard. I'll take the piece."

Blanchard lifted the back of his shirt tail and pulled out a 10mm Glock semi-automatic that was stuck under his belt.

"Lay it on the running board…Now get in."

Buck climbed in and turned toward Janssen. Janssen picked up Blanchard's gun and climbed inside.

"Sit down," Janssen said.

"Fuck you!"

"Your vocabulary is as big as your brain, Buck. Sit down, and I'll let you keep your gonads and maybe some of the cash."

Janssen parked himself in the swivel seat opposite Blanchard.

"Give me your cell phone, Buck."

"Go to hell."

Janssen rose and stuck his .45 just above Blanchard's left ear. Before Blanchard said another word, Janssen swung his left arm and slammed his cast into the man's nose.

"Ah, shit! You crazy son of a bitch, you broke my nose."

"The phone, Buck!"

Buck reached out with the cell phone, and Janssen, with his cast hand, slapped a handcuff around his wrist.

"Now take the other cuff and clip it to the bar underneath the arm rest."

Blanchard eyed Janssen as he secured the cuff. Janssen jumped out of the van, walked over to Buck's car and closed the driver side door. He proceeded to the fifty-five gallon drum of a trash can on the other side of the dirt lot. He stuck his .45 in his belt, slid on a surgical glove, and lifted the briefcase from the bottom of the container. He raced back to the van, jumped in, slid the door closed, and sat back down opposite Blanchard. Janssen took a hammer and screw driver and removed the handle from the briefcase and placed it into a plastic bag. He'd check it later for prints. Then he turned to Blanchard. "Time to talk, Buck."

"How did you find me?"

"I'll ask the questions, you give the answers. Now, let's start with who has the knife?"

"I don't know."

Janssen opened Buck's cell phone and looked at both outgoing and incoming calls. The last number was a New York area code.

"Is this the guy who left the briefcase?"

"Fuck you."

"Ok, Buck, let's do Drug Dealing 101. Nice address book, Blanchard, all church-going people I'm sure. After the cops bust up your apartment, they'll have a field day with these numbers in your phone."

Buck stared out the window toward the Hudson River and squirmed in the seat. Janssen lifted the case onto his lap and opened it up.

"A lot of money, Buck. Time to play truth or consequences. Here's how it works. Each time I ask you a question, and I don't like the answer, you forfeit one of these ten thousand dollar bundles. I figure that gives you ten wrong answers before you're out of cash."

"All right. What do you want?"

"Who gave you the money?"

"I don't know."

"Brilliant, Buck—that's one."

"You dumb fuck, I'm telling you the truth. I've never met the guy. He called and offered me a deal. I picked up the cash, just like now."

"How did he know you had the knife?"

"How the fuck should I know? How'd you find out?"

"You're down to eight—Buck."

"You son of a bitch."

"Seven."

"All right, all right, he didn't know at first."

"Go ahead."

"He said someone was looking for information about a murder forty-six years ago. They suspected my old man had been involved. He said a man could get rich with the right information. I asked, how rich? He said it depended on the information. I said someone's hard up. He told me it wasn't my business. So I asked him how much the murder weapon would be worth. He said a hundred thousand. I said what? He said a hundred thousand. So I came here and picked up the cash and left the knife in the plastic bag that my old man had it stowed in. That's all I know. I have no idea who he is, or what he looks like. I never met the man."

"Is this the number you called from your house?"

His eyes squinted as he stared at Janssen.

"How do you know 'bout that?"

"Six."

"Shit, yes, that's the number."

"Is this the only one?"

"Yes."

"Does he have a name?"

"I don't know."

"Who else knows about this?"

"No one."

"Buck?"

"That's all I know."

Janssen studied Buck's face. Blanchard's eyes shot side to side.

"You've taken a lot of my time, Buck. You should have come clean the first time we met."

Janssen pulled out one more bundle.

"You son of a bitch that's my money!"

"Fifty – fifty, Buck. That's life. I suggest you take what you have left and do as you were told, get the hell out of Dodge."

Janssen closed up the briefcase and slid open the door. He handed Buck the key to the cuffs and trained the .45 at his head. Blanchard unlocked the cuffs and got out of the van, and Janssen kicked the case out the door toward him. He escorted Blanchard to his car.

"Adios," Janssen said, "now get!"

Janssen drove to the end of the street and stopped. He watched the computer screen to make sure Blanchard was moving in the right direction. The red dot had traveled quite a distance in a short time.

"Buck Blanchard could buy a lot of drugs in South America with fifty thousand," Janssen mumbled. "The son of a bitch will probably be dead by the end of the year."

CHAPTER 23

It was the first time Deborah would see her mother since Shelter Mountain Park and dinner was set for six. Ramone headed to the garage to pull out the car as Deborah smoked a cigarette by the front door and tried to calm her nerves. The bottle hidden in her mother's garden had not been discarded, yet, and the personal pledge to tell Ramone stood on shaky ground. On the outside, she leaned against the porch column and flicked the ash off her cigarette and blew the smoke out of the corner of her mouth. On the inside, a war raged on. One side fought for the merit of sobriety, while the other side fought for the solace of a drink.

As Deborah waited for the car to appear, her mind wandered to the concrete bench in her mother's garden. From there, it was a short reach to the bag hidden beneath the bush. She closed her eyes and imagined the twisting of the cap in her fingers, the crunching of the bag in her hand, the pouring of the cool liquid into her mouth. Her eyes rolled as sobriety took a left hook and went down.

The back-up lights beamed off the concrete floor, and the car rolled out of the garage. Deborah noticed the creased rear panel that matched the height of the missing wood stop on the garage door jamb. The car damage was just another embarrassing casualty from her pre-dry out days—which was only visible through sober eyes. She flicked the ash off her smoke as sobriety got to its feet and cold cocked Smirnoff with a left hook. She crushed her cigarette and walked to the car.

Halfway to her parents' house, she blurted out the truth about the hidden alcohol. Ramone looked stunned.

"Your parents' azalea bush!" he said. "Is that the last?"

She surprised herself again when she gave up the last hold-out, the one saved when all else failed, when every other bottle was empty, and the car didn't start.

"There's one in the attic tucked in the bottom drawer of the bureau, under your mother's old table cloths."

Ramone rubbed his forehead with his left fingers as he turned into the Williams's driveway. He located the azalea bush with the bag underneath and a half-empty Smirnoff bottle inside. He poured the vodka onto the stone gravel and went inside the house.

They were in the living room when Janssen rang the bell. He insisted on meeting with them before dinner. Nora had escorted him into the living room, and he sat down next to Robert. Janssen was guarded and brief in what he said, and the future direction of the investigation. Ramone kept his mouth shut this time. Deborah stared out the window. She observed the conversation like some floating spirit hovering above the room. Their mouths moved up and down, muted voices slid by her ears—a strange sensation at best. Then the name John slammed her back into reality.

"He hasn't called back," Nora said. "But he will. John will be there if we need him."

Hearing her brother's name brought Deborah's thoughts back to years before. Cutting all communication with his parents reared its head as early as his first year of prep school. John had displayed a sharp edge of anger that year. He became totally engrossed in his studies and distanced himself from his fellow students. Even though he wasn't physically big, his classmates knew not to mess with John. He was a loaded cannon ready to go off. He excelled at his academics and was at the top of his class, but he was considered an eccentric loner. He literally had no friends.

She understood now. Her father, being a pragmatist, dealt with John's behavior with an intellectual approach. All problems, he often said, can be reasoned out. The decision to send John away to school was a product of exactly that. It backfired, and John became resentful of his father's solution to the turmoil at home. She knew that. He never initiated a phone call to his parents, and he failed to respond to their letters that he received by mail. And even though he didn't physically cut himself off and he came home for the holidays, those visits were marred in arguments and John's abuse.

"Mom, you're in such denial. John could care less about this family. I guarantee he won't call back."

"Deborah, that's enough, I won't have you talk like that in this house."

"Mrs. Williams, with all due respect, you have less than three weeks. Without John's help, it's going to get messy," Janssen said.

"Mr. Janssen, did you have anything else you wanted to tell us?"

"Jesus, Mother, do you understand what Hans is saying?"

"Is that all, Mr. Janssen?" Nora asked again.

"Mother, wake up."

"Mr. Janssen?"

"I wanted to give this back to you, Mrs. Williams." Janssen handed Nora a piece of paper. She examined it.

"Mr. Janssen, what is the meaning of this?"

"What is it?" Deborah asked.

"It's the check I wrote Mr. Janssen."

"Hans, what's going on?" Ramone asked.

"Well, let's just say there's been an anonymous donor," Janssen replied.

"And who might that be Mr. Janssen?" Nora asked.

"Can't say directly, but be assured you no longer have to worry about expenses."

Deborah, suspicious, watched as Ramone escorted Janssen to the front door. She walked toward the front entranced and listened.

"Hans, what's going on here?"

"Good night, Ramone."

She watched out the front window as Janssen drove away. As she moved back toward the living room, the question rang out in her head. *Where did he get that kind of money? What's Janssen up to?*

She stopped near her mother as Ramone walked back into the living room.

"Enough Sherlock Holmes," he said. "We need to go to the authorities. Let them handle it from here. This whole affair is larger than us, not to mention dangerous and perhaps illegal. We are common folk trying to do other people's business. This is not going away. Five million dollars in exchange for the murder weapon is absurd. It's blackmail, and is a serious crime. John is not going to bail you out."

"No," Nora said, "Mr. Janssen will handle it."

"Nora, these are dangerous people trying to extort a lot of money over a crime Robert didn't commit. Robert is not going to jail, and you will not lose your home. Using his compelling investigative charm, Hans Janssen has done nothing but convince you otherwise. John won't pay that kind of money; he won't even return your calls. What happens when your time runs out, and you don't have the cash, what then? You need to contact the police."

"Mother, Ramone is right. This is getting out of control."

"Can either of you tell me for sure Robert won't go to jail, or we won't lose everything we own—can you?"

Deborah glanced at Ramone.

"No, but the chances—"

"Then it's done. And stop picking on John. He's a good boy, who runs a big business, and he works very hard. I've heard enough of this now. Drop it."

Robert sat in his wheelchair looking at the floor.

"Dad, do you understand what's going on here…Dad?"

His eyes looked around the room, and then he moved his fingers on his left side off the arm of the chair.

"Did you see that, Deborah? Your father moved his hand. He's really doing better. Ms. Labronski is doing wonders with Robert; he will walk again very soon. He will. Did you know he held himself up on the walker last Thursday? Even Ms. Labronski said it was a miracle." Nora turned to Robert. "We're all very proud of you, dear. Oh the roast must be done. Why don't you make yourselves a drink? Dinner will be ready in ten minutes."

"A drink," Deborah said. "A drink?" she said to Ramone. "I'm afraid my mother's gone daft. A drink, Jesus Christ. And this crap about John. He's a selfish, egocentric asshole."

The Eco-Star EC-130 landed on the Cheyenne tarmac and concluded John's second trip in as many weeks out west. He climbed aboard his Bombardier accompanied by Pamela Thurston, who, in a matter of moments, was about to be a half million dollars richer. The forty-five hundred acre ranch in Johnson County, snuggled in amongst the Big Horn Mountains, was a cool eight point five mil. And Thurston was the listing and selling broker. She had both ends of the deal.

John sat at his desk, signing papers as she shuffled one after another to his awaiting pen. She insisted on playing attorney over Dubach and Stoddard's objections. The steward poured Cristal Champagne into flutes and delivered them as the last of the contracts were signed. Thurston packed up the bundle and placed them into her leather pouch. Then she took a sip of the expensive champagne. When the glass pulled away from her lips, the curl of her mouth revealed the conceded smirk of an arrogant victor.

John reached for her hand and escorted her into his private compartment at the rear of the aircraft. Even though her four-carat wedding ring shot sparkles of light onto the cabin walls, Thurston put up no resistance. Half a million, plus expenses, has its rewards, and John Williams had been studying her "cleavage by design" all day. Of course Thurston had rules. She always waited until the deal was complete before her clients got their just deserts. She called it smart work ethics—no deal, no fling with Thurston—it was as simple as that.

Williams closed the door and placed his champagne on the small table by the bed. She unbuttoned her silk blouse and slid it off her shoulders exposing the absence of lingerie. Pamela Thurston worked the sale, and when it closed, she loved the feeling of the climax that came as the result of her diligent work.

The Bombardier Challenger 605 screamed off the Cheyenne runway and began its climb at four thousand feet a minute. By the time it reached ten thousand, daylight had faded, and the sky on the horizon had orange-fired clouds providing the only light. John Williams sat at his desk and checked his Blackberry and then called his secretary in New York. He leaned back into the soft leather and watched out the window as Martha told him Kursman had called. Kursman had said it was urgent.

As he dictated orders to his secretary, he sipped his Crown Royal and looked down to the horizon below. There was a certain godliness that came with conducting business at forty thousand feet above the Earth, and John took command as if he was the man himself.

"Have the Bell fired up at 6:35 to take me to Greenwich," he ordered Martha. "Call the house and tell Stangler I'll be arriving at 6:50. I want a '61 Chateau Margaux at 7:45. Cancel my appointment with Bennett at eight tomorrow morning and tell Bateman I want to see him in my office at seven. Tell him to bring the work up on Tritech Instruments."

"Sir, Mr. Bateman is in Indiana at the Tritech plant."

"Seven, Martha!"

Williams dialed Kursman himself.

"Congrats, Williams, the board voted unanimously on the deal. Cochran gave me the verbal confirmation at four thirty this afternoon. I guess you can buy another jet."

"Bullshit, Kursman, get your head out of your ass and sober up. Nothing is on paper yet. There's still work to do. You better be two steps ahead of Cochran, or I'll have you roasted on a spit. You make damn sure you have the votes until the ink is put to paper. The board may have second thoughts about a German firm buying the biggest satellite company in the world. Keep your God damn eyes open, Kursman!"

The Challenger rolled up to the hangar and the engine's whistle slowly began to fade. John walked the twenty feet to his Bell-429 already humming and ready to lift off. He wasn't on board more than two minutes when the outside door was secured, the back end lifted slightly, and the ground let go its grip. John pulled out his cell phone and called Senator Ballicose on his private line.

It rang twice and the senator picked up. Two million funneled into his re-election campaign saw to that, not to mention the fifty thousand in cash as a bonus. Ballicose knew the phone number well.

"John, how are you?" he asked.

"Larry, I need a favor."

"Certainly, John, what can I do for you?"

"I have a deal that's about to come up before the feds. I don't want any problems. Hastings's Satellite, Larry, it's a done deal, and I don't want some American pie fucking this one up."

"I'll see to it personally, John."

"Oh, and Larry, you might want to pick up some Hastings's ticker symbol, HAS, in your overseas account. It's a forty percent premium to today's close."

"Let me know when you're in town, John, we'll have lunch and a round at Congressional."

"I want this one on fast track, Larry—got it?"

John hung up and text messaged Hansfetal. He typed in "done," and then after that "all bases covered, will talk a.m."

As the helicopter zoomed over White Plains, John loosened his tie and made one last call. It was to a man named Kyle Feinstein out of Manhattan. Kyle was a private investment whiz who managed twenty-five percent the year the market lost eighteen. He was the unknown Warren Buffet and could boast of only twelve clients. Kyle's financial wisdom came at a fee of three percent while most funds charged one. The catch, unless you had a minimum of one billion to invest, Kyle would turn you away. John Williams fit the bill.

"Kyle, John Williams."

"Hello, John."

"Kyle, a woman named Pamela Thurston is going to contact you tomorrow. She will give you instructions on where to wire eight point five next week. Oblige her if you will."

"Certainly, John."

"Good night."

John hit the pad at exactly 6:49 with Stangler opening the door to the cabin. His routine landed him in front of the fireplace, with his book, as always, twenty minutes after his arrival. The first glass of Margaux would be consumed in front of the fire and then he'd take the ride to the wine cellar below. The bottle would be waiting on the café table a hair before 7:45.

The dramatic outbursts began almost immediately, just as they always did. "It offends me too, Peter, nothing is more offensive than that!"

He took another sip with his left hand while his right hand held the book off the table. His eyes never left the words. The wine found its way without sight.

"We have fun, don't we?" John's hand almost hit the wine glass as it swept through the air. "That's right, Peter. What more could there be?"

The food arrived, but the servant didn't speak. The words echoed up the twisted stone stairs when he left.

"What else is there? Oh yes, you're right Peter, no one can make you!"

John carried on through dinner, with the book propped up in its reading chair. Something was different, though. The servant had seen it but acted as if it didn't exist. It was the hat on John's head. It wasn't just any hat; it matched the one in the book to the stitch.

"I got my hat back, you see?"

John finished his meal and about three quarters of the bottle of wine. He rode the elevator up to his room and got ready for bed. When he climbed in and pulled up the sheets, he removed the hat and placed it on top of the book which sat on the night table to his right. He rolled over on his side and looked out the open sash. He shuffled his feet until they reached out from under the covers, and his head settled into the goose down pillow. And he whispered to himself over and over.

"Second from the right, straight on till morning. Second from the right, straight on till morning."

Nora opened the kitchen door and looked at her daughter on the cement bench.

"Dinner's ready, Deborah," she said.

"I'll be right in."

She took a draw on the smoke and stared at the bird bath, which was empty and discolored. Then she turned her eyes toward the bay window, exhaling upward. Robert sat in his wheelchair parked at the table with a blank stare on his face. In the background, behind the counter, she spotted her mother cutting the roast. Ramone walked to the side of Robert and sat down. The end of the cigarette went bright red. She reached into the bushes, and then she remembered…it was gone.

CHAPTER 24

Janssen sat in his office surrounded by electronic equipment and downloaded all the records on Buck Blanchard's cell phone. It was a treasure trove of information: the call logs, video games, text messages, photographs, and the address book filled with dealers and users all within a fifty-mile radius of his illegal drug store. Upon completion, he opened his email and clicked on Leaf Hamlin's address. Then he pasted the call log and address book in the body of the email. Before he clicked send, he scrolled down to be sure they were all included. Then he typed a note at the top.

"Leaf, I need your help. I'd appreciate you running a reverse lookup on the numbers—particularly the first one with the New York area code. Also, any information you can find on the man's name, address, social etc. Thanks, Hans."

Leaf Hamlin worked for the FBI. He was Janssen's second wife's brother. The marriage hadn't worked, but his brother-in-law's friendship had. They did one stint in Vietnam together, in the DMZ. They were stuck for three nights alone together with Cong swarming all around them. Janssen rarely asked Hamlin for help on a case, because he knew Leaf could lose his job. Janssen, though, had hit a dead end, and all he had was the hope of a phone number to keep the trail alive. Three days later Hamlin called and had a calm but serious tone in his voice.

"Hans, the dog's loose. I saw him running down the street," he said.

It was code, something they had thought up in Nam. It signaled a warning. Janssen knew exactly what it meant and didn't say another word except thanks. He hung up, grabbed a pencil and pad that fit in his top pocket, and left the house.

Janssen climbed in the van, backed out of the drive, and turned left on Saddle Brook Road. He went two blocks and turned right onto Chisim, another block and turned left onto Stagecoach. Then he pulled to the curb. He waited a moment and checked to see if he had been tailed. It was all clear.

Janssen drove back down Stagecoach until he reached a stop sign and turned right onto Saddle Brook and made a left onto Route 1. About a half mile on the right, Janssen breezed by an old Exxon station and swerved left into Chuck's Diner. It was a 1950's style diner with spinning stools, large booths, and a juke box stuck on the wall above each table. But he wasn't there to eat. In the back, at the far end, was a phone booth. It was a safe location from which to make his call.

He waited in the van until he checked both directions of traffic. It was still all clear. He slipped out and went inside. Jack, the owner, was behind the counter talking to a customer. He waved. Janssen ate breakfast at Chuck's at least three times a week. He liked their hash browns, eggs over with bacon, and the second cup of coffee free. He walked past the turning stools to the end of the counter and opened the door to the phone booth. He slipped in and closed the door. Janssen dropped in a quarter, punched in the numbers, and waited. Hamlin picked up on the second ring.

"Janssen, what the hell have you gotten yourself into?" he asked.

"Why?"

"Your home and cell phones may not be secure. I didn't want to take the chance."

"What's going on?"

"It's a throw-away phone, Janssen."

"What are you talking about?"

"The phone number you gave me, it's a throw away. You pay thirty bucks for sixty pre-paid minutes. Terrorist use them all the time; the owner can't be traced. This one was bought at a Walmart in Baines County. We ran the calls for locations. The last one was made from a small town in New Jersey called Malcolm Village. It's on the edge—"

"Yeah, yeah, I know where it is," Janssen said.

"Anyway, we're running the locations on the other numbers in his phone, but I need more time. We did get a fix, though, on that throw-away phone. Four calls from the same location in Manhattan. You got a pen?"

"Go ahead."

"2001 Park Ave. and 71st. We got a video from the Walmart where it was purchased and printed the image of the man. No name, he must have paid cash, but I'll send it via email."

"Thanks."

"One thing, Janssen, that location of the four phone calls…"

"Yeah?"

"There's an office building located a block away. Inside is an organization made up of international ex-intelligence men, six to be exact. We've been watching them for three years now. They hire out, and they're not particular as long as it pays. I'd compare their expertise to that of the CIA, and here's the kick, five thousand an hour. Every time we think we have a jump on them, we end up chasing a ghost. If you're messed up with these guys, I'd be ten steps ahead. They're not someone you want to meet head on."

"Thanks, Leaf, I'll take that into consideration."

"I mean it, Janssen. If you want something done, and you want it done right, that's who you hire. I'd start with a complete sweep of your house and check the car for a tracer."

"I don't have the car anymore. Someone ran me into a tree."

"That someone might have been them. Maybe this is just a long shot, maybe not, but I'd watch my ass if I were you."

"Thanks, buddy."

"Listen, I don't know what you're involved in, and I don't want to know, but if these guys are mixed up in it, it must be something big. I didn't save your ass in Vietnam to have it shot up here."

"I'll keep that in mind."

Janssen hung up and stuck the palm of his hand on his forehead. *Shit, the son of a bitch saw the whole thing. He was there at Malcolm Village when I surprised Blanchard, shit!*

Janssen stopped at the library on the way home. He pulled up his email and printed out the picture from the Walmart where the phone had been bought. It was blurry and grainy, but it was good enough to identify the man if seen. He printed a smaller version to keep in his pocket and headed home.

Janssen did a clean sweep. He started on the first floor and worked his way through the house beginning with the phones, the computer for hacking software, and the attic for video cameras. Then he checked the van, the perimeter of the house, and the shed in the back yard. He found a U-3 satellite tracer under the back bumper of the van, a stage 2 audio bug inside the van, a macro-phone interceptor in his land line, a camera cut through the ceiling in the back corner of his office, and another stage 2 audio bug underneath his work station.

His computer, cell phone, and laptop were clean. After discovering the camera in the attic, he took his RAB 500-watt halogen work light, placed it in the corner of the office on the floor, and directed the bright light into the lens of the video camera until the sweep of the office was complete. When he was done, he left all the surveillance devices in place.

Then Janssen walked to his neighbor's house and asked to borrow his car. He drove to Best Buy and purchased a new laptop, a laptop connect card, portable printer, and a throw-away phone with sixty minutes. He rented a room at the Sheraton on Hallmark Street which he paid for in cash. He set up the equipment on the desk near the window and created a new email account with MSN.

He connected to his home computer using remote desktop and downloaded all his relevant files and emails. After that, he called Enterprise and had them deliver a rental car to the lot out front. Janssen then locked up the room, returned the neighbor's car, and when he arrived home, he grabbed a beer and went straight to his office. It was time for the Hans Janssen reality show. He popped open his bud, pulled a slug, and went to work.

CHAPTER 25

Now that Buck Blanchard was out of the picture, Janssen figured he was two levels short of solving the case. The lower tier was the one responsible for delivering the note and running the day-to-day operation. The upper tier was the master mind. Someone who had the clout to find a firm like the high paid ex-intelligent men and had the ability to pay five thousand an hour—not your average chump change.

As he told Nora, he believed the real target was John Williams, not Robert. It made perfect sense. It was someone on the inside of John Williams's firm. It had to be an upper-echelon disgruntled employee of Williams Investment Bank. He figured it was a person with access to a large expense account. A person with a grudge who wanted justice, but instead of a gun, they were going for cash—going postal for profit. He had deduced this from day one, but now his instincts and the evidence had started to back it up.

Janssen worked the internet at his new motel office and found nothing at the address Hamlin had given him: no names, businesses, or nonprofit organizations as a front. He was not surprised. Men of that level of skill don't advertise. They depend upon autonomy—phantoms that operate in the dark—and success, like Hamlin said, was dependent on the ability to disappear. Janssen knew the only way to get out in front of these high-priced thugs was to make them believe they had the upper hand. And he believed he already had the infrastructure in place.

He printed out a map of Park and 5th, put a pin point at the address, and with a pen he drew a line around the surrounding streets. After he closed up the laptop, he pulled out the wad of cash from inside his coat pocket and counted out the remainder of the ten thousand dollar stack—eight thousand two hundred. He stuffed the cash back into his pocket and called Chase Rutherford, his old mentor. Of course, he used the throw-away phone.

Chase had broken Janssen in as a rookie, and they remained friends after Rutherford retired from the force. But Rutherford missed the excitement. He wasn't the retirement type. Janssen had learned Rutherford was a valuable asset when the circumstances fit. So he instructed Rutherford to meet him at his motel office, and he worked out the details as he waited for Chase. By the time Rutherford arrived, Janssen had everything in place.

They drove to Janssen's house and parked a block away. He handed Rutherford the keys to his van and gave him a sheet of instructions. It told him to drive to I-95 and head south. As he did, Janssen tailed from behind in the rental car. When they crossed the Queensboro Bridge, Janssen and Rutherford looped onto the FDR and headed south. Janssen stayed two to three car lengths back. Rutherford slipped off the FDR as instructed at exit 13 onto East 71st Street and drove down 71st crossing Park Ave. He took a right on Madison, then another right onto 72nd , two blocks down a right onto Lexington, and then back onto 71st. Janssen maintained his distance. Chase repeated the square loop around 71st and Park three times as it said on the sheet. After completing the third, Rutherford found a parking spot on 71st in sight of the entrance to 2001 Park Ave. He shut off the engine and slipped into the back of the van.

In the back, he flicked on a remote transponder and then exited and locked the van. Then he walked three blocks to 74th Street where Janssen picked him up. Janssen circled two times before he found an empty slot about six cars down from the van. He turned off the rental car, opened up the laptop, and brought the computer to life. The windows of the van were dark and impossible to see into. He could, however, record any outside movement within sight of the lens. With the laptop fired up, Janssen tested the zoom on both cameras and tried the lateral movement as well.

"God, I miss this shit," Rutherford said. "What's next?"

"We wait. If they're in there, we got their attention."

Hans pulled out the surveillance photo taken at Walmart and stuck it on the keyboard of the computer.

"This is the target," he said. He zoomed in on the entrance using the doorman as a means to focus. He set the second camera to an open lens out the back door window of the van.

"Just like old times," Rutherford said. "How about a cup of Joe?"

"I'm buying."

"Just milk, right?"

"Just milk," Janssen said.

Rutherford stepped out of the car and walked down 71st toward Lexington. He had spotted a deli when he turned his loop around Park. Janssen sat in the car and waited.

The doorman with his white gloves, hat, and fancy uniform, reached for the front door handle and opened up the wide glass door. Janssen turned off the split screen. He concentrated on the front entrance and picked up the photo of the man. A tall, thin, smartly dressed gray haired man walked past the outstretched arm of the doorman. Janssen glanced at the print and back to the screen and back to the print. No match. He followed him with the camera, but the man had no interest in the van. He focused back to the front door, flipped on the split screen, and laid the photo back on the keys. The side door of the car opened and Rutherford slipped in.

"Any action?" he asked.

"Nothing yet."

They drank their coffee and reminisced for the next forty-five minutes. Rutherford never shut up. He was giddy like a rookie cop, not a veteran of forty years. Then Rutherford slid back his sports coat.

"Look," he said.

Janssen looked down and saw Rutherford's .38 strapped to his belt. "What the hell do you think you're going to do with that?" Janssen asked.

"Don't know, but it sure feels good packing a piece again."

"Hold on."

He singled out the camera in the back of the van and zoomed in on the man who turned the corner of Park and 71st Street. He followed him with the camera and zoomed in.

"Nope," Rutherford said. "That's not him."

Janssen reset the camera and settled back in his seat. He handed Rutherford a bunch of quarters and asked him to go feed the meter and watched as it ate the change like a hungry wolf. Hans looked in all directions, making sure no one watched Rutherford outside on the street. Chase emptied his overturned hand and walked back to the rental car.

"Lucky it didn't eat your hand too," Janssen said.

"That damn thing makes more than a retired cop."

"No shit," Janssen said.

He played with the zoom for a moment and then turned to Chase. "I've got to take a leak, keep an eye on things."

Rutherford shook his head.

Janssen was aware whoever was in that Park Avenue building knew his face, so as he exited the car, he abruptly turned away from the front entrance. He walked down 71st toward the Hudson River and took a left on Madison, and then a left on 70th Street and found a French restaurant about a half a block up. He did his business, washed up, and walked back out to the street.

When he turned onto 71st Street, he zoned in on the rental car. *What the hell?* The rental was empty. He peered up 71st and down Lexington. Rutherford was gone.

He rewound the video from the entrance and saw nothing except the doorman. Janssen examined the video of the area toward Park, nothing. He pulled back the second camera and took a wide angle view of the street on both sides, still no sign of Rutherford. He set both cameras back to the original setting, jumped out of the car, pushed the fob to lock it, and with a steady gait headed to the corner of Park and 71st. He searched both ways. He picked up his pace and scrambled one block to 72nd Street—again nothing.

He climbed back into the rental and waited five minutes more. He searched the tapes again. Only two people had passed: a woman walking her little white poodle and an old lady who entered the building on Park. It suddenly struck Janssen that the photo of the man had disappeared too. He checked his pockets, and looked on the floor, but it had vanished along with Chase.

The sun started to set. He pulled his .45 Smith and Wesson from his shoulder holster and checked the clip. He slid it back under his arm. He pulled out the pad from his top pocket and read some of the notes he had scratched. He played with the cameras, twitched around in his seat, checked his pocket for the cash and checked his 45 again. The street lamps came on. He decided to wait five more minutes, and if Rutherford hadn't shown by then, he would take another look around.

The knock on the glass startled Janssen. The face outside the passenger window grinned like a little boy. He gestured his hand to unlock the door. The locks flipped, the door flung open, and Rutherford slid inside.

"I found him," he said.

"Jesus, Rutherford, where the hell have you been?"

"Janssen, I found him!"

"Found who?"

"The guy in the photo." He pulled out the picture and pointed. "Him."

"Where?"

"Walking right by the car."

"He didn't come out of the building, I checked."

"You're looking in the wrong place," Rutherford said.

"All right, back up, what happened?"

"I'm sitting here watching the screen, and I see this guy walking down 71st toward Park. He's trying to act nonchalant, but he's checking out the van as he walked. I looked down at the picture, and then back to this guy, and bang it's him. He figures you have no idea what he looks like so he's pretty brazen and approaches the car but keeps his distance from the van.

I figure he doesn't know who the hell I am so I get out of the car acting like I'm going toward Park. He circles around for a couple of blocks, making sure he's not being followed, and then he goes back to a deli and goes inside. About twenty minutes later he comes out with a bag and starts down Lex. He turns up 70th Street, walks to the corner of 70th and 3rd and goes inside a high rise. His apartment building, I figure, so I wait awhile to see if he comes back out, but he doesn't."

"Why didn't you call me?"

"I didn't want to take any chances in case your phone was tapped."

"I told you my phone's a throw away. It's not bugged."

"Jesus, right, I've been stale too long. Anyway, I watch the front door and a couple of people come and go, but he's still inside. Here's what I figure: the guy followed the tracer, and when it landed in his neighborhood, it freaked him out. When it parked and didn't move, he waited awhile and decided he was safe and came and had a look. He doesn't know me from Adam, 'cause he's looking for you, which lets me run a tail on him. The calls you traced were all made from his apartment a block away. Forget Park Avenue, the man's on 3rd."

"Shit, maybe these ex-intelligent geeks aren't my mark."

"What's that?"

"Never mind, Listen carefully. I want you drive the van back to my house. That way he'll think I'm gone. Grab a bug setup and a U–3 Tracer out of the back of the truck, I'm back in business."

Rutherford walked back to the van and opened it up. He climbed inside and retrieved the equipment Janssen wanted and then returned to the rental car.

"Listen," Janssen said, "when you get back to my place use the key and go inside. In the second floor hall closet grab a towel. Take off your shirt and put the towel over your head like you just took a shower and your hair is wet. Go to the computer in my office and pretend to be working online. Be sure to do it without showing your face to the back wall. I'm going to call you from my throw-away phone and when it rings, pick up your cell phone and pretend to take a note."

"Then what?"

"Nothing, don't say a word, act like someone just gave you information and hang up. Then pretend to make a phone call using your cell. I will be logged onto my home computer, read the two lines I typed on the screen into your phone, with your hand over your mouth as a disguise. Just say what I typed. When you see four periods in a row on the screen, hang up. Exit the room with your face covered, get dressed, and proceed to your car parked down the street."

"What's this all about?"

"I'll get to that later. Here's the eight hundred for today's work and don't forget to watch your face. The camera's behind the computer in the ceiling. Always face toward the computer."

"Got ya."

Rutherford started to climb out of the car. As he was about to close the door, Janssen stopped him.

"Remember," he said, "only call me on the throw-away phone!"

CHAPTER 26

Deborah paced the kitchen thirty minutes prior to her appointment with Dr. Reed. The cabinet doors slammed, the refrigerator opened and closed, and the pantry was ripped apart. As a last act of desperation, she bolted up to the attic to the bottom drawer of the bureau. She looked underneath the table cloths, ripped the faded linen sheets from the open drawer, and hurled them behind her onto the plywood floor. As the last cloth flew across the attic and landed in a crumbled heap, she dropped to the floor and sat with her head sunk into the palms of her hands. Ramone had thrown it out.

She grabbed the keys to the car and bolted out the kitchen door. It was the worst day she had experienced since leaving Shelter Mountain Park. It had started after Ramone left for work and then built to a psychotic crescendo by nine o' clock. Deborah was ready to crawl out of her skin as she fumbled with the key and tried to slip it into the ignition. The engine finally turned over, the wheels screeched as she backed out of the garage, and the car sped down the length of Summit Avenue.

The five white lines in front of the liquor store were empty. So was the store inside: It wasn't open until ten. She slammed the car into reverse, backed into the curb behind her, and then snapped the stick into drive.

The abrupt stop at the traffic light shook her head forward. She cursed out loud at the car in front of her. She mouthed a "Jesus Christ" to the guy crossing the street on his bike because it made the car in front of her stop. Somewhere between Al's Liquor Store and Dr. Reed's office, Deborah found some strength and with it the courage to abstain. She lit a cigarette and mouthed the "F" word sandwiched between Jesus and Christ. When she arrived at the row of one story wooden offices, and parked in front of G-3, she took a deep breath, pulled the visor down, and applied some lip gloss.

The waiting room was empty. She chose the chair by a stack of magazines and nervously clutched her pocket book in her arms at her chest. She stared at the wall across the room. A long minute passed and then another. The door finally opened and Dr. Reed stood in the hall behind it.

"Mrs. Sanchez, please come in," he said.

Deborah followed him to his office, and as she stepped inside, he closed the door behind them. She felt claustrophobic. She wanted to bolt. Instead she examined the room. Two leather chairs faced each other and to the left was a large leather couch. She sat in the chair, as she had the previous meetings, and crossed her legs. Her pocket book was clutched to her side. Dr. Reed sat down in his chair in a calm and gentle manner. He was relaxed more than his blue bow tie would have implied. His soft, calm voice melted away the rigid feeling of the stacked bookshelves and formal prints on the walls.

"How are you, Deborah? You look distraught."

Deborah rolled her eyes and turned away.

"Why don't we begin where we left off in our last session? You were talking about your fear of being alone. You described the terror you felt out at Crab Point a few weeks ago. How you secured the room, and you drank and smoked all night. Does the alcohol make it go away, Deborah?"

"No!"

The doctor turned his head slightly, and his forehead wrinkled in an inquisitive way. "Tell me about that."

"It's always there. It was worse out at Crab Point, but even at home when Ramone has school board meetings or a school event at night, I sometimes start to panic. I felt that way this morning after my husband left for work. I almost took a…well…a…well…you know."

"What's that, Deborah?"

"You know what I mean?"

"Yes, I do, but what's stopping you from saying it?"

"I guess I don't want to say it….a…Jesus, a drink?"

Deborah's eyes looked down to the red and blue oriental carpet beneath her. "What's the matter with me, Dr. Reed? Why am I so pathetic?"

"Is that how you feel?"

"When I act like I did this morning I do. Not when I'm out of control but afterward, like now. I've felt this fear most of my life. I started drinking when I was thirteen, not all the time, but when it got really bad. Then in high school it got worse, and in college, I'd sometimes pass out and not remember anything about the night before. I want it to go away. I'm tired of being scared. I'm tired of drinking because I'm in a panic. I want it to go away!"

She grabbed a tissue from the box next to her and blew her nose and then took another and wiped her eyes. "I'm sorry I'm a mess. I guess you keep the tissues here for a reason?"

"Sometimes the truth is very painful."

"It sucks."

"You said you've felt like this most of your life, Deborah. What's your earliest recollection?"

"I guess around seven or eight. I don't remember much before that."

"And what happened?"

"I don't know. I just remember it started then and just got worse and worse. My brother and father would argue all the time. I hated it. My mother would cry and ask my father to leave John be. My father didn't know what to do, so he sent John away. I missed him at first, but then when he came home he was mean and said horrible things to me. I was glad when he finally went back to school. At least it was peaceful and quiet in the house."

The session, which lasted fifty minutes and cost one hundred sixty dollars, went quickly for Deborah. She felt more confused when it ended than when it had begun. At the end she made a vow to call Alcoholics Anonymous, as Dr. Reed had suggested, but wasn't sure if she really would.

"Group stuff isn't my thing," she said, "besides, I'm doing just fine on my own."

On the ride home, Deborah thought a lot about what she had said. She stopped at the grocery store and picked up a steak for dinner, but she didn't really register being in the store. She didn't notice the traffic, or the cop with radar, or the work crew she had to drive around. When she arrived home, Deborah put the steak in the refrigerator, changed her clothes, put on her sneakers, and went for a walk—a long walk. It lasted an hour and a half. When she arrived back home, she breathed a sigh of relief at the sight of her husband's car. She had dreaded coming back to the house, alone, after her long, pensive walk.

CHAPTER 27

Rutherford, as instructed, walked into the office with a towel draped over his head, rubbing it with both hands. He sat at the computer, logged on, and then punched a "Y" to let Hans know he was ready. Janssen called Rutherford as planned and then Rutherford pretended to make a call on his cell phone. As he did, back in New York, Janssen had Buck Blanchard's cell phone glued to his ear. He listened as the phone on the other end rang twice and then a man's voice cut in.

"You stupid son of a bitch, I told you not to call me again. You're a dead man, Blanchard."

"This ain't Buck Blanchard, asshole, and you ain't as smart as you think."

"Who the fuck are you?"

"Welcome to my world, dickwad. I know where you live, and the prepaid phone you're talking on, the one you bought at the Walmart in Baines County, it's bugged. I'll be in touch!" Janssen hung up.

It only lasted seventeen seconds and four periods popped up on the screen. Chase flipped his cell phone shut, pretended he was still studying the computer screen, and walked backward out of the room. He went upstairs and retrieved his clothes, got dressed, and left the house out the back door. He sat in his car with it running and pulled out the crisp one hundred dollar bills. He fanned them out so he could examine all eight together.

"Shit," he said with a grin, "I would have done that pro bono!"

He put the bills back into his pocket, put the car in gear, and drove down Summit Avenue.

Back in Manhattan, it happened fast. Janssen watched amused. The man in the photo walked out of his building and crossed the street. He headed straight for the pay phone about twenty yards to the right and made a call. It lasted about a minute, and then he walked back down the sidewalk to the cross walk, waited for the light, and breezed into his building and disappeared. Janssen exited the rental car and ran across the street. As he bolted toward the door, his right hand reached inside his left coat pocket. The doorman looked alarmed as Janssen approached. The doorman slid out the door onto the sidewalk.

"Detective Strand," Janssen said as he flashed a badge out of his wallet. "I'm chasing a car thief, and he headed toward this building. I just saw someone go inside."

"You did, but I can assure you Mr. Philippe is no car thief."

"Did anyone else enter?"

"Why do think I'm here, to let car thieves in?"

"Did you see a man about thirty, dressed in blue jeans and a hooded top run by?"

"No."

"Shit," Janssen ran off. He waited until the doorman went back inside. Then he crossed the street and got back into the rental car. "Dumb shit," he said, "I knew that call would flush him out." He took Buck's phone out of his pocket and placed it back into his satchel. He turned on the computer and examined the reading on the recording program. It recorded the entire conversation from the pay phone. He left the bug in the pay phone, started the rental car, and pulled out.

The laptop was open and sat to the right of where dinner had taken place. The battery was low so he plugged the cord into the wall, brought up the recording program, and played back the call from the pay phone. The person Philippe called was not identified. Hans rewound the beginning several times to become familiar with the identifying properties of his voice. The fourth time he let it continue.

"I told you not to call," the man's voice said.

"I think this investigator's on to me. I tracked his van into New York and it stopped two blocks from my place. Then later he called using Buck's cell phone and told me he knew where I lived. I watched him on the video feed make the call from his office. So I figured it was safe to call you from a pay phone."

"You don't figure shit, Philippe. You do what I instruct you to do, that's it! The next time an idea falls into that mentally impaired brain of yours, you ignore it. You don't contact me again unless I instruct you to, is that understood?"

"Yes, sir."

"Now go do your fucking job, or you'll be peeling farm raised shrimp in some mangrove forest out of Minh Hai, Vietnam."

Janssen took a long swig on his Bud and pulled up a search of "Philippe" using the address where he lived—nothing. Then he punched in the last name on his private investigator's paid subscription program and had more people with that name than he bargained for. Janssen checked the apartment address through the property appraiser's office and found that it belonged to a Charles Progane whose primary address was listed in Florida. He ran a check on Progane to see if there was a connection between the two, but there wasn't. He closed up his laptop, finished his beer, and headed home.

CHAPTER 28

Nora helped Robert into the handicapped-accessible van and then headed to her car parked in the lot. The prospect he might walk again with the help of an aid was on the forefront of her mind when suddenly she felt her legs buckle beneath her. She grabbed the driver side mirror with her left hand as her body collapsed against the car door. Her breaths were short and weak. She regained her balance, stood upright, and stared at the envelope tucked beneath the wiper blade. She leaned against the front fender of the Volvo as her right hand lifted the black metal blade, and her left hand slid the beige envelope free. Then she opened the car door and climbed inside.

The envelope was clutched in her right hand, which rested on her right thigh. She felt her body quiver as her eyes froze upon the name, Nora Williams. As if the envelope was tainted in poison, Nora's hand exploded open and the latest communication fell to the floor. It sat at her feet upside down for almost a minute.

Dazed, she started her car and let it idle with her hands clutched to the steering wheel. When she gathered the strength to pick the envelope up, she felt physically ill. She looked out the windshield afraid the man who put it there may still be around but the parking lot was empty.

She tore apart the back of the envelope with such force it ripped the paper in half. A photograph sailed through the air and landed sideways on the inside of her leg, resting on the seat. She reached down and flipped it over, and she caught sight of the image on the face.

It made her gag and her hand shot to her chest and her fingers clutched at the lapel of her coat. It was a picture of the bloodied murder weapon inside a plastic bag. Nora tossed it onto the passenger seat and looked over to make sure it landed face down. Her eyes caught the words printed on the back. Two words, "ten days," were written with magic marker in thick, black letters. She put the car in drive and sped out of the lot.

She drove down Route 1 with her hands glued to the steering wheel. When she turned left onto Route 4, she heard the quick blurb of a siren. Blue lights flashed in the mirror above her. The controlled short yelp of the siren squelched again. She pulled to the side of the two-lane road, and a police car parked behind her. On the verge of tears, she reached the gear stick and pushed it into park. The officer arrived at the driver side window. He bent over and looked in. Nora rolled down the glass.

"You went through a red light back there, ma' am."

"I did?"

"Yes, ma' am, may I see your license, registration, and insurance card please."

Nora fumbled through her pocket book and pulled out her wallet. Her hand shook as she took out her license and laid it on the dash. Then she reached over the photograph and opened the glove compartment. She lifted out the car manual and placed it over the upside down print. She was scared to death the officer had seen the writing on the back. What if he asked to see what it was? She retrieved the card and registration and handed them to the awaiting officer.

"I'll be back in a minute, ma' am. Please remain in the car."

Nora exhaled and watched in the rear-view mirror as he talked into a microphone and then looked down toward the seat. She suddenly realized Robert would be home waiting, and the driver couldn't leave until she arrived. The officer took his time. He looked down, then up, then picked up the microphone again and then finally opened the cruiser door. He walked toward her car.

"I'm only going to give you a warning this time, Mrs. Williams. Please be more careful."

"Thank you, officer."

The cop walked back to his cruiser and pulled out and around her. Nora put back the insurance card, registration, and manual and closed the compartment door. She slipped her license back into her wallet. Then Nora grabbed the photograph and placed into her pocket book. She proceeded with caution and drove slowly home.

When she arrived at the house, she pushed Robert inside and got him settled in front of the TV. Then Nora called Hans Janssen, left a message, and made a cup of tea.

As she sat at the kitchen table, Nora looked down to the phone. *Please call*, she thought, *help us...please!*

The Bell-429 lifted off the roof top with the ringing of John's cell phone echoing inside. He looked at the number and answered the call.

"This better be good, Kursman."

"It's done," he answered. "He accepted the offer, John, and the contracts are signed."

"What was the closing price today?"

"Ninety and change."

"That's a thirty-percent premium when it opens tomorrow. Some lucky peons are going to feel big. What time's the press release?"

"It hits the wires at six in the morning."

"You keep your mouth shut, and your eyes open. It'll get regulatory approval within sixty days."

"They're not going to fast track a satellite company to a German in sixty days, John."

"That's not your concern, Kursman. You just tell Cochran to be ready."

Williams hung up. A voice sounded on his blackberry.

"Jesus, what is it Martha?"

"Mr. Williams, your mother's on the line. She said she has to talk to you."

"God damn it, Martha, I told you not to bother me with that."

"But Mr. Williams, she said your father is in a real mess. There's a threat he could be incarcerated. She needs your help."

187

"Well, I guess he won't have to worry about food, clothing, or health care, then, will he, Martha?"

John looked out the window at the Manhattan skyline as he slipped his phone in his side coat pocket. A steady stream of car lights crawled down I-95 bumper to bumper. Williams cracked a smile. He just made more in one day than the whole stretch of highway made in a year. He brought his vision back into the cabin, closed his eyes, and pictured the zeros in his head. As the helicopter banked left and made its turn for Rolling Hills Estate, John opened them and rolled his eyes to the bag on his left. He studied the twine tied in a bow which rested on top, and he reached out with his hand and touched it.

He picked up the package and laid it on his lap. His hands clutched it tight to his chest. Its contents had been hand made by his tailor, delivered to his office that afternoon, and had taken six weeks to complete. As the Bell-429 landed, and Stangler opened the door, John held the bag tight in his hand and walked briskly into the house.

He climbed the winding staircase, zipped down the long hall, and disappeared behind the closed door to his bedroom. He pulled the contents out of the bag and held them up. The craftsmanship and the soft texture of the green-colored Plonge Cowhide was exactly to his specifications. In front of the mirror, he held it up to his chest and checked the size for fit. Pleased, he placed it without a wrinkle on the bed.

The frenzy began. His suit coat landed on the bed. His tie shot straight up in the air and landed in the doorway to the master bath. His shirt floated down to the floor at the bottom of the foot board and one of his shoes hit a wall. By the time he was stripped naked, the bedroom was a chaotic mess. He turned toward the bed, bare as the day he was born, and carefully lifted the garment in the air. He slid it up his legs and over his left shoulder and turned to the mirror for a look. He moved side to side then turned around and examined the back.

"Perfect," he said rubbing the material with the palm of his hand. "Perfect!"

He sprang over to the night table and picked up the hat sitting on top of the book. He placed it onto his head and walked back to the full-length mirror. With his left arm stretched into the air, he spoke.

"I'll teach you to jump on the wind's back!" he said. He danced around the room swinging his arm back and forth, while his eyes were glued to the reflection in the mirror. "'Tis time," he said. He picked up his book, walked to the elevator and pushed the "C" button for the cavern.

When the door opened, he pranced over to the café table, which had a flute filled with 1985 Krug Champagne next to a small bowl of caviar. He sat down and lifted the book level with his eyes and pulled the pages apart. As John Williams sipped from the flute, his eyes focused on the words, and his mind climbed inside the scene in the book. His head moved back and forth with the orchestrated rhythm of his hand, and his lips moved but without a sound being spoken. When his hand stopped, it glided to the open book, turned the page, and then back into the open air.

The sound of leather soles pounded on the stone steps and echoed from the twisted stair well. First one, then another, then another as each foot landed on the tread below, but John's head did not move. The servant paced formally toward the table. Without a sound, he removed the dinner platter from the tray and placed it onto the table. The servant remained silent and expressionless when he saw how John was dressed. Then the noise on the steps commenced again as the leather soles slid on the stone steps and John's voice echoed as he shouted from below. "Then go home, yes, yes, then go home and take your feelings with you! Go, by God, then go!"

He sipped the last of the Krug from the flute and picked up his book and walked over to the elevator. He turned at the door and eyed the French swords that hung above the old tavern door. They were crossed one upon the other. John tilted his head back and off to one side as he studied them from handle to point. He hustled over to the café door. He reached up and lifted one of the French naval officer's swords off the hook, held it in his right hand, and examined the etching on the silver blade. Then he plunged, and he jabbed it into the vacant air.

"Put up your swords, boys," he cried, "this man is mine."

The sword cut through the air as Williams lunged forward, driving the point of the weapon into his visionary target.

"I am the best there ever was!" he yelled. He stepped into the open elevator backward, and the door slid closed.

Nora took the photo in the envelope and stuck it into the kitchen drawer. She could not bear to look at it again. It had been cloudy most of the day and outside the window, the snow had begun to fall. She watched the peaceful calm of the flakes as they landed on the garden bench out back. The words of John's secretary were still fresh in her head.

"I'm sorry, Mrs. Williams, Mr. Williams is out of town. He can't be reached." The snow came down harder now, and the oak tree disappeared in the whiteout.

CHAPTER 29

Janssen picked up his Dunkin' Donuts coffee and slurped the last of the cold liquid as he sat in the rental car on 70th Street. It was a long shot, but Janssen lived on long shots. Some called it luck, some called it a gift, but back on the force his fellow detectives were stunned by the way it always played out. He had built a reputation on beating the odds because he never lost when he placed a bet.

He stared at the cell phone and punched in the numbers he had gotten off the internet. He eyed the pay phone half a block away as he waited for the call to go through. As the first ring came up, he felt that old familiar rush that came from pushing the investigative envelope when the deck was stacked dead against him. That's when Hans Janssen was at his best.

A lady's voice cut in. "Williams Investment Bank, how may I direct your call?"

"Ah, yes…uhm…shoot, I don't remember the fellows name. I'm an associate of Mr. Philippe who is working on a deal with ah…I'm sorry. I'm in my car, and I don't have his name, but Mr. Philippe asked me to call. I have some information on a deal they're putting together. He said they needed the numbers this morning."

"Who's calling?"

"I'm with Mansford Consulting, miss. Mr. Philippe is caught up in meetings all morning, so he directed me to make the call."

"What project is this on?"

"They don't tell me that; that's insider information. I just run the numbers: how many cars are rented a day in the U.S.? Which state has the largest market? What model car is preferred? You get the picture."

"I'm sorry, sir, but I need a name."

"Look, ask around, they said they needed the numbers this morning. Mr. Philippe is not to be disturbed. His secretary is out sick, and I'm three hours from the office on the highway in traffic. Find out who is working with Mr. Philippe and call me at 904-332-4545 with the right fax number or email account. I'll send it from the car. If I don't get these numbers out this morning, heads are going to roll, and if they find out I talked to you, it could be yours."

Janssen figured he had some time to kill so he got out of the rental car and walked a block and bought a cinnamon raisin bagel and a second cup of coffee. On the way out of the deli, his cell phone rang. Janssen shifted the bag to his left hand and held it in the little bit of fingers that stuck out of the cast. He pulled out his phone, looked at the number, and flipped it open.

"Rutherford," he said.

"Janssen, are you sitting?"

"What's up?"

"I had a friend in intelligence run Philippe's name. Juan Philippe worked for the DINA in the late eighties under the Chilean dictator General Augusto Pinochet."

"Chase, speak English."

"DINA, Hans, the Direccion de Inteligencia Nacional, the intelligence agency built to gather information on any threat to the dictatorship and then carry out strong-arm enforcement, which, in this case, was torture or a permanent vacation to places unknown."

Janssen laid the bag of coffee and roll on the hood of his rental car. He held the phone against his ear and shoulder, pulled out his keys, and pressed the fob to unlock the door. The phone started to slip.

"Rutherford, hold on," he said.

Janssen grabbed the bag off the hood and got inside the car. He settled in, picked up the phone, and resumed the conversation with his old partner.

"Ok, go ahead."

"Philippe was a small fish, but he had the training: you know, surveillance, interrogation, torture, and in some cases murder. He's probably the guy who ran you off the road whether he was told to or not. My contact is checking out how he got into the country, and who he's working for…Janssen…"

"I'm listening."

"This is getting pretty deep, international and all. You may want to get the FBI involved."

"Not yet, I've got more work to do."

"It's your call, pal, but I'd watch my back."

"Right."

Janssen laid out his roll on the seat, on top of its paper wrapper, opened the tear-away lid on his coffee, and put it on the console between the seats. He checked his watch, noted it had been forty-five minutes since his phone call, and ripped off a piece of the bagel. He pulled the morning paper from the door slot and studied the NFL scores. After an hour with no action, he dialed up Rutherford.

"Chase, you know the drill. Make sure the camera can't see your face. Sit there until I call you on your cell phone. Play solitaire, blackjack, I don't give a shit what you do just make it look like I'm in the office at the computer."

Janssen waited. He checked his home computer and saw that Chase was actively online. By noon it finally happened.

"Bingo," he said to himself. Janssen watched Philippe look up and down 70th Street, making sure it was clear. He crossed the street and headed straight for the pay phone. The phone booth was occupied, and Philippe stood for a minute nervously looking around. His hands were in his pockets and he turned toward the phone booth and stared at the man inside. Then he looked at his watch, then back to the booth, then he started to walk away ready to turn up 3rd.

"Shit," Janssen said. "He's going to another booth."

He took two more steps. He stopped and turned. The phone booth door opened, and the man stepped out. Philippe hustled into the booth and closed the door. Hans pulled up the recording software and turned the volume up. He listened as the phone rang through.

"You signaled for me to call?"

"You dumb son of a bitch, how'd he know to call here?"

"What do you talking about?"

"He called the office and asked to speak with the person working with Philippe. The main secretary all but put it over the loud speakers, you Chilean asshole."

"He knows nothing. He's guessing, trying to shake things up, relax."

"You ignorant son of a bitch, he knows your name."

"Yeah, but..."

"But nothing, you get the ball back in your court or you're history. Do I make myself clear?"

"What do you want me to do?"

"Finish what you started. He's got Buck's phone, your number, and your name. Use it to your advantage. One more fuck up and you'll be swimming back to Chile with weights around your waist—you dumb shit!"

The phone went dead and Janssen fired up the car. As he drove back to White Plains, he worked on a scheme to flush out the Williams Investment Bank con. He was close, he knew it; he felt it in his gut.

The traffic slowed to a crawl and then stopped. Janssen looked at his watch, two-fifteen. He remembered he hadn't called Rutherford back. "Ah shit," he said, "he must be getting saddle sores." Janssen pulled out the throw away and dialed him up.

"Rutherford, go up to my bedroom closet. You'll see a blue blazer, left center, with brass buttons. Inside the coat, in the pocket, is a wrapped bundle of cash. I want you to count out twenty-five hundred and put what's left back in the coat. Meet me at the motel in," Janssen looked at his watch, "in about twenty minutes."

"What's this about?"

"I'll tell you when you get there."

CHAPTER 30

Ramone listened as he lay still in the dark. He half opened his eyes to a squint with his head still on the pillow and looked at the alarm clock, 1:22. The back door squeaked downstairs and then there was a muffled thud as it closed. A flicker of light danced outside the bedroom window, then it went dark. He rolled over on his back and stared into the darkness with his arm lying across his forehead. *Every night,* he thought, *she's driving herself crazy.* He pulled the sheets and blanket back, slid out of the warm bed, retrieved his bathrobe from the chair, and went downstairs.

Ramone looked out the kitchen door. His wife was sitting on the garden bench in her flannel nightgown underneath a heavy hooded snow parker. She had Bear Paw 436 Eskimo boots on her feet. In her hand sitting inches from her mouth was a lit cigarette that glowed in the dark. Ramone rubbed his forehead with his fingers as he watched her through the glass. Then he opened the door a crack.

"Deborah," he said, "come inside, it's freezing out there."

He waited, but she didn't move. She was sucking the life out of the cigarette and was determined to burn it down until it reached the filter. She took two consecutive draws and then stuck it in the small bucket filled with sand and went inside.

"What are you doing up?" she asked.

"I heard you."

"Why don't you go back to bed, Ramone? I'll be up in a minute."

Ramone put his arm around his wife's shoulder and nudged her toward the family room. "Come, sit down, please?" he asked.

"What?"

"Can we talk?"

She sat on the couch, against the arm, with her coat and boots still on.

"Deb, why don't you take off the snow gear?"

She didn't respond. He sat in the chair beside her. Her eyes had dark black circles under them, and her hands were scrunched between her legs. The short stay in bed had flattened and tangled her long dark hair, and the downward arch of her mouth made her look like a sad soul who'd lost her way. Ramone leaned forward and placed his hand on her thigh.

"Deb...Deb?"

She raised her head. "What?"

"Talk to me, is Dr. Reed helping you?"

"I don't know," she said. She lifted her legs and put her dirty boots on the cushion of the couch and wrapped her arms around them.

"Deb...Deb, talk to me."

"I can't stand myself. I'm crawling with demons; they're eating at me from the inside—driving me crazy. I don't know if I can do this, Ramone, do you know how bad I want a drink?"

"Let's go upstairs and talk, Deb." He reached out and helped her up. "Come on, let's go to bed."

She slid her coat off and left it on the couch. They walked upstairs, and she sat on the edge of the bed and took off her boots. Ramone shut the lights out and laid his bathrobe at the end of the mattress. He brought his wife to his side. Her body stiffened and recoiled at his touch. He leaned over and kissed her forehead. "I'm here, right by your side."

"Ramone?"

"Yes."

"Something's wrong with me. I don't know what it is, but something's not right."

"What do you mean?"

"Something inside," she said.

"What is it?"

"I don't know."

They were quiet for a time. The warmth had returned to the sheets. He had taken her hand, but it felt empty and limp and didn't respond to his touch. She blew out a deep sigh.

"What do you think I should do, Ramone?"

"What does the doctor say?"

"I should talk to my mom."

"About what?"

"My childhood."

"Why?"

"Because there's a lot I don't remember."

"And what do you think?"

"I think I should."

Ramone rubbed her hand. He waited for her to say something more, but she didn't. In the silence, they both drifted off to sleep.

Deborah slept until four-thirty when she slid out of bed and went downstairs. She started a pot of coffee and read the morning news. She waited until six-thirty and then she made the call. She left the house by seven.

When Deborah walked in, her father lifted his left hand and wiggled his fingers hello. His movement took her by surprise, but her mother's voice snapped her back.

"Hello, dear, you seem to be a stranger these days."

"I've got a lot going on."

"So much you can't visit your own mom and dad?"

"Mother, I'd like to talk to you, alone."

"Is something wrong, dear?"

"Besides drinking myself to death, smoking two packs of cigarettes a day, and thinking I'm going crazy? No, Mom, everything is great. Let's go to the living room. We need to have a talk."

Deborah sat on the couch opposite her mother. Nora looked at her concerned. "What is it, Deborah?"

"Do you understand what's going on here?"

"You're upset?"

"Jesus, Mom, upset? I'm a drunk. I had to go dry out, and I'm trying to stay sober every day. I'm killing myself with these cigarettes; I can't sleep at night, and I'm scared to death to be alone."

"Deborah, you're overreacting. It's probably hormones, dear. I went through the same thing when I was your age."

"Hormones, I'm seeing a psychiatrist because of hormones? I don't think so."

"Deborah, don't say that so loud. Someone may hear you."

"Like who, Mom, the walls?"

"Deborah, what's gotten into you?"

"Jesus, Mom, have you heard anything I've said?"

"Yes, dear."

"I need a smoke. Put on a coat, Mother. We're taking a walk."

"I can't leave your father alone."

"Then we'll sit out in the garden and talk. Grab your coat."

Deborah stormed to the kitchen, picked up her jacket, and slung it onto her shoulders. Outside, she marched over to the concrete bench by the oak tree and plopped down on the cold fabricated seat. With her eyes, she followed her mother's movements on the other bench as Nora positioned herself with her hands on her lap and a blank stare on her face. She was irritated by her mother's denial, and her unwillingness to acknowledge what a mess her life had become.

Deborah spoke with a sharp tone in her voice. "Don't you have anything to say?"

"About what, dear?"

"About what I said."

"What was that?"

"I can't believe you, Mother. Do you think I'm normal? Do you understand what I'm admitting to? I'm an alcoholic, Mother, a lying drunk. Talk to me damn it, say something!"

"Deborah, there's no need to be nasty and upset."

"Nasty and upset…"

"Deborah…"

"Did something happen to me, Mother, something very bad?"

"What in heavens do you mean?"

"I mean like did someone hurt me, or try to take me away, or did I almost drown, anything. Did something traumatic happen to me? Something that I can't remember?"

"My goodness, Deborah, I've never heard you talk like this. Is that psychiatrist putting these thoughts in your head?"

She took a draw on her smoke and looked at her mother. "Answer me. Did something happen to me?"

"Deborah, you had a wonderful childhood. You were a very happy child, and your parents loved you very much."

"Then why can't I remember it? Why is there a blank in my head where there should be a memory?"

"I don't remember much of my childhood, Deborah, but that doesn't mean something happened to me. I'm afraid this doctor is planting ideas in your head, dear."

Deborah pulled another cigarette out of the pack and lit it up with the one she had been smoking. She inhaled and blew the smoke toward the ground. Nora turned her head and looked perplexed.

"Why was John always at sleep-away camp when we stayed at Crab Point?"

"Jonnie loved summer camp; he begged to go each year. We asked you, but you said no."

"Why wasn't he ever at home when I was young? How come he always went to boarding schools?"

"Your brother, Deborah, was very mature for his age. He wanted to excel, even then. He thought public school wasn't good enough. He had straight A's all through prep school, then at Harvard, where he got his MBA. And look, Deborah, look at how he has excelled. You see him in magazines, on television, on the news. John is a very successful man now. Your father and I are very proud of your brother."

Deborah squinted as she examined the look on her mother's face. It took a few moments, and a couple of inhales, before she decided to push it further. "Horse shit, Mother."

"Deborah, that's enough."

"No, it's not, Mother. I want some answers. I want to know the truth. Your loving son hasn't talked to you in ten years…is that normal? Give me the truth!"

"And what truth is that, dear?"

"What are you saying, Mom, I had a normal childhood? So did John? I took to drinking. He removed himself from the family, but we grew up like normal kids?"

"That's right, dear, just like normal children."

"Talk to me, Mom, the truth."

"Why would I lie, dear?"

"Mom."

"You're upsetting me, Deborah."

"Good, because I've been upset for a long, long time. No, not just upset, a God damn wreck."

"Deborah, please, I think that's enough now."

"Talk to me, Mother."

"Oh dear."

"Talk!"

"Please, I have enough to deal with, with your father."

"Why, why am I so fucked up, Mother, why?"

"Oh sweet Jesus, Deborah, oh my, I must go look in on your dad. He's been alone far too long, dear."

Nora walked off to the house. Deborah threw her smoke into the bucket. She sat on the bench with her head down for a moment and then looked up at the house. She stared at the back door. After a long while, she stood up, snapped a disgusted look at the image of her mother in the kitchen and stomped off to her car.

CHAPTER 31

Janssen waited for the walk light on the corner of Williams and Beaver as his brain ran a mental check list of how it was going to go down. He was oblivious to the morning rush hour traffic that sped by, or the sirens that yelped down Water Street or the helicopter that flew overhead. Janssen was focused on the order of the events he had carefully planned out the day before. Everything needed to happen in the exact sequence he had mapped out or his scheme to uncover his mark would fail. And failure, for Hans Janssen, was not calculated into the mix.

The light turned, and he proceeded down Beaver Street. A block down Beaver, Janssen took a right onto Broad Street. He stood on the curb and looked toward the row of buildings. The one that housed Williams Investment Bank was not hard to pick out. It was the tallest on the block. At thirty-five thousand a month, the twentieth floor belonged to John Williams with his Bell-

429 parked up top. And as Janssen eyed the granite façade, his mind entered the massive structure, and he envisioned the workspace inside. Somewhere on that floor this whole charade had been hatched, and he was going to enjoy every step of this last maneuver. After all, the ex-homicide cop had again cracked another tough and seemingly unsolvable crime.

He stood amongst a crowd of financial district suit coats with the Wall Street Journal tucked under their arms. As he waded through the herd on their way to the opening bell, he reached in his side coat pocket. The recording device was set and just needed to be turned on. His left arm was hidden under the long formal coat in a sling, and the empty sleeve hung limp in front. He checked the microphone on the lapel of his sport coat and then slid his hand to the inside pocket. Janssen touched the wad of crisp one-hundred dollar bills and then removed his hand from his jacket. Everything was in place.

The light turned green and the suits began to move. Janssen stayed in stride. He separated himself from the pack on the other side of the street and eased against a building on the left. His eyes locked onto the rotating front glass door of the office building across the street. He looked at his watch, 8:55. He nodded his head and started to walk. Suddenly, he felt a jerk on both of his arms. The force pulled him backward and turned him away from the building.

"Resist and we stick you with this needle," a voice said.

Before he had a chance to think, a van sped up to the curb. It had black windows, no markings, and the side door slid open and stopped. They shoved him inside. Two men climbed in behind Janssen, pushed him into the first seat, and pulled a hood over his head. The door crashed shut as the van took off and barreled down Broad Street.

He sat in darkness and felt the motions of the van turning left, then right, then it stopped. A moment later, his head jerked back, and the van moved again. His body tilted from the pressure of a hard right turn. Horns beeped, sirens sounded, car engines roared past, but no one said a word. He felt the hood move in and out with each breath he took and sensed warm moisture forming next to his mouth. He grabbed the armrest to steady his body as the van made a hard left turn. It stopped.

The noise had changed. Janssen knew they had left the street. He heard a heavy metal door begin to close behind them and with a hard thud, it hit the concrete. The side door of the van slid open. They pulled on his arms and dragged him out of the van and escorted him up four concrete steps. *A service garage,* he thought, *a loading dock.* They nudged him forward, one on each side. He heard the ding of an elevator bell, then the sliding of the doors, and Janssen was pushed inside. The elevator continued to rise. Both his arms were still secured by the grip of the two men. *How many floors up? No way to count.* Then with a jerk it stopped.

The echo of the doors as they opened signaled a sparse and empty hall. He heard a door open, he was led forward and then pushed down into a chair. When the hood was lifted from his head, he squinted as the bright florescent light poured into his eyes. As they adjusted, he caught his first glimpse of his abductors.

Janssen examined the two men sitting across from him. They were dressed in dark suits—like the rest of the

Wall Street zombies—and looked like they belonged on the floor of the exchange. One of the men had gray hair and looked mature and distinguished. The second, a younger man with jet black hair and a dark clean shaved beard, looked like a subordinate. The dark-haired man leaned forward in his chair. His jacket separated, and Janssen eyed a Glock strapped to his belt. *CIA, FBI, mob hit men, who the hell are they?*

Janssen examined the room. Big, white cloth sheets hung over the windows to disguise the outside skyline. The empty office looked old and worn. The cheap linoleum floor tiles were faded. The walls needed paint, and a number of the discolored sound-proof ceiling tiles above were missing.

"Who are you?" Janssen asked.

"That doesn't matter," the dark-haired man responded.

"What do you want?"

Neither man answered. The man on the left, the one with gray hair, took a small pad out of his coat pocket and turned the pages a few times. Janssen thought it odd they hadn't secured his hands, but he still had no intentions of trying to flee. The dark-haired man looked at the older man and raised his eyebrows, as if to say, "You or me?" The gray-haired man looked at Janssen.

"You've gotten too close," he said.

"To what?"

The younger man burst in now. "To the core of the operation."

"What the hell are you talking about?" Janssen asked.

The older man took control. "What do you know about Williams Investment Bank?"

"What do you know?"

"I'll ask the questions, Mr. Janssen."

His eyes opened wide at the use of his name. "How do you know my name?"

"Answer the question."

"Nothing."

"Then why were you headed there?"

"I was just going for a walk."

"With a recorder and a wad of cash?" the young man asked.

The older man held up his hand to his partner, signaling for him to stop. He pulled out an 8 x 10 brown envelope from a small briefcase sitting on the floor. He tossed it over, and it landed on Janssen's lap.

"Open it," he said.

Janssen looked at the two men and then down to the package.

"Go ahead," the younger man said. "Open it!"

Janssen picked it up and untied the string. He opened the flap and slid out a small pile of colored photographs. The first was a picture of him sitting in the rental car on 70th street. The second pictured Rutherford as he walked down the street after Philippe. He continued to flip through the prints. It was a documentary on Hans Janssen, private investigator, from the beginning of the case to the present. Every move he'd made in the last thirty-five days. He stared at the two men with his head cocked to one side.

"Who are you guys? These aren't amateur pics. Some of these are satellite."

The gray-haired man went back into the briefcase and pulled out another 8 x 10 brown envelope and tossed it to Janssen.

"Open it," he said.

Janssen uncoiled the string. He kept his eyes trained on the older man and slid out the contents. A stack of papers fell on his lap. He pulled his stare from the man down to the pile. It was written transcripts of various conversations that had taken place in the course of his investigation. They knew every conversation he'd had.

"Who the hell are you guys?" Janssen asked again. "CIA, FBI, covert? You're not local or state. That's for damn sure."

"We're not," the gray-haired man said.

"Why'd you stop me?"

The two men looked at each other and the older man nodded his head. The younger man took over. "What do you know of Juan Philippe?" he asked.

"I know he's from Chile and worked for DINA."

"In 1973, after the coup in Chile, the self-appointed dictator General Augusto Pinochet appointed a man named Colonel Manuel Contreras to rid Chile of all political opponents: by means of arrest, torture, and ultimate death. DINA or the—"

"Departamento de Inteligencia Nacional," Janssen said.

"Very good, Mr. Janssen, you've done your homework. It was never acknowledged that DINA actually existed, but later proof, and Colonel Contreras's hand in murdering a man in Washington, landed him in jail for seven years. Still in prison in his home land, his reach extends to the U.S. and a group who wishes to re-establish a new reign of terror in Chile.

Leaf Hamlin warned you about this group. Their purpose is to raise cash and funnel it back to the underground to finance a new coup. They do white-collar dirty work and get paid millions. Juan Philippe is one of their leading producers. Last year alone he took in two million seven hundred and fifty thousand."

"He's in a different building," Janssen said.

"They all have separate offices, and no one knows what the other is involved in. The money is given to a runner with four hand offs on the way to the home land. We have all the pieces except the last: the man who takes the money on the other side."

"Why not just take these guys down?"

"Because we're close to getting the entire organization, not just the bank roll."

"So why are you telling me all this secret agent shit?"

"Because we need your help."

"My help?"

"You've been in on this from the beginning," the older man said. "You just didn't know it. Leaf Hamlin was instructed to give you the information. We needed the scam intact."

The older man nodded to the younger and he turned to Janssen. "We'll take the ball from here. You just keep up your PI stuff, but only for the cameras—stay out of the mess. When we're done, we'll hand you the man behind the blackmail scheme."

"What about the knife?"

"You can do whatever you want with it. Throw it in the Hudson River, take it to the police, or keep it in a display case on your mantel. It doesn't matter to us. We know the perpetrator is dead."

"How do you know you can trust me?"

"You wouldn't be sitting here if we didn't."

The two suits leaned into each other. The young man listened, eyes trained on Janssen, and nodded his head yes. Then something else was said, and the younger man looked up toward the ceiling as the older man pulled away.

When the younger man's head came back down, he spoke. "That was a ballsy move, calling Williams Investment Bank, Janssen. We all got a kick out of that."

"Happy to entertain you."

Janssen looked into the older man's eyes. "Who's behind this?"

Again a nonverbal nod and a head shake and the older man took over.

"We'll tell you when the time is right. Just know your client is safe. There won't be any payday. You keep quiet about this meeting, continue to play along, and the fifty thousand you took from Buck Blanchard is yours."

"Jesus Christ, you all got pictures of me pissing too?"

"We do."

"Figures."

"Just do your part," the older man said. "When it's over, I'll show you the picture of the man taping the first note on Williams's front door out at Crab Point."

"You guys could have saved me a lot of work."

"We needed you sniffing around, Janssen. It brought out the fleas."

The younger man threw the hood to Janssen. "Put it on, can't let you see where we work."

He slid the sack over his head, and they led him back to the van.

"You'll be taken to your car, Janssen. Remember, you're just a decoy, no tricks. You'll find your gun, bugs, wallet, and cash in a box in the van."

They helped him into the van. He worked his way over to the seat unable to see. As they started to slide the door closed, it stopped before it snapped shut.

"Oh, by the way," the older man said, "it was Philippe who ran you into that tree."

"Son of a bitch," Janssen mumbled as the door slammed shut.

CHAPTER 32

Something had been bothering Robert all morning. It started at breakfast when Nora was feeding him. He continuously spewed his food out from between his lips and tapped the metal support of the arm rest with a spoon. He wanted Nora's attention. When she rolled him into the bedroom to begin his workout, he refused to cooperate. He stared at his wife defiantly when she attempted to coerce him to stand. By ten-thirty she was frustrated, and tired, and asked Robert what was wrong. He made a circle with his left finger, and he looked straight at her twitching his lips.

"What is it, Robert?" she asked. "You're upset aren't you, Robert, you're upset with me?"

Nora was at her wits' end. She knew he was trying to communicate with the only means he had—his eyes—but she had no clue what he was trying to say. He started to bang the spoon on the metal chaise again.

"Robert, stop that, please!"

He continued until she looked at his eyes. He blinked once, and Nora's blank expression commenced another round of tapping.

"Robert, stop it!"

The clanging ended. Robert closed his eyes and his head tilted toward the floor. She looked at her husband, who now looked defeated.

"You need some fresh air," she said.

She grabbed his coat from the closet, wrestled it onto his body, took his Yankee's baseball cap from the hook by the garage door, and put it on his head. She slid a blanket over his lap and tucked it in around the sides and rolled him to the door. When they got to the end of the driveway, she took a right, and she continued to push her husband down the sidewalk toward the park.

"Look, what a beautiful day. A little chilly but sunny and beautiful, isn't it?"

As the chair rolled down the concrete walk, Nora continued with her conversation from behind. "Remember, Robert, we used to take little Jonnie to the park with Deborah in her stroller. Doesn't it seem so long ago, dear? John so loved to swing on the swing set, and Deborah would sit in her little stroller and laugh as you pushed John from behind. Remember that cute laugh?"

They passed the old one-door fire station, restored by the historical society, and turned down the road on the right. Coyote Street led down behind the old fire station. Two Little League ball fields were located in the back, with chain link metal fencing surrounding and separating the two fields. A small park beyond the fields was enclosed also. It had swings, slides, a couple of see saws and hippo head riders on one side. Nora stopped for a minute adjusting the blanket on Robert's lap, then continued past the fenced in fields. She pointed as they passed.

"Look, Robert, the scoreboard you donated years ago is still there. Remember your advertisement on the fence below? You were a great coach, Robert. Even when John stopped playing baseball, you still continued helping those young boys for years. You made it all the way to the Little League state finals. Everyone in town was so proud. No team had ever gone that far."

Nora looked into Robert's eyes. They were moist and expressed the pain he felt inside.

"I know what you're thinking, Robert. You were a good father. You tried to help John, but he pushed you away. He was a troubled boy and it tore all of us apart, but it wasn't your fault, dear. It just wasn't your fault. I know we agreed to never talk about this, but it's why I don't sleep at night. We all hurt because of it, but we can't change that now."

Robert closed his eyes.

"Look at me, Robert…Robert. You were a dedicated father and husband. In spite of it all, we've had a wonderful life. John was a very confused boy. That's why he stole Deborah's undergarments and took them back to prep school that one year. You didn't make him feel ashamed. You had long talks with John, and whatever you said to him, it helped. He never did it again. You did the right thing, dear, and look at John now. He turned out to be a great success. I just hope…all right, Robert. I won't talk about it anymore."

Nora eased the chair inside the fence and over to the dugout. She turned Robert so he faced the field and sat on the bench beside him. She put her hand on his as he stared at the pitcher's mound.

"Mr. Janssen stopped by last night," she said. "I didn't tell you because I didn't want to upset you before bed. He gave no details, but he said he was close to solving the case. Mr. Janssen also told me we didn't have to bother John anymore. I'm so glad, Robert. He doesn't need to be bothered with our problems. Mr. Janssen said he'd have enough evidence to go to the police and clear this whole thing up. He said that whoever was responsible for the blackmail and the notes would spend a great deal of time in prison. I'm so thankful this whole nightmare is over."

Nora squeezed his hand and looked into his eyes. "I always knew you had nothing to do with that woman's death. I know you too well to think otherwise."

Robert banged the metal of the chair with the commemorative letter opener in his hand. Nora ignored it. She swept her eyes away from his. He banged again.

"It's ok, Robert."

He continued this time hitting metal on metal and would not stop.

"Robert, please stop that."

She looked into his eyes again. "I know. Yes, Deborah and I did talk."

The look in his eyes changed from insistence to anger.

"We just talked about her seeing a doctor, that's all. She said she was drinking too much so she stopped. That's why you're angry with me today, isn't it, Robert? You knew Deborah and I talked. You were afraid of what we talked about. I understand now. Come on, dear. Let's go home."

Nora pushed the chair back to the road in silence. Before she continued toward the old firehouse, she leaned down and adjusted his blanket. Then at the main road, Nora took a left and pushed Robert down the sidewalk toward home. She raised the collar on her coat as a breeze started up as she stared at the empty sidewalk ahead. Nora looked like the life had been sucked from her soul and her face looked tired and frail. And as Nora approached the driveway to their home, with her husband slumped in the chair, she could no longer ignore the truth about her son's behavior, and how callous he had been not returning their calls.

"Martha, I want Compton in my office, now!" His feet touched the Brazilian Azul Guanabara granite and John pushed with the ball of his left foot. His high-back swivel chair spun in a half circle, and it stopped as it faced the Hudson River. He lifted his right hand under his chin and propped up his elbow on the soft leather arm of the chair. With a squinting stare, he pierced the distance between Broad Street and the stiff current of the murky river, and in a semi trance, he gathered the office behind him into his complete command. The door to his office opened and his concentration remained undisturbed.

"You asked to see me, John?" Compton said from the other side of John's desk. Nothing but the rich brown leather back of Williams's chair could be seen from where he stood. A big dark mahogany desk sat in front of the swivel chair. Compton knew John was there even though he couldn't see him. He waited in the tense silence until sweat formed into little beads just above his brow. Francis Compton's eyes moved side to side around the elaborate interior of King John's throne. As one of John Williams's top executives, he knew all too well the bleak cold stare from the back of his chair. And as is expected, he waited for the faceless voice to begin its denigration of his Williams Investment Bank soul.

"Explain to me, Compton, this one hundred-thousand dollar expense?"

"John, I thought we agreed, whatever it took on the Bryant deal. You said that yourself."

"Itemize it!"

Compton stared at the dark leather confused. "John, I can't do that. You know how these deals work: cash payoffs, expensive women. Those aren't the kind of things you get receipts for."

"Two times in one month, Compton? That adds up to a lot of cash."

"The first hundred, John, was for the politicians, the second to get the deal done."

"How close is it?"

"It's practically on paper."

"You fuck this up, Compton, you'll be cleaning bathrooms on the first floor."

"Yes, John."

"You pull another stunt like this without my knowledge, I'll have you castrated—understood?

"Understood, John."

"Finish it. I'll instruct Martha to take the two hundred thousand from your commissions!"

John waited until the door shut and then turned his chair back around. He picked up the phone and called Bollen West, his real estate attorney and asked about the ranch deal.

"Monday of next week, John, the contractor is slated to begin first thing Tuesday morning. The contractor said approximately nine months to completion. The wine cellar with the authentic Tombstone saloon was going to run an extra 750k, John. Should I ok it?"

"I don't give a shit what it cost."

"And the elevator to the second floor?"

"Just get it done. Tell him there's a fifty-thousand dollar bonus for each month it comes in early."

"All right, it'll be put in the contract, and we'll fax it out tomorrow. I'll call you when it's signed."

"Martha, I want the Bell ready in fifteen minutes. I'm going to Greenwich early. Get me Baxter on the phone, and tell Matkins if he doesn't have the Haskell deal done this week, he can clean out his desk."

"Yes, sir."

"Where's Baxter?"

"I'm getting him now, sir."

About ten seconds went by and her voice perked the intercom. "He's on the line, Mr. Williams."

"Baxter, what's the story on the offshore account?"

"Can we talk?"

"Christ, Baxter, just tell me what I want to hear."

"You got three million shares before the announcement, and the buy came from the Emirates. John, it will look like some camel drank crude and shit out gold."

"What's the bump?"

"The average…let's see…it's thirty five-twenty-five in; it's sitting at forty seven-fifty. That's twelve twenty-five a share profit!"

"Sell, and ship half the thirty six mil to Zurich and half to the account in Dhabi. Leave the principle there until I tell you otherwise."

"Got it."

"Martha, is the 429 ready?"

"Yes, sir."

"I don't want to be disturbed. Is that understood?"

"Yes, sir."

John slipped on his suit coat and pulled the pile of papers on his desk together and slid them into the leather case. He locked his desk, logged off the computer, and walked to the elevator on the other side of the room. On the way up, John checked his watch, four-fifteen. He had plans for tonight, and the early exit had been on the agenda since the flight in this morning. The elevator stopped, and the door opened. The Bell–429 hummed just to the left. The transport girl stood at the steps. He climbed in and she closed the door. The copter lifted off and headed toward Rolling Hills Estate.

John called Stangler at the house.

"Did a package arrive?"

"Yes, sir, first thing this morning."

"Excellent, put it on my bed."

"Your selection, sir?"

"I want Wild King tonight. Have the chief select the wine."

"Very good, sir."

The Bell landed and John bolted up the stairs and straight to his room. The package lay on the bed wrapped in brown paper addressed to John Peter Williams. He tore back the paper and pulled open the box.

"Perfect, the final piece, what took you so long, Peter?"

He sat in his leather chair next to the bed and untied his Ferragamo derby shoes. One shoe flung to the left and one to the right, and then the Hermes silk socks ended up on top of the lamp by the bed. He held the new custom made moccasins in the palm of his hand and admired the soft leather and exquisite stitching up the sides. He poked the toe with his finger. The finest top grain leather in the world, under the pressure of John's touch, collapsed. He placed one on the arm of the chair and slipped the other onto his barefoot. He picked up the second and placed it on the other foot. It felt like part of his skin, and he stood and danced first on one leg then on the other until he remembered the rest of the outfit hanging in his walk in closet.

He ripped off his Kiton suit, Hermes tie, and handmade shirt and walked to the closet, removing his boxers on the way. When he reached the closet, stark naked, except for the moccasins on his feet, he jumped into the air shouting quotes from his book. The closet door flew open, and the hat and garment were taken carefully off the hangers. He climbed into the handmade outfit, placed the hat on his head, and leaped over to the full-length mirror.

"You're back," he shouted, "I knew it, just like you said; all it took was faith and trust."

He ran to the night table and retrieved his book and vaulted in the air on his way to the elevator. As the door closed, and it descended to the cavern below, yelping sounds bounced off the walls and echoed in the emptiness of the darkened elevator shaft. When the elevator stopped, John Williams vaulted again into the air and out through the open metal doors.

Nora pushed Robert up the handicap ramp and into the house. She parked Robert next to the cooking island and locked the wheels. "There, Robert, you can watch me make lunch."

CHAPTER 33

"One move and your history," the voice said.

Janssen moaned and rolled over. He'd thought he'd been dreaming. He heard a click, and then a painful flash of light shot into his eyes. The voice came back again.

"Get your sorry ass dressed, now!"

Janssen squinted and tried to focus in the direction of the command, but his night eyes were still in control. He lifted himself upright and sat on the edge of the bed. A cold chill shot through the right side of his neck. The man pressed the barrel deeper into Janssen's skin, and Hans flinched as he regained his sight. Then his shirt and pants landed in his lap.

"Put them on," the voice said.

Janssen, totally awake now and fully aware of a .45 aimed at his head, struggled with his one good arm to get his left leg inside his pants.

"Hurry up," the man said.

Janssen pushed the other leg in the pants, stood up, and buttoned the waist. He slid the sleeve of his shirt up his cast.

"Faster," the man said, and he took the side of the gun barrel and whacked Janssen in the back of the head.

"Shit," Janssen said, "Ah, shit." He grabbed his head with his good hand. "I only got one good arm for Christ's sake."

A coat flew through the air and Hans caught it by the sleeve.

"Let's go," the hooded man said. "Now!"

"What do you want?" Janssen asked.

"Move."

Janssen, still groggy from the hammering of the gun barrel on his skull, walked down the stairs and into the front hall.

"Outside."

Janssen opened the door and proceeded down the three steps to the walk. His van was the only vehicle parked in the driveway. He scanned the landscape to access if the hooded man had an accomplice, but there was none. The man waved the .45 toward the van, and the head underneath the hood nodded in the same direction.

At the van now, the man opened the side door and ordered Janssen to get in. Janssen sensed the presence of the gun just inches from his head as he climbed in.

"Get in the driver's seat," he said. Then the man tossed the keys onto the dash. "Go out the driveway and take a right. Any bullshit and your brains will be part of the windshield."

The van backed out onto Saddle Brook Road and drove north toward Route 4. The clock on the radio display read 2:35, and the street was empty and the houses dark. Janssen rubbed his face with his right hand. His head felt like it was split in half. The blood had dried on his scalp. As he put his right hand back on the wheel, he thought of spare gun he kept strapped under the driver seat. It was well within reach. The left arm under normal circumstance could get away with the move, but things hadn't been normal since he'd been run off the road by the Chilean hood. He turned his attention for the moment back to the road. Then as ordered he took a left onto Route 4.

"Where are we going?"

"Just drive."

About a half mile on Route 4, Janssen was instructed to turn right into the strip mall next to the Hess station and go around to the back. The van pulled to a stop next to a fenced in dumpster. The man opened the side door and stepped out backward, still training the barrel of the .45 at Janssen's head.

"Get out slow and easy. Any tricks you spend the night in the metal coffin behind the fence."

Next to the parked van sat a khaki-colored Ford Explorer. The lights blinked as the man pushed the fob and unlocked the doors. With the gun to Janssen's head, he pushed him face first against the SUV, pulled his hands behind his back, and put a plastic tie around both wrists. Then he opened the back hatch.

"Get in and lay down. If I see your head above the seats, I'll blow it off."

The hatch shut, then the front door slammed, and the Explorer started to move. Janssen heard his van start up. The headlights flashed through the windows as the Explorer began to roll. Janssen, on his side, could feel the turn to the right and then the Explorer accelerated onto Route 4. He wiggled to the side and tried to find a comfortable position. The cast against his right arm was heavy, and it hurt as it pressed against it.

About forty minutes from the strip mall, Janssen felt the SUV turn off to the right. Then a short time later another right and then a left and the street lights disappeared. His right arm had fallen asleep from the weight of the cast. The SUV took a left and the road made a drastic change. The dirt potholes bounced the truck and slammed his cast against his back. The Ford snaked left, then right, and Janssen could hear the sound of the tires against gravel and dirt. The trees looked like skeletons against the half-moon in the cold October sky. He could see them from the side back window as he lay still. *Where the hell are we?*

The crunching of the tires slowed, and the SUV pulled off to the right and stopped.

"Stay down," the man said, and the Ford's engine shut down.

The back hatch flipped up, and the hooded man ordered Janssen to climb out. Janssen struggled to his feet. His body was cramped after the hour ride on his side. A log cabin stood ten feet beyond the Explorer with a front porch, a railing made of tree branches, and stone steps. The hooded man turned on a flashlight, and they walked the short distance to the house. He took out a key and unlocked the door with the gun trained on Janssen's head. They went inside.

The man flipped a switch and two lamps on each side of a couch lit up. The old worn green couch sat in front of a big stone fireplace. A cheap imitation bear rug covered the floor in front of it. On the mantel sat a half empty bottle of Wild Turkey bourbon and two shot glasses sat to its side. The inside of the cabin felt cold and unused.

With the gun in one hand, the man turned the thermostat with the other. After a few moments, Janssen heard crackling from the baseboard radiators, and he smelled the odor that permeates the air the first time the heat is used after a long rest. Janssen figured they were someplace in the Catskills, out in the wilderness, where men come to hunt and drink.

"This way," the man said as he pointed the .45 toward a door.

As Janssen moved, he could feel the barrel of the gun between his shoulder blades.

"Hold it," he said. He reached around Janssen and turned the knob and pushed the door open. "Inside!"

Janssen shuffled to the middle of the dark room. The man flicked a switch on the wall. A light on the night table next to a single bed went on. The bed had a metal brass frame and it was located to one corner of the room. A dark wooden dresser with three drawers stood against the opposite wall. A single wooden saloon chair sat against the wall near the head of the bed, and on the wood paneled walls were faded spots, bleached from the sunlight, probably where trophy pictures had been removed to protect someone's identity. Janssen studied the room in the light. He took note of the window centered over the bed— a possible way out.

The man cut the tie behind Janssen's back.

"Get on the bed," he said.

Janssen slouched on the edge facing the man.

"Lie down."

Janssen looked at the old worn white cotton spread. He noticed some sort of dark stains, like burn marks, at the crease of the pillow on the bed.

"Down," he said again.

"The bed stinks."

The man lifted the .45, and Janssen slid down on his side.

The man took out a pair of handcuffs. He tossed them next to Janssen on the bed and told him to clip one side around his right wrist and the other to the bed frame. When Janssen had finished, the man walked over with the gun pointed at Janssen's head and checked both cuffs with his free hand. Then he shut out the light and left the room.

Janssen dozed in and out. The one arm chained to the bed made it impossible to sleep for long periods of time. By daybreak, he heard sounds from behind the locked door. He listened to distinguish if it was still only the one man. Whatever was going on someone believed he was better alive than dead—but for how long?

The door unlocked, and the man walked in with a cup of coffee in one hand, and the .45 in the other. The hood was again over his head.

"I have to piss," Janssen said.

He handed the key to Janssen and nodded his head. They walked to the bathroom off the kitchen.

"Don't close the door," he said.

"Who are you working for?"

"Keep your mouth shut!"

"Kidnapping's a federal offense, did he tell you that?"

"Shut your fucking mouth, or I'll shut it for you."

"A little edgy—no?"

The man cocked the .45.

"All right, all right, back off," Janssen said.

Janssen did his business, locked himself back up to the bed frame, and drank his coffee with his cast arm, trying to manipulate it to his mouth. Outside his locked door a cell phone rang and a muffled conversation ensued. Then the front door closed and there was silence. A few minutes later, the front door opened and closed again, and he heard the man walk into the front room and pull a chair free from the table in the kitchen. And then silence again. Janssen examined the cuff locked to the brass bed frame and shook his head. *I've been abducted twice in a day and a half; I must be losing my edge.*

CHAPTER 34

The sound of a car approached in the distance. Janssen listened as the blunt thud of tires bounced in and out of the pot holes. It was early evening. The room had grown dark after sunset—a good half hour before—and the constant sound of the car grew louder until it slowed and came to a stop. Janssen, strapped to the bed, turned his head toward the noise. Footsteps from the man in the kitchen began on one side of the room, crossed at the opening to Janssen's door, and then faded as the front door opened and closed. A car door slammed shut, and then another, and then mumbled voices started up. Janssen leaned his head closer to the bedroom door. He strained to see if he could recognize the signature of the tones and couple it with a face. They were too distant and inaudible—just a mixture of noise—and soon the front door opened, and he could tell more than one person entered the house.

Shoes pounded on the wooden floor as they passed by the door and stopped in the kitchen. The smell of cigarette smoke drifted into the room. Then the footsteps continued back to the front door, and the door opened and then closed with a thud. The car engine turned over and then he heard a short crunching of dirt and rock. It stopped, and then the familiar rumbling started up again, and then it faded off.

The bedroom door popped open, and Janssen's eyes suddenly hurt from the flash of light. He squinted and looked at the dark silhouette of a figure coming through the open door. As it moved closer, he recognized it was the man with the hood. Janssen had surmised he must be one of Philippe's cronies. He was carrying a tray, and as he approached the bed, Janssen could see it was something to eat.

"I have to go to the bathroom first," Janssen said.

The man turned his head to the right and placed the tray on the night table. Then he took the key out of his pocket and threw it on the bed. He pulled out his gun from his belt and waved it toward the door. Janssen unlocked the one cuff, slowly rose to a sitting position, and then carefully tried to stand. His legs were stiff and awkward, and he needed a minute to get his balance back. It had been an entire day since he'd been on his feet. The man waved his pistol again. Janssen got up slowly, and he stumbled off to the bathroom.

"Leave the door open!" the man said.

"I have to take a shit."

"Do as I said!"

"Jesus Christ," Janssen said. "You going to stand there and watch?"

The man waved the pistol in the direction of the bathroom.

"Get going," he said.

He positioned himself to the side of the door where Janssen's bare legs were visible. As Janssen sat down, he scanned the bathroom for an object he could use to unlock the cuffs. The bathroom had been stripped of everything but the shower curtain. When he finished and stood up, the man waved the gun again and they proceeded to the bedroom. Janssen sat on the edge of the mattress and showed him his cast.

"I can't eat with my left hand," he said.

The man picked up the saloon chair from the foot of the bed and placed it by the door. Janssen picked up the tray and placed it on the bed. Then he took a bite of the sandwich. It was Tuna fish on white bread, but it tasted like filet minion. As he chewed, he looked over to the man in the chair.

"Who are you, and what do you want?" Janssen asked.

The hood stared back at him.

"How much is Philippe paying you?"

Still nothing.

Janssen chomped on the tuna sandwich and washed it down with a some milk.

"How about we make a deal? I'll double whatever Philippe is paying you, and you say I escaped."

"Shut up and eat!"

"Philippe's in it for himself. You think he cares what happens to you? What do you think will happen when it all comes down? You're American. I can tell from your voice. Philippe, he's got a contingency plan just in case. He'll be off to Chile and you'll be left answering to the feds. You ever done time…huh…you know what it's like on the inside?"

"Close your trap!"

"Think about it…double… and it will be cash."

"Put the cuff on."

"I'm not done."

"Put the cuffs on, or you'll need a cast for the other arm."

"Think about it."

Janssen cuffed his right hand and the man waved the gun. Janssen threw the key over, and the man caught it and put it in his pocket. He slipped the .45 in his belt, picked up the tray, and snapped the switch before he closed the door. Janssen was left alone in the dark.

Janssen knew that they intended to kill him when the time was right. The question that puzzled him, though, was why had they waited to take him out? It made no sense. What was the benefit of keeping him alive? He shook his head. None of that mattered. Not if he was stiff. He had to work fast. It wasn't a question of if, it was a question of when and Janssen knew if he hung around to find out the answer to that, he'd be dead.

His right side hurt. His back hurt, and his head hurt. Janssen rolled onto his stomach and slid his legs off the bed so his knees landed on the floor. He pulled himself up and used the space between the horizontal bars in the bed frame to slide the cuff up and down. It allowed enough slack to reach underneath the bed frame with his immobile arm. The cast had been applied above his elbow which left his arm at a ninety degree angle inside the plaster cast. It turned out to be the perfect angle for reaching underneath, but the little bit of fingers sticking out restricted how much he was able to grip.

The cloth material underneath the box spring was thin and old, and his finger popped through the cloth with ease. He made a long tear and maneuvered his hand inside the cloth to one of the metal coils and began to pull. His head rested on the mattress. The bed smelled like old clothes shut up in a box in a wet and humid basement. He took short and shallow breaths. His right hand clutched the metal bars of the head board as his left hand worked a box spring back and forth.

After five minutes, his right shoulder cramped from the strained position, and he had to stop and roll his head and stretch his joints. Janssen pushed and pulled again, but the coil would not budge. After a few more minutes, he raised his body up and sat on the edge of the bed and wiped the sweat from his brow.

Janssen worked the coil most of the night. The hooded man had check in once, and when he heard him coming, he hopped up on the bed and pretended to be sleeping. It worked. He went back to the coil after the man had left. His fingers were raw and sore, and one had started to bleed from the constant rubbing on the metal. He ripped some of the material completely off the box spring and wrapped it around the bleeding hand like a bandage. He clutched the material between his two fingers and slid it under the wrapped cloth as to fasten it. That gave him an idea.

Janssen pulled the blanket off the bed and ripped the top sheet out of its setting. He knelt back onto the floor and grabbed one corner of the sheet with his thumb and first finger and dragged it under the bed. When it got to the coil, he began to push the material around the metal, but each time he tried to grab it on the other side, it fell to the floor. His cast arm ached from the weight of the plaster, hanging for so many hours. He knew the hooded man would be back. And, with the bed pulled apart, he was probably as good as dead.

With the sheet around the coil, Janssen got up off his knees, stood straight up, and holding the metal bed frame, stretched his back. Facing the bed, he maneuvered the looped sheet onto the back of his shoe and pushed as hard as he could. It didn't budge. He tried kicking motions, like a horse, and applied as much pressure with each lunge as he could. The coil started to loosen. One more tremendous thrust and the bottom part of the coil let go. But the top was still attached. Janssen pulled the sheet until taught and pushed with everything he had. The coil popped.

CHAPTER 35

Deborah stared at her hair color in the mirror and scanned down to her face. The image she saw disturbed her. She examined the dark caverns beneath her eyes, the cat whisker wrinkles on the sides of her temples, and the weathered look of her face. The years of drinking and smoking had taken its toll. She looked more in her late fifties than forty-two, and she was disgusted by how far she had let herself go. As she locked onto her reflection and looked into her own eyes, she vowed to make a change.

It was time to get a job, too. It had been ten years since her last employment. She had taught art at a middle school where Ramone had been a very young assistant principal. That's where they met. Her drinking was still under control back then, although on weekends she had begun to hone her craft. After one year of dating, Deborah and Ramone got married and Ramone took a job at the high school. His career had advanced and they felt the time was right to try to have a family. Twelve months passed and Deborah failed to become pregnant. That's when she went for tests.

She was diagnosed as having idiopathic hypogonadotropic hypogonadism: a rare condition in which certain hormones are under-produced and prevent the development of functional ovaries. She was told she could never have a biological child. That realization became the excuse to take the cap off the vodka bottle for good. She functioned for the next year teaching art, but that soon changed too.

Ramone was making enough income to support the two so she gave her notice and became a substitute. It all went downhill from there and hide and seek became her new vocation. She had the propensity to drink too much coupled with a lot of time home alone. It was a formula that resulted in Deborah becoming a functional drunk, and now it was clear to her, she needed to get out of the house.

So Deborah spent the morning looking for opportunities in the world of art. She looked for employment on the internet and started a list of where to apply. The phone rang several times, but she ignored it. The fourth time, aggravated, she picked it up. It was her mother and she sounded distraught.

"Deborah, Mr. Janssen is missing."

"How do you know that?"

"He has a friend, Mr. Rutherford, who contacted me. What do we do?"

"About what?"

"Mr. Janssen."

"When did you talk to him last?"

"Yesterday, he said he was close to solving the case and that we didn't have to worry about getting the money from John."

The Challenger 605 headed east with an arrival time at Teterboro airport of 1:22 p.m. In the back of the Bombardier was Senator Les Stanton—a good old boy from Abilene, Texas. He was Chairman of the U.S. Senate Committee on Energy and Natural Resources. Next to him was Charlie Butterman, one of four commissioners on the Nuclear Regulatory Commission (the NRC).

John Williams had a mega deal between Independent Power Producer TTY Energy and Atom Inc. in the works, but he needed one obstacle cleaned up. Atom, the largest nuclear power producer in the United States wanted to build two new nuclear power plants in Texas. The NRC had rejected every new nuke build since 1977, thirty-one years ago, but John Williams was about to change all that.

As soon as the 605 hit the tarmac in New Jersey, all three would be swept into the Bell-429 and flown across state to Williams's mansion in Connecticut. Also arriving by helicopter was Adair Stevens, CEO of Atom Inc. He was expected for a fortuitous late afternoon of drinks, food, and expensive women brought in via limousine.

The estate was far from the peeping eyes of the public and the press, and John Williams had assured the dignitaries their afternoon jaunt would be private and safe. And as the Bombardier descended to ten-thousand feet and awaited clearance to land, loud mouth Les Stanton was entertaining Williams and Butterman with accounts of his heroics on the senate floor.

The Bell landed at exactly 1:52 p.m. and the two guests were escorted down the massive hall to the lower level swimming jungle. They had both heard of it, but nothing could have prepared them for the one and a half acres of gardens, swimming rivers, ponds, and a tributary which led underneath a retractable wall to an outside twelve foot hot tub that overlooked the Rolling Hills estate.

John had arranged the proper size bathing suits, optional of course. The three women entered out of the lush green cover of southern Selma wearing grass skirts and a Lei, nothing more. Adair Stevens, who had just landed, was expected to join them momentarily. The girls handed the senator and commissioner an exotic drink with umbrellas and fruit and put a Lei around their necks. Senator Stanton pulled the big old fat Romeo and Juliet from his mouth, with his first finger wrapped around the tobacco, and shot off one of his enthusiastic Texas greetings.

"Well howdy girls, my name's Les Stanton, when you want more, you take Les!"

In the second floor master bedroom suite, John stripped down to his shorts. By the time he arrived at the walk in closet, he was buck naked. The clothes lay in a trail behind him separated by the time it took to take them off. He reached for the hand-made outfit on the hanger and slipped it on, then the shoes, then the hat. He vaulted in the air toward the mirror and stood for a moment and admired the look.

Then he ran to the bed, and his body shot in the air in one swift push off the floor. He landed on the mattress and jumped up and down chanting. "There it is, where all the arrows are pointing." He hopped off and landed on his feet and ran with his arms stretched outward. "Come," he cried out imperiously, "come."

He scrambled to the mirror and turned sideways looking back over his shoulder with his hands resting on his hips and shot a defiant stare at the figure that reflected back. Then, like a general inspecting his troops, he examined the image in the glass. His eyes shot down the glass to the feet, then slowly rose up the torso and finally to the hat slightly cocked to one side on his head. His posture was strong and combative as his head tilted upward, and he intimidated the image with his look. Then he spoke as if addressing his troops. "There are pirates asleep in the pampas just beneath us, if you like, we'll go down and kill them."

He twirled around once and stopped in the position he had started. He demonstrated his power and his control as he lifted his head from his chest just an inch or two. "To die will be an awfully big adventure," he said, and then he suddenly dashed off.

He ran to the elevator and pinged open the door. He pressed the "C" and yelped all the way to the cavern, and when the doors opened, he jumped as if to catch air. As ordered, the Krug was chilled, and a flute was poured next to the wine bucket in front of the cafe. He scurried over to the door and pulled a sword from its catch and eyed the blade down its shiny shaft.

He strutted to the flute and stuck the blade in the floor boards, leaning on it with his hand balanced atop the handle and drank a sip of the champagne. The sword plunged and jabbed through the air as he jumped and danced around the cavern like an old time swashbuckler in the heat of battle. With the flute held outward in his left hand and the sword in his right, he carefully practiced the quick and fatal lunge. Then, in imaginary victory with the blade tilted downward, he toasted with his glass hanging in the air and then drank to the fallen warrior.

He stopped and listened, but there was only silence. He turned his head for a minute to be sure, and then he drank what was left in the glass. With an air of invincibility, he jerked the bottle out of the bucket and downed a hearty slug, then another, and then thrust it back into the ice. With the champagne dripping from his chin, he swept his arm across his face wiping his mouth with his bare skin. The sword swept through the air once more, and the bottle was yanked from its berth. He worked his way with the bottle and the blade toward the open elevator. When he arrived, he pushed the button for the master bedroom chambers, and as the door slid closed in front of him, he took another drink.

A yelp rang out in the compartment as the elevator headed up the shaft. The echoes grew louder and wilder until it stopped at his bedroom, and John Williams vaulted out. He had rehearsed this in his head for years, and he was prepared for whatever he'd face. He stopped and took one last look in the mirror and quoted from the book—again.

"Discipline," he said. "That's what fathers believe in. We must spank the children immediately before they try to kill you again. In fact, we should kill them."

He cracked the door to his chambers and carefully spied the massive dark hall. Assured it was clear, he slipped out the door, and the shadow of a seasoned combatant slithered down the open hall until the second-floor sitting room came to view. With his back glued to the tapestry covering the paneled mahogany wall, his head turned left, then right. In three quick lunges, he landed just to the left of the columned opening on the other side of the eight foot wide hall. John slid his head around the marble column and determined the room was clear.

The soft leather of his custom made shoes landed in silence as he stood in front of the walnut book shelves on the opposite side of the room. He pulled a lever and the cabinet turned. He slid into the dark opening and pushed a button on the other side. It illuminated dim lights lining the stone treads. He pushed another lever, and the book shelves swung shut.

The stairs turned downward winding their way undetected through the inner living space of the eloquent mansion. Only John knew they existed, and he had used them many times before. Sneaking quietly down the treads, he heard the voices as they penetrated the walls of the stairwell, and he was careful not to let the metal blade hit the cold stone steps. Down further, a stone platform had been constructed, and before continuing, John paused. He slid his sword through the leather straps of the tied belt and turned to the wall and carefully slid a four inch by six inch panel sideways. The light from the jungle room shot through the wall.

He leaned his head against the wood and peered through the opening to the tropical forest below. Senator Stanton stood in the stone river gully that flowed through the Selma bushes. He was leaning against the stones with champagne in his right hand and his elbow resting on the bank. Next to him sat a naked woman, with her legs in the water. The senator was rubbing her foot, which slid up and down his chest. John followed the tributary with his eyes and spotted four figures in the hot tub outside. On the laps of Adair and Butterman sat the two naked woman, and the dim garden lights reflected off their bare breasts. John swept back to Stanton with the smoke rising from his big fat cigar. He decided Stanton was the mark. He was too far into the tropical forest to be seen, and, he was separated from the others outside.

John worked his way down the remaining steps and at the bottom spied out the little peephole to make sure it was clear. The clip lifted without a sound, and the small door with the fake rock façade on the outside opened just a crack. He slid out from the secret stair well with his sword pinned to his side, and then he pushed the door closed with his soft leather shoe.

He slithered to the granite boulder surrounded by lush tall Selma and whispered quietly to himself, "To die would be an awfully big adventure."

As he spied over the rock, he tried to reassure the twitches in his stomach and the tightness in his throat. He studied the position of the senator and whispered again, "To die would be an awfully big adventure!"

Deborah walked over to the desk in the kitchen.

"Do you have Rutherford's number?"

"Yes, dear."

"Well, give it to me."

Nora dictated the number and Deborah wrote it down.

"I'll see what I can find out, Mother. I'll call you later."

CHAPTER 36

Hans Janssen managed to place the bedspread back over the bottom sheet. He rolled onto the bed, and his body collapsed into a lifeless heap. His cast hand was raw, cut, and cramped. His back ached from kneeling on the floor and stretching to reach underneath the bed. Janssen reached to his side and picked up the metal coil, lifted it to the cuff, and attempted to pick the lock. The coil's flat flange on each end was too thick to fit into the key hole. He placed the coil in his cuffed hand and tried to bend the metal with his cast hand, but it was too thick. His head fell back onto the pillow, and he exhaled and closed his eyes. .

As he lay on the bed half asleep, he listened for any sound from behind the door, but there was nothing. The noise he had made loosening the bedspring had gone undetected. Janssen slipped the useless tool between the mattress and the wall and thought about what to try next. Within moments, he drifted off to sleep.

Not long after sunrise, footsteps pounded outside the door. He could smell the scent of fresh brewed coffee floating into the room. Then the door unlocked and the man stepped in. He placed a cup on the night table and threw the keys on the bed. "Go piss," he said. He waved the gun toward the door and stood aside. Janssen unlocked the cuff and rubbed his wrist with his fingers. He walked through the living room and into the bathroom.

"Leave the door open," the man said.

Janssen stood at the toilet with his head reared back. As he did, he noticed the metal clips that held the shower curtain to the plastic pole. They were like safety pins, except bigger. He reached over with his right hand and squeezed a pin together without making the curtain shake. He maneuvered it away from the pole, stuck it in his cast at the palm of his hand and zipped his pants shut. He flushed the toilet, and the hood escorted him back to his room.

Handcuffed back to the metal head board, he slid out the clip and stuck the one end into his cast and pried it open. When it was at a forty-five degree angle, he slipped it into the key hole and worked it side to side. The cuffs remained locked. He slid it in and out, round and round, back and forth for almost an hour, Janssen soon realized he was as good at picking locks as he was at picking wives. The only difference was with marriage he had no trouble getting unhitched. He put his head back and thought about the shape of the key.

He started talking to himself in his head. *Hand cuff keys were universal, you dumb shit. Think about it, one key will open any pair of cuffs. It was easy to pick a lock, remember what Rutherford had said. Think, Janssen! He said the key had a pin that released the ratchet gear of the opening arm; get the pin in between the ratchet and notches and it releases the grip.*

Janssen stuck the pin back into the keyhole and felt it slip into the notches. He yanked the cuff with his secured hand and slid the pin in what he thought was the right spot. The cuff sleeve started to move. He pulled harder, and the cuff popped open, and his hand went free.

Released from the cuff, Janssen moved to the closet and searched the contents inside: two wool overcoats, a pair of wading boots, some hangers and a camouflage hat. Then a cell phone rang outside the door. The man answered it. Janssen listened.

"I'll take care of it right away," the man said.

Janssen froze. The click of an ammunition clip released from the handle explained the "I'll take care of it" part. Then there was silence, and then the clip snapped back into the stock. Janssen stuck the wooden saloon chair under the door handle, leaning the feet on an angle to jam the door.

He heard the man cock the .45 and the sound of his footsteps drew toward the door. Janssen lifted the small night table with his right hand and balanced it with the left. He turned toward the bed, across from the shuttered window, and threw it into the glass. The crash of broken glass and splintered wood exploded into the room. The door immediately unlocked, the door knob turned, but the door was jammed.

Janssen moved to the side of the door. The man's shoes pounded on the wooden floor and then there was a tremendous crash. The chair splintered, and the door flung against the adjacent wall. With the bed vacant, the cuffs hanging empty, and the window smashed to bits, the man rushed in with his gun pointed toward the bed. As he cleared the door jam, a tremendous thud knocked him backward and into the next room. The force of the blow had shattered Janssen's cast, and he held it in his right hand. As he quickly moved from the room toward the hooded man, he felt an intense pain shoot up his arm.

He rushed toward the unconscious man and Janssen picked up the gun off the floor. He stuck it in his belt. Then Janssen searched the man's pockets for the key to the handcuffs, and when he found them, he slid them out. He unlocked the cuff chained to the bed and dragged the man to the chestnut post. He cuffed his hands behind the six by six support beam, as he sat upright, still out cold. He cleaned out the man's pockets, staggered to the kitchen table, and fell backward into a chair.

After he collected himself, he returned to the bedroom, ripped the sheet with a steak knife, and made it into a sling. He hung it around his neck and slipped his arm into the support. He returned to the kitchen and rummaged through the kitchen drawers. He found matches, a flashlight, ten rounds of ammo, and a church key. In the refrigerator were five cans of Bud, a half a loaf of bread, a jar of peanut butter, and a quarter of a tub of tuna fish. He loaded up his arms, dropped it on the kitchen table, popped open the Bud, and downed half the can. Then he looked at the busted up cast. *The dumb son of a bitch broke my arm.*

CHAPTER 37

John Williams climbed on top the back of the manufactured glass fiber reinforced concrete hill that simulated a natural outcrop of solid granite. The sword lay against his left side held in place by the tied material functioning as a belt. As he reached the top of the mound, from which all the forest and rivers could be seen, he raised his head above the highest point and spied the two couples still in the hot tub. Then he swept his eyes to Stanton and the girl who were now in the water together. As her hands massaging his scalp and her breast stimulating his face, Stanton's cowboy slang fell into quiet moans. Williams slid down the incline toward the river and advanced to a Selma tree on the right.

He lifted his legs with an intentional vigilance, mocking the movement of a stalking cat. One foot set down, the other eased up as his body worked toward the thick oversized leafs of the mature Selma trees. His eyes gazed out between the foliage and focused on his prey—unaware in the river ahead. Crouched in a thicket of three tree trunks, his left hand pushed one of the thick stems aside. He studied Stanton now lying on the bank. The women's mouth was working the senator's mid-section, and her legs were wrapped around his head.

Williams crept undetected and edged closer to his mark. His left hand squeezed the blade to his side, and he lowered to one knee. Now only six feet from Stanton and the girl, Williams lowered onto his belly. He froze as Stanton's excitement rang out.

"Yee ha, little lady, you sure are a gifted mare."

Laughter echoed from the hot tub. Stanton turned his head, but when he realized he had the cover of the jungle, his attention settled back to the lovely lady at his waist. John watched from the shrub as the senator lay back on his towel smoking his Cuban cigar making sounds cowboys make when they rounded up cattle. Six hours earlier Senator Stanton sat in the Senate Chambers passing a law to make stiffer penalties for prostitution. Now, the good ole boy from Texas was on recess testing the wares. He raised his flute of champagne into the air as his enthusiasm reached a sexual crescendo.

"You bess tie the bell on your bull rope, little lady, cause Les Stanton's gettin' ready to ride!"

John Williams had seen enough. It was time to move in. On his stomach, he lifted his body up by his elbows and crawled to the six foot boulder a few feet away. The river current slapped against the manufactured rock walls and made a steady splash as it ran by the bend. It drowned out the sound of the disturbed soil as Williams maneuvered through the crop of ferns. He reached the rock, arranged the sword by his side, and pulled his body up the boulder and peered over the edge. Only four feet separated the new look out post from the delirious Senator Stanton.

A thicket of Florida Bottlebrush Threeawn grass lined the riverbank about two feet back from its edge. Between the rock and the grasses, a thirty-inch wide gravel walk ran parallel to the senator. John pulled the sword from his belt. He reached behind his back with his arm and held the belt away from his body and slid the sword point up through the cloth. He pushed it up until the blade lay across his back, and the handle rested on his back end. After surveying the landscape one last time, he lifted his body onto his hands and toes, just off the soil, and crawled around the rock and into open ground.

He inched sideways, instead of straight forward, making sure before he put full weight on either hand or foot the rocks would not move under his weight. He stopped at the sound of Stanton's voice.

"You bring that Texas rump roast up here, little lady. Old Les Stanton's gonna put you on the spit."

John pushed across the walk to solid ground. He weaved in and around the gaps of the grasses as the sounds of moans from Stanton's mouth grew closer. Just short of the edge of the river, John laid flat on his front and reached behind his back and slid the sword out from under the belt. He rolled over on his back and inspected the blade.

At the tip, where it had settled in the dirt, a line of powder covered the metal. He wiped it on his stomach and checked both sides to be sure it was clean. Then he rolled back onto his stomach and wiggled to the last plantings and looked around a clump. The woman now on her hands and knees faced away from John. The good old cowboy rode her from behind. He was on his knees upright holding her sides with his hands.

He's mine, John said in his head.

John brought the sword up and out from the grass. Stanton howled again. "Yee ha, ride 'em, Stanton."

It caught John off guard, and he pulled the blade back into the grass. He felt his heart as it pounded in his chest. A rush of excitement overtook his body. The kill lay only inches away. John glanced back around the reeds of grass. Les Stanton was playing rodeo as the woman egged him on.

Her hands reached behind him and smack his butt. "Giddy up," she yelled.

John raised the sword once more and eased the blade out of the grasses. He pushed himself up with his left hand as the sword rested in his right. Inches off the ground, motionless, his inner voice prodded him on. "You can do this, you can, you, Peter, you can." His head barely above the seeds of the stalks, he reached out farther as Stanton's head leaned back and faced the ceiling.

Then John Williams screamed in his head, *Die pirate, die!*

He rose to his knees, and reached out with the sword, and as it approached Senator Stanton, he thrust it into his butt cheek and retreated. As John lay in the shelter of moving grasses, Stanton went wild.

"Yee ha, little lady, your nails are like the claws of a Texas Grizzly. I'll be your Davey Crocket!"

John peered through the grass. Stanton's right hand waved in the air, and a tiny stream of blood ran out the cut in his back end and down the inside of his leg.

"Yessss," John said, "Yessss!" He slithered off.

He retreated to the boulder and then the Selma and to the mountain and the secret door. John bolted up the stone stairs as if shot from a cannon, waving his sword in the air triumphantly. When he reached the top step, he scanned the room out of a peep hole in the secret door. It was all clear, and he pulled the lever. He closed the bookshelf door on the room side and vaulted across the hall and into his bedroom.

The elevator doors opened and John rushed in. He danced as the compartment slid down the shaft, and when it hit bottom, John stood in front of the door, with the point of the sword in the ground, both hands atop the handle. He had one leg across the other, and his head was cocked to one side.

He scanned the cavern toward the café façade and stopped at the orphan sword that hung above the door. A new bottle of champagne had been placed in the bucket. He strutted to the table, poured the liquid into the glass flute, leaned on his weapon, and gulped the entire glass down. He hurled the flute at the café door, and it shattered into a million pieces. "I'm the best there ever was, and the best there ever will be," he said. "Now ride the wind, Peter, ride the wind!"

He stood at the side door that led to the helicopter pad. Dressed in his Kiton suit and Hermes tie, he greeted Adair, who was the first to leave. The smile that stretched from ear to ear on Adair's face made it clear the party had been a huge success. And if anyone got cold feet, John had the video tapes of the Les Stanton show. When Stanton and Butterman arrived at the door together, they embraced each other like old friends.

Stanton, of course, couldn't keep his mouth shut long enough to breathe through his nose. "That's quite the spread you got here, Williams. Take it from a good ole Texas boy, that's one of the finest Texas barbecues I've been to since I saw a coyote and wolf howling at the moon holding hands. Just one thing short of hog tying a steer though, Les likes more poontang than can be found on one mare—that's more for Les, if you know what I mean."

John walked them to his Bell-429 and watched as they climbed inside. Stanton moved to his side as he sat down, and his eyes scrunched together. His lips moved as his back end hit the seat. John noticed, and a great sense of pride ran through him. When they settled in their seats, John handed them each a yellow envelope that sealed the deal.

"Boys, you forgot your party bags," John said.

He ambled back to the mansion calculating the number of zeros this one would bring in. He stood at the door as the Bell lifted off and smiled at the thought of Stanton and Butterman staring inside the envelope at a hundred thousand in crisp new c-notes. The Bell shot forward toward Manhattan, and John looked up at the departing transport and as he watched it level off and shoot forward, he whispered in his head. "Second from the right, straight on till morning, boys, second from the right, straight on till morning!"

CHAPTER 38

Janssen finished the last of the Bud staring out the window at the lake behind the house. Then he got up and walked through the kitchen and over to the man chained to the chestnut beam. The blood had dried on his face and shirt, and his nose was black and blue and bent sideways to the right. The man didn't look at Janssen as he approached. His head hung down toward his waist, and his chin rested on his chest.

Janssen dragged the wooden chair from the kitchen, placed it in front of the cuffed man, and sat down just short of the man's feet. With the gun in his right hand pointed at the man's head, he started his interrogation.

"Who are you working for?" Janssen asked.

"Go fuck yourself," the man said.

Janssen pulled out the cell phone taken from the man's pocket. He opened it up, pulled down the menu, and went to recently made calls. The last number called was Philippe's. It was the same number as the one on Buck Blanchard's phone. Janssen had it memorized now. He scrolled through the remaining numbers and then to the man's address book: Buck Blanchard, Juan Philippe, Robert Williams, Hans Janssen. He looked at the man.

"You dumb son of a bitch—putting in real names."

Janssen strolled back to the kitchen table. He examined the items collected from the man's pockets: a wallet, an extra clip for the .45, and a key which looked like it belonged to a pad lock. He pushed them aside and rubbed his forehead. His broken arm throbbed. He found a bottle of Advil in the medicine cabinet and ate three after struggling with the child proof top. He stuffed the bottle in his shirt pocket, walked back to the living room, and slid the hood back over the hand-cuffed-man's head. "You look better with it on," he said.

He examined the wallet, which contained receipts, credit cards, a hundred and fifty in cash, a driver's license, a piece of paper with Janssen's license plate number, and a storage locker receipt for a rental in Newburg, New York. The license identified the man as Colt Buchanan, and his address was listed as Boise Falls, New York. The storage locker receipt disclosed it was rented using an alias, Steve Dunkirk, of Kruger Falls, New York. Janssen scanned through the various receipts.

Most were related to purchases for electronic devices which he recognized as surveillance oriented—all paid for in cash. Janssen set them aside, put the cash in his pocket, picked up Buchanan's cell phone, and dialed up Jack Rutherford.

"Rutherford it's me, Janssen. I need you to look into something."

"Jesus, Janssen where the hell are you? I've been trying to reach you for the past two days."

"I'll explain later, see what you can find out about a man named Colt Buchanan, Boise Falls, New York."

"Forget that, Janssen, listen to me. John Williams has been taken into custody by the feds. I was at your office trying to dig up clues to your disappearance and two guys surprised me on my way out. They looked like FBI dressed in suits and claimed they needed to talk to you. What the hell are you into, Hans?"

"Did they leave a contact number?"

"Yes."

"Give it to me."

"Janssen, did you hear what I said about John Williams? It's all over the national news?"

"Chase, the number."

Janssen hung up and made the phone call. The older man answered, the one from the abduction episode in Manhattan. He instructed Janssen to leave the cell phone on and sit tight.

Janssen turned on the TV in the living room and was surprised it had cable. He popped on CNN. It was their top story, and Wolf Blitzer was in the news room pulling in the latest from correspondents all over New York.

Behind him ran a tape of John Williams handcuffed, being escorted out of his office building by two men in suits. Each man had a hold of an arm. It was the same two men he just spoken to on the phone. In front of the video was Blitzer, who was reading from sheets of paper in his hand.

"This just in: this morning John Williams was taken into custody immediately after his Bell-429 landed on the roof of his office building on Broad Street. This is the building where Williams Investment Bank is located. The FBI has refused to answer questions but has scheduled a news conference for three-fifteen this afternoon. According to an affidavit filed in federal court this morning, John Williams is charged with multiple counts of bribery, extortion, conspiracy to influence federal regulators, and insider trading. According to one source, the charges involve hundreds of millions of dollars in illegal trades. We will bring you more on this story as it develops. This is Wolf Blitzer for CNN breaking news."

Janssen looked over to Buchanan, awake but with his head under the hood hanging down toward the floor. He went back to the kitchen and found a small paper bag in the pantry closet, to the right of the refrigerator, and placed the items taken off Buchanan into the bag. He brewed a pot of coffee and sat at the kitchen table and drank from a mug and waited. He knew what to expect. The agent had told him to leave the cell phone on so they could triangulate his location using the signal. About twenty minutes later, he was right.

In the distance, he heard the sound of a helicopter as it approached the cabin. It grew closer and louder and even Buchanan lifted his head. When it reached the cabin, it circled in a radius from the lake to the field in front of the house. Janssen got up and walked over to the front door. After the second pass, it hovered over the swaying brown grasses of the field and slowly descended toward the ground. Janssen opened the door, leaned against the jam, and watched the Black-colored Bell UH-1H float down with the white FBI letters painted on the side. The wind from the rotors bent the grasses toward the ground as Janssen sipped his coffee, and the chopper touched down.

The motor shut down, and the blades began to slow then stop. The side door slid open, and two men in suits jumped out. The gray-haired man and the younger man from Manhattan walked toward the house.

When they reached the door, the gray-haired man put out his hand and spoke. "My name is Special Agent Brent Thomas, and this is my partner, Special Agent James Blake. Let's go inside."

Halfway through the door Blake turned to Janssen. "Looks like you've been busy Janssen. Is that Buchanan?" Blake asked.

"It is. You know him?" Janssen asked.

"He works for Philippe," Blake said. "We brought them all in this morning before we arrested Williams. We've been looking for you since yesterday. We found your van abandoned in a parking garage in White Plains. We thought we were too late."

"I don't understand," Janssen said. "What did Williams have to do with Philippe?"

Thomas looked to Blake. "Jim, read him his rights," he said as he nodded his head toward Buchanan. Then Thomas turned back to Janssen. "We'll go over all that. Let's get outta here first."

Blake pulled the hood off Buchanan's head. "What the hell happened to him? He run into a wall?" Blake asked.

"Something like that," Janssen said.

Blake unlocked one cuff, stood him up, and re-cuffed his left hand behind his back. Then he read him his rights and escorted Buchanan to the helicopter. Janssen turned to Thomas and shot questions rapid fire.

"Where am I?" Janssen asked.

"About an hour outside of Peekskill," Thomas said.

"What the hell's going on, Thomas?"

"It's over."

"My investigation?"

"Over."

"And the knife?"

"Yeah, the knife, that's got us all shaking our heads. Come on," Thomas said, "we'll give you a lift."

"What about the car?"

"We'll have people all over this place in a matter of minutes—let's go."

Thomas took the evidence bag and the .45, and the two walked to the UH-1H. The blades started to spin as they climbed on board. Thomas slid the door closed and the Bell lifted off. It spun around in the air and climbed with its nose pointed downward. Inside the passenger cabin Janssen was eating Advil, and Thomas and Blake were busy making calls. Buchanan sat in a single seat handcuffed to a hook on the wall, with his nose bent, two teeth missing, and his head hanging down toward the floor. The Bell's nose rose slightly and the UH-1H sped off.

CHAPTER 39

The media circus had obstructed access to the driveway and to the street in front of the house. Ramone maneuvered between the long row of parked vans, which lined the street, and the crowd of reporters huddled into small groups with their lights, umbrellas, and cameras. They were cutting their news clips for the six o clock report. As the crews realized the approaching car was working its way into the driveway, throngs of microphone-holding field reporters encircled the vehicle. Ramone eased forward through the crowd.

Ramone's head flipped right to left as he inched up the drive. Reporters banged on the windows and scurried for positions as the car came to a stop. He turned to his wife. "Deb, stay put until I open your door. When I do, slide out under my arm and don't say a word, just keep moving forward toward the front door. Remember, stay hunkered down beside me and keep moving!"

Ramone took a deep breath and pushed his door open. He was instantly smothered in a claustrophobic circle of screaming reporters. He slid one side of his body against the car and moved to the front. He pushed a microphone out of his face and forged a path around to the front fender. The mob pressed in closer and his movement stalled.

"Stop—now!" Ramone said as he held up his hand. "Move away from the car. I will only say this once more—move away from the car!"

The crowd edged back and he opened Deborah's door. She jumped out, and she slid under his arm, and he pushed their way through the crowd. They reached the front door and Deborah slipped her key into the lock. When they got inside, they both fell against the closed door and tried to grasp what had just happened. It was hard to believe her parents' house was under siege, all because of John.

Nora was sitting next to Robert in front of the TV staring at the screen. She had just witnessed the whole scene of Ramone and her daughter arriving in the car, getting out, fighting the crowd with each step, forcing open the front entrance, and closing the door behind them. It had all been live on the flat screen in front of her. When they entered the living room, Nora turned and looked at Deborah and Ramone with tears rolling down her cheeks.

"Why are they doing this?" she asked.

"It's what they do," Ramone said. "They're like hungry animals waiting to be fed."

"It's on every channel," Nora said. "I can't believe what they're saying about John."

"Mom, they're not making this stuff up. John's in serious trouble, and he won't get out of this one. I guarantee it."

Nora looked up to her daughter. "Do you think it's true, Deborah? Do you think he did all those things?"

"What's wrong with you, Mother? Do you ever face the truth about John? Look at the way he's treated us, his own family. He has no conscience. He has no heart. He wouldn't help out his own father. I believe everything the press has said, and I wouldn't be surprised if there's lots more to come out."

"Let's all calm down and take a deep breath," Ramone said. He turned to Nora. "Nora, we contacted the authorities. No one is allowed to see John until they finish the interrogation. He's probably got ten of his big time lawyers already sitting by his side, holding his hand, circling the wagons. Have you heard anything from Hans?"

"Yes, he called just before you arrived," Nora said. "Mr. Janssen said he'd be coming by in an hour."

"Now he shows up. What happened to him?" Deborah asked.

"He didn't say. All he said was he needed to talk."

"I'll make a pot of coffee. It's going to be a long night," Ramone said.

Ramone went off to the kitchen. As Deborah sat on the couch, the news broke across the screen.

"This just in: these are live pictures from the Channel Four news helicopter flying over John Williams's estate in Greenwich, Connecticut. As you can see, there is a massive search being conducted inside Mr. Williams's mansion. I've counted over twenty law enforcement vehicles presently on the estate. We've been told the search began sometime early afternoon and it may continue well into the night."

"Jesus, Ramone come out here. That's where he lives, that's his house? Ramone," she yelled out. "He lives in a God damn castle. Mom, press the record button. I don't want Ramone to miss this!"

The anchor man continued. "We are going to a live report from Michelle Parks who is flying over the Williams's estate. Michelle?"

"Yes, Dan, as you can see this is the large circular entrance in front of the mansion. I estimate as many as twenty-two cars parked outside. Two large delivery size trucks are backed up to the entrance and for the last three hours authorities have been loading evidence into the trucks. The scale of the estate, as you can see from these pictures, is astounding. We will try and get a shot of what we believe are the riding stables. Marty can you get us over there...yes, there. That, we have been told is the stables to this sprawling fifteen-acre estate."

"His barn is six times bigger than this house. Did you know he owned all that, Mother?"

"No, dear."

"That son of a bitch...his own family has to see it for the first time on TV."

"Deborah!"

Forty-five minutes passed as they sat huddled in front of the flat screen learning about John's life, and the massive amount of assets he owned. They covered his new spread in Wyoming, no pictures yet, but the size and cost were all disclosed. They had a reporter at Teterboro Airport and showed John's Bombardier Challenger parked by a hangar, lit up by security lights. A chopper flew over Manhattan, over his office building on Broad Street, and got a shot of his Bell-429 sitting atop. Then they reported back to Rolling Hills Estate.

"We're going to fly a circle around the entire mansion so the viewers at home can get an understanding of the size and scope of John Williams's stone mansion."

The news camera started with a shot of the massive hot tub Butterman and Stevens had their frolic in. As the chopper started around the south side of the stone facade, the phone rang. It went unnoticed. They were spellbound witnessing the inside world of a reclusive billionaire, and it seemed surreal that the man who owned all of it was actually Deborah's brother and Nora and Robert's son. The phone rang a second time and Ramone picked it up.

It was Janssen calling from the street out front. His car was entangled in the crowd of reporters. He asked that someone let him in the main entrance as he approached the front of the house. When he arrived at Ramone's car, he parked, fought his way to the front door, and pushed his way inside. Janssen sat down in the living room and asked them to turn the television off.

Then he recounted his investigation from the beginning, most of which they had not heard. He started with Barton La Barge, and the incarcerated man's explanation of the blood on the knife. He continued until they understood the complete scope of the investigation. Then Janssen wrapped it up with a colorful expose on Juan Philippe, his Chilean mafia, his side-kick Colt Buchanan with the nose job and dental work, and, of course, Special Agents Thomas and Blake.

"In a few days," he said, "I'm scheduled to meet with Agents Thomas and Blake. I was told they would disclose the individual responsible at that time. The reason for the delay was due to the execution of multiple warrants that would be served over the next two days. This part of the ordeal for you is over, and I have been assured by Thomas and Blake that the threat to your family has been successfully neutralized."

Then he turned to Nora. "I'm sorry about your son, Mrs. Williams. I understand how you must feel, but you need to give the media something to settle them down. They're like a pack of hungry wolves, but if you throw them a bone, they'll back off. I'll handle that. It used to be my specialty a few years back."

"What a bunch of crap," Deborah said. "We know nothing of his life. He screws up, and they come to us for answers—that's bullshit."

"That's how it is," Janssen said. "I'll handle the press for you—no charge."

Janssen went to the front door and told the press he would talk to them in twenty minutes. Deborah poured him a cup of coffee, and he made a list of what he would say. He asked for some Advil for his arm, finished his coffee, then stepped outside and waited until he had complete command of the crowd. Janssen had experience. He knew how to work it, and he knew when enough had been said. He began.

"Good evening. I have been asked by the Williams family to read a short statement. My name is Hans Janssen. I will briefly answer questions after my opening comments. John Williams has been estranged from his family for many years. They know less about his life, and his actions, than you all do. They are learning about their own son through you, the media, as it unfolds on the national news. John Williams's father, Robert, is disabled, and his wife, Nora, spends all of her day attending to his needs. There is nothing this family can offer you. John Williams was a stranger to them, and they ask that you respect their privacy and leave them alone. Now, I will answer a few questions."

"When was the last time they saw John?"

"I am told many years."

"How many?"

"More than ten."

"Did they have any knowledge of John's illegal activities?"

"Of course not."

"Do they think John is guilty?"

"No comment."

"Why were they estranged from their son?"

"He was estranged from them. That's all I'll say. I ask you please to leave them alone. They know nothing of John's life or his activities—thank you."

Janssen turned and headed toward his car.

"Mr. Janssen, what is your relationship with the Williams?"

He pressed the fob and unlocked the door.

"Mr. Janssen!"

CHAPTER 40

A day and a half had passed and Janssen had a new cast, six more weeks of lugging it around, and a meeting with Thomas and Blake. When he arrived, they walked Janssen to John's cell. John Williams sat huddled in a corner, rocking back and forth, and talking gibberish to the walls. He looked more like a ten-year old kid, scared out of his mind, than a big-shot investment banker barking orders and making deals.

"What is that?" Janssen asked.

"You got me," Blake said. "Every time we asked him a question, he either says that or, 'brimstone and gall, say that again and I'll cast anchor in you.'"

"What the hell does that mean?"

"It means John Williams wants us to believe he's lost his mind," Thomas answered. "We have a room down the hall. We'll talk there."

They stopped at a coffee station and poured what gave true meaning to the word "mud"—even after two sugars and enough milk to fill a cereal bowl. Thomas led the way. About three doors down from the recessed coffee terminal, he reached into his sports coat and pulled out a key and unlocked a thick oak door. The barren room had a long four by eight table, a bunch of shuffled chairs around it, and paper files covering the entire top.

"This is your office?" Janssen asked.

"For now," Blake responded.

"Have a seat, Hans," Thomas said. They all pulled a chair and sat in a circle. Thomas started his briefing. "I can't go into details because it's an ongoing investigation, but I will tell you this. The scope of the Williams's investigation includes a laundry list of illegal activities. Offshore accounts, numbered Swiss bank accounts, buying politicians, insider trading, you name it, he was into it."

"Sounds like you've nailed him."

"Perhaps," Blake said.

"What do you mean?"

Thomas took another slurp of his coffee and leaned forward and placed his arms on his legs with both hands holding the paper cup. He looked at the cup in his hands and then to Janssen.

"Either John Williams was a reckless fool, or a God damn genius, and we're not sure which."

"I thought you were investigating an international ring of bad boys?"

"The CIA would have handled that."

Blake chimed in. "The whole group was deported. The government was more than happy to have them back on Chilean soil."

"So your investigation was centered on John Williams?"

"John Williams is the God Father of Wall Street corporate corruption. You just happened to walk into the largest investigation in the history of the Securities and Exchange Commission. His hands are in politician's pockets, CEOs of some of the most influential and security sensitive companies in the world, and the most sophisticated far-reaching violations of securities fraud this nation has ever seen."

"What the hell is going on?" Janssen asked. "Why are you guys talking to me?"

Thomas nodded to Blake, who stood up and walked over to a map hanging on the wall. His hands rested on his hips with his suit coat pulled to each side. Janssen waited for him to say something, but he didn't. Blake's head fell back as if he was looking at something on the ceiling and one hand left his hip and rose up to his chin with the finger outstretched. The pause was long enough for Janssen.

"Well?"

"Have you ever seen the movie *Primal Fear*, Mr. Janssen?"

"Yes."

"Do you recall the defendant, the young man accused of killing an archbishop? In the movie Richard Gere defended him on an insanity plea?"

"Yes."

"And then found out he'd been duped?"

"What does that have to do with Williams or my investigation?"

Blake looked to Thomas to take the lead. "His behavior, as exhibited by the documents in his personal file, interviews with his staff, the incoherent ramblings in his cell, is in line with an insanity plea. It was written all over his lawyers' face in the indictment hearing. Williams put on quite a show."

"Are you saying this was all planned as a defense in case he was caught?"

"Yes," Blake said.

"And you have enough proof to show it was all enacted from a sound mind?"

Blake stood up and walked over to the cluttered table and shuffled through a pile of files. He picked up one labeled "Williams personal file" stenciled on the front. He rummaged through a couple of papers and a photograph and ambled back to his chair and handed them to Janssen. Blake didn't say a word. He looked at Thomas, then back to Janssen.

"What the…are you saying?" Janssen asked.

"Makes it pretty convincing," Thomas said.

Janssen studied the papers and the photographs. He held one up, shook his head, and then looked to Blake.

"Has his attorney seen this?" Janssen asked.

"Not yet, but I can guarantee he knows," Blake said. "It sure makes an insanity plea pretty tight."

"It doesn't make sense."

Janssen stood up and handed the papers back to Blake.

"Keep them," Blake said. "You may need them to plead your case."

"What case?"

Thomas nodded to Blake again, and he took out his cell phone and made a call. Janssen walked over to the water cooler, in the corner next to a small refrigerator, and pulled out a paper cup. He pushed the handle down. He lifted the cup to his mouth twice, crumbled the cup, and tossed it into the metal basket next to the cooler.

"What the hell is all this about?" Janssen asked.

"Like I said before," Thomas said, "either John Williams is a reckless fool or a God damn genius and this sure makes it look like the latter."

The oak door opened and a man in his thirties with a suit and briefcase walked in.

"Hans Janssen, meet Eugene McCarthy, lead prosecutor on the case. He works directly under the Attorney General of the United States." Thomas looked to the attorney. "Eugene," Thomas said. At that Thomas and Blake stood up and left the room. McCarthy pulled up a chair in front of Janssen and put out his hand.

"Nice to meet you, Mr. Janssen, you've had quite the ordeal. How's the arm?"

"It'll heal," Janssen said. "Let's cut the small talk and get to the reason you're here."

"You're direct, Mr. Janssen, I like that. You've seen the file I take it?"

"Yes."

"Makes a hell of a statement, yes?"

"Get to the point," Janssen said. His distaste for lawyers went back to his days as a patrolman. He testified in a case that involved a shooting. It happened at a bar in down town Manhattan, and he was the first on the scene. He was a young rookie on the force, and he overstepped protocol and contaminated the crime scene. On the stand, the defense made a fool out of Janssen. He never forgot it. He didn't trust lawyers of any kind, federal prosecutors or not.

"We need your help, Mr. Janssen."

"To do what?"

"To be a liaison between the United States Attorney's office and John Williams's family. They trust you."

"How do you know you can trust me?"

"We don't, but we have no choice."

"I'm listening."

"We need you to convince the Williams family to testify before a competency hearing. We want to convince the judge that John Williams needs a maximum of four months confinement to consider whether or not he is competent to stand trial. That time will prove Mr. Williams does indeed retain all his faculties, and he will not walk free on an insanity plea."

"And what if he's deemed incompetent, Mr. McCarthy?"

"If he is not competent, Mr. Janssen, the court will proceed with a civil commitment trial, and he will be placed in some God awful institution taking medications for the rest of his life. One way or another John Williams will never walk the streets again."

"You think I can convince the Williams family to cooperate with you?'

"After they see what you're holding in your hand, I have no doubt."

"What about John's attorneys, you think they'll stand by and allow that?"

"Mr. Janssen, I am fully prepared to handle an insanity plea, only one percent are ever successful. John Williams is on borrowed time, and he's about to start paying it back."

CHAPTER 41

The news crews had multiplied. Stanton, Butterman, and Adair had been arrested, along with a herd of other prominent figures. The onslaught had begun. Janssen's rental car stopped six feet from the driveway, mobbed by reporters, and he beeped the horn and proceeded to push ahead. He attempted to enter the driveway and almost ran over a news reporter's foot. As he stepped out of his car and turned toward the house, Janssen was attacked by a flock of waving microphones. He raised his hand in the air and waited until he had full control of the crowd.

"We have no further comments to make. You need to direct your questions to the Attorney General's office. The Williams family has nothing more to say."

He called Ramone on his cell phone and instructed him to unlock the door. When he slipped inside, Janssen looked to Ramone.

"You may want to help your in-laws relocate. This will get worse before it gets better."

"They refuse. I've already tried."

They walked to the family room together, and Janssen sat down in a chair facing the couch. Before he had time to say a word, Nora asked Janssen if he had been allowed to see John. He said he had, and he went into a description of John's behavior while in confinement. They listened without interruption as Janssen reported on the multitude of illegal activities John had been involved in, summarized the details of the arrest, and explained the possible consequences for his crimes. Then he finished his report with an observation on John's mental health.

"The federal prosecutor," Janssen said, "views John's behavior as a well thought-out scheme of legal intent and not a genuine breakdown. Mr. McCarthy has vowed to either expose John's fraud or have him institutionalized."

Nora finally looked up. "And what do you think, Mr. Janssen?"

"I'm not a psychiatrist, Mrs. Williams. I'm afraid I can't answer that."

Nora's thin frame sat rigid on the couch with her hands glued to the cushions as if braced for Janssen's next round of ominous news. Robert sat in his wheelchair moving one finger up and down as Janssen let Nora catch her breath. He looked to Ramone in the chair to his left. Their eyes locked. Then he leaned slightly forward in a comforting gesture toward Nora. He connected Ramone once more then spoke.

"Whatever the case, Mrs. Williams, John needs a great deal of help."

Nora exhaled. She appeared distant, and her stare seemed far from the content of Janssen's words. Deborah sat frozen on the hearth studying her mom's reaction. Janssen glanced down to the folder at his feet and then back to Nora.

"Mrs. Williams..." Janssen hesitated. "Mrs. Williams, your son is incoherent. He says some very strange things that no one can make out. Having been questioned by the agents, his servants described some very disturbing behavior that they witnessed inside his mansion. The prosecutor has filed a petition and is asking the judge for a competency hearing. Mr. McCarthy wants to have John committed for a mental evaluation. That confinement could last as long as four months."

Nora came back from wherever she had been. She refocused on Janssen. "John is not crazy, Mr. Janssen. Robert and I both believe that."

"Well, I can only give you the facts, Mrs. Williams. The prosecutor would like you and your family to testify at the hearing. They want you to testify that in your opinion John's behavior is and has been abnormal for many years."

"I will not testify against my son, Mr. Janssen, and neither will anyone else in this family."

Janssen reached under his chair and picked up the 8 x 10 brown file and placed it on his lap. He opened it up.

"Mrs. Williams, I know this is going to be difficult, but please take a look at these documents."

Nora turned her head to the side and studied the file in Janssen's hand. She looked at Robert.

"Please, Mrs. Williams, you need to see these documents."

Nora reached out and took the papers from Janssen and laid them on her lap. Lifting her reading glasses onto her nose, she opened the file. She examined the photo, the papers underneath it, and made some sort of gasping noise with her mouth. Her eyes rose and glared at Janssen seated across from her.

"What is the meaning of this, Mr. Janssen?"

"It was John, Mrs. Williams."

"Whatever do you mean?"

Deborah jumped up from the hearth and bolted to the back of the couch behind her mom. She prop her hands on the back of the couch and studied the papers on her mother's lap.

"Jesus Christ, how do you know these are his?" she asked.

"They found them in his mansion," Janssen said.

"What did they find?" Ramone asked.

"They found everything, Ramone, even the God damn knife. That sick son of a bitch…it was him." Deborah's face turned bright red. "Why?" she asked. "What kind of animal would do this to his own family? He made his own father have a stroke."

Ramone jumped up and grabbed his wife. She flailed her arms and wept.

"My son would not do this to his family, Mr. Janssen." Nora's face turned stone cold as she stared at Janssen and continued. "Someone who works for John put those papers in his house. Someone's out to get my son, and I want you to find out who!"

"Jesus Christ, Mom! Wake up. Your fucking son almost killed Dad, tried to blackmail his own father, for what? What would make anyone do something like that?"

Deborah rushed to the hearth and lit up a cigarette. The smoke hung in the air and turned in circles by her sudden move back to the couch.

"Let me see those," she said. She ripped the file from her mother's hand. "Look at that, even the notes that he sent—every one of them." She examined the photo of the knife, the phone records from the throw away phone, and the hand-written log of the cash transactions to Buck Blanchard and Juan Philippe. She tossed them over the back of the couch onto her mom's lap. The papers slid off her legs and onto the floor. Janssen leaned over to pick them up.

"John wouldn't do anything like this, he—"

"Mrs. Williams, they found all the notes he sent. They were saved in his document file on his home computer. It wasn't even password protected. It was as if he wanted them to be found. The FBI believes he had orchestrated this whole charade as an insurance policy. He was so entangled in illegal activities he probably knew eventually he'd be caught. If so, this would prove he was not of a sound mind. His actions would be all the ammunition his defense team needed."

Deborah pulled away from Ramone. "I'll testify, Mr. Janssen. That son of a bitch sacrificed his family to save his own skin. I'll tell them anything they want to know."

"Hans," Ramone said, "what did he say to the FBI? Did John give any type of explanation?"

"He's incoherent. He hasn't said anything anyone can understand."

Ramone pulled his wife tight to his body with his arm around her.

"What's your best guess, Hans?"

Janssen shook his head. "I don't know."

CHAPTER 42

The competency hearing lasted two days. Deborah testified. Nora did not. She sat in the back of the court room next to Robert, in his wheelchair. He watched the proceedings as Nora held his hand. John Williams sat at the defendant's table, disinterested in the whole affair, blabbering nonsense and looking mentally impaired. The judge had warned John's team of lawyers on numerous occasions to control his client or he would be removed from the court room. When it was over, John Williams was sent to the psychiatric hospital for a maximum of four months. Eugene McCarthy saw it as a win for the prosecution and a loss for the defense.

John's lawyer, Stephen Townsend, asked the judge for a separate evaluation, with psychiatrists appointed by the defense. The judge granted the request. When they escorted John from the courtroom handcuffed and shackled in an orange suit, he was shouting his nonsensical phrases all the way down the hall.

Last to leave the courtroom was the law firm of Townsend, Bogart, and Stipple, spearheaded by Brick Townsend. Townsend was a renowned Manhattan attorney whose reputation for representing the rich and the famous was as legendary as his exorbitant fees. Three years into his practice he successfully defended Wall Street legend Samuel Patterson who was charged with securities fraud, insider trading, and conspiracy.

Known in lawyer's circles as The Brick, he rarely lost a case. His defense, they said, was as thick as a brick. Some believed the tag referenced Jethro Tull's album back in the seventies when The Brick attended Harvard Law School. It was rumored a fellow student pinned it on him, and it stuck.

Townsend's firm received a quarter of a million dollar retainer from Williams Investment Bank, and they prepared the Wall Street firm for monthly requisitions of the same. When the five lawyers exited the Foley Square Federal Court house, in Manhattan, a large black limousine pulled up in front. The press wanted a statement from Townsend, and, of course, The Brick obliged.

Flanked by his team of six attorneys, The Brick spoke for ten minutes, and when he concluded, the reporters had no more information than when he began. Afterward, they all landed at Smith and Wollensky's steak house for a late afternoon dry-aged 14-ounce rib eye, a few matured bottles of Lafite, and a good old Cuban cigar.

John Williams, however, found himself at Bellevue Hospital in a sixty-eight bed inpatient lock up. He settled in his unit pacing the corridor amongst the other wondering souls, talking his gibberish, jumping in the air and crying out, "I've lost my garments, can you help me, please?"

The next day he would start his first session with the prosecution's psychiatrist. McCarthy believed, beyond reasonable doubt, John Williams was not insane. His ploy to destroy his family, McCarthy had said, was a brilliant but flawed attempt to recreate mobster Vincent Gigante's escapade of strolling around Greenwich Village in a bathrobe and slippers. Only John Williams's bathrobe was not a garment; it was family-related blackmail.

Brick Townsend, on the other hand, thought Eugene McCarthy's theory was absolutely absurd. He was anxious to get his legal sword into McCarthy's case. The law firm of Townsend, Bogart, and Stipple was prepared to slice the young prosecutor into a hundred legal bits.

Their client, they contended, was suffering from some fancy psychiatric word, which no one understood, and John Williams's behavior supported his diagnosis one-hundred percent. And, as John Williams sprinted down the halls of Bellevue Hospital waving his arms and shouting phrases that made no sense, even the orderlies agreed with Townsend's assertion...John Williams was many cards short of a deck.

The evaluation started the next day. Townsend hired two separate psychiatrists with impeccable credentials. The first, Dr. Wilhelm von Kempt, was a professor from the University of Chicago. He arrived that afternoon and had a two-hour session with John. The second, Dr. Martin Bruchel, was a private psychiatrist from Boston, who was world renowned for his bestselling novel *The Therapeutic Relationship and the Role Symbolic Imagery Plays in*

Coping with Post Traumatic Stress. He was not scheduled to begin for five days.

The states evaluation would be performed by the lock-down shrink—Dr. Madhya Pradesh who was educated at Jaipur University in Jaipur, India. He had been the lead psychiatrist at Bellevue lock down for ten years. In a shoot-out on the stand, the government was out-gunned by money, expertise, and reputation. Brick Townsend made sure of that.

After one and half months, the written reports were submitted to the court. The competency hearing began on a Monday morning, with the prosecutor's psychiatrist, Dr. Pradesh, taking the stand first. Brick Townsend drilled the man into the ground. Townsend wanted the court to understand the difference between a layman and a seasoned professional. When he finished with the lock down shrink, Pradesh looked like John Madden playing running back for the Pittsburg Steelers. Townsend rendered Pradesh's findings useless and shelved the ammunition in case John Williams's case ever went to trial.

Nora, Robert, and Deborah sat in the back of the court room as the prosecutor, Eugene McCarthy, questioned the firm of Townsend, Bogart, and Stipple's first psychiatrist, Dr. Wilhelm Von Kempt. Von Kempt was brilliant, and made the young McCarthy stumble, stutter, and stop in confusion with each answer he gave. McCarthy looked like a fumbling intern, not a federal prosecutor under the Attorney General of the United States. Smugly, Townsend questioned Von Kempt and Von Kempt meticulously laid out his diagnosis. And as an exclamation mark on the report, John Williams interrupted the court with delirious outbursts and had to be escorted from the room. Then the third psychiatrist was called.

Dr. Martin Bruchel sailed a different tact in his evaluation of John Williams, and Townsend's line of questions had the young McCarthy up in arms. McCarthy believed Townsend was positioning himself to broad-side the court. Neither of the other two psychiatrists had done an historical background on John Williams or any of the events leading up to his arrest. So when Townsend questioned Bruchel about John's childhood, McCarthy objected four times. Each time he was over ruled. At the fifth objection, the judge asked both attorneys to approach the bench.

"Mr. McCarthy," the judge said, "in light of the charges against Mr. Williams, and that this hearing is a fact finding proceeding to determine if Mr. Williams is competent to stand trial, I am going to allow Dr. Bruchel's testimony." Then the judge looked at The Brick. "Mr. Townsend, wherever you're headed with this, you better make your point."

"Your honor, I am only trying to show the court there is mitigating circumstances for my client's present behavior that have a direct impact on the possibility of future competence."

"Then do so, Mr. Townsend, my patience is running thin."

Surrounded by his small army of lawyers at the defense table, Townsend questioned Dr. Bruchel. He paced back and forth in his twelve hundred-dollar suit, and drove Dr. Bruchel just short of the intended destination at which point he stopped, put his hand to his chin as if in deep legal thought, took an extra moment to emphasize the drama, and then floored the court.

"Dr. Bruchel, would you please explain to the court, clinically, the difference between incompetence and insanity?"

McCarthy exploded. "Your honor we object, this is a hearing to determine whether or not John Williams is competent to stand trial, not a medical class on the different gradations of mental health."

"I want to see counsel in my chambers," the judge said as he banged his gavel. "This court is adjourned until one this afternoon." He stood and exited the court room.

Townsend and McCarthy followed the judge out. They sat in the chairs in front of the his desk as Townsend thought about lunch, and McCarthy eyed The Brick wondering what he was up to. After a minute the judge arrived without his robe, sat down, and looked at Brick Townsend.

"Mr. Townsend," the judge said, "two of the three psychiatrists have given testimony as to Mr. Williams's prognosis for reclaiming competence. I could rule civil commitment on that basis alone. What do you hope to gain by wasting the courts time?"

"Your honor, Dr. Bruchel believes there is a forty-percent chance John Williams could regain competency given the proper treatment. In light of Dr. Von Kempt's and Dr. Pradesh's testimony, it is in my client's best interest to show the court this possibility exists."

"What are you up to Stephen?" McCarthy asked.

The judge interrupted before The Brick could answer.

"What difference does it make at this point, Mr. Townsend? One way or another Mr. Williams would still face involuntary commitment for treatment."

"In a state institution, your honor. Dr. Bruchel is considered at the top of his profession. If…"

"I am aware of Dr. Bruchel's credentials, Mr. Townsend, get to the point."

"We have an unusual request to ask the court."

"Go ahead, I'm listening."

"Given the circumstances, and a better than forty-percent chance of successful therapy, we would like that he be remanded to a different location for treatment."

"Why would I do that?" the judge said.

"Williams Investment Bank has had two legitimate offers to be bought outright. The board of directors, and acting CEO, both feel it is in the best interest of all parties involved to proceed with the sale. We would agree to a seventy million-dollar escrow account to assure the state and federal government adequate money for future fines and penalties, anticipating the possibility my client's case is tried, and my client is found guilty of the alleged charges against him. We think this is a generous offer.

"In return, we are asking the court that John Williams be committed to a private institution outside of Boston where Dr. Bruchel has agreed to work with John. He has asked the family, and they have agreed, to participate in my client's therapy. We are asking additionally that Deborah and Nora Williams be appointed conservators of the estate. Under this arrangement the government would not have to bear the cost of institutionalizing Mr. Williams. The trust would incur the total cost."

"Why should the government agree to this?" McCarthy asked.

"Because it's a win/win for the government. If John Williams goes to a state institution, he will spend the rest of his life drugged up, with inadequate treatment, of which the government will incur the cost. If he is allowed to be treated by Dr. Bruchel, there is a better than average chance he responds to treatment. Thus, the government gets exactly what it wants: the opportunity to hold John Williams accountable for his alleged crimes with seventy million sitting on the sidelines as compensation."

"Are you going soft, Townsend?" McCarthy asked.

"If Mr. Williams becomes competent to stand trial, Eugene, Townsend, Bogart, and Stipple are well prepared to defend our client successfully."

"And what about conservator of the person?" the judge asked.

"May I remind your honor, as a federal court, jurisdiction breaches state boundaries?"

"Mr. McCarthy, if I were to rule in favor of Mr. Townsend's proposal, what is the government's position?"

"We would agree, your honor."

"Given the circumstances the court agrees."

McCarthy and Townsend started their exit and halfway to the door the judge summoned The Brick. "Mr. Townsend?"

"Your honor?"

"What are those incessant phrases your client spews out?"

"We don't know."

CHAPTER 43

Just short of a twenty-five minute boat ride, between the towns of Marblehead and Manchester, Massachusetts, sat a five-mile private island owned by Dr. Martin Bruchel. Joanna's Island, so named after Joanna Bickerworth, wife of wealthy industrialist Hackford Bickerworth, had been transformed into a psychiatric treatment center utilizing the best-selling therapeutic model of Dr. Martin Bruchel.

Tactfully spread throughout the secluded shores were quaint cottages used to house the less supervised inpatient population. In the center of the island, the Bickerworths had constructed a twelve thousand-square foot stone mansion. It had been renovated by Dr. Bruchel and was now employed as a twenty-bed inpatient facility for those who required confinement. It was the hub of all psychological services for the Bruchel Institute and where John Williams was presently locked up.

The supply boat ran three times daily, once in the morning, once at lunch, and once in the late afternoon. Nora, Robert, and Deborah boarded the boat at half past eight in the morning. Dr. Bruchel requested the initial session take place at the treatment center as John had to be confined and could not leave the island. He wanted to observe John's behavior when confined in a room with his mother, father, and sister, alone. When the idea had been proposed, Deborah had refused to cooperate. She insisted she would have nothing more to do with John, but Dr. Bruchel had convinced her to attend the session.

He explained to Deborah that her addictions were only symptoms used as a mechanism by which she attempted to cope. That the deep rooted issues that remained unresolved would only continue to haunt her, and he believed that her emotional disorder was manifested in the underlying dynamics of her family. It was an opportunity in the safety of the therapeutic setting, he had said, for Deborah to begin her search for the truth. He concluded by saying, "Making the trip to Joanna's Island would be a positive step toward your own mental health." She had thought about it and decided Dr. Bruchel was right.

When the boat arrived, they were escorted to Dr. Bruchel's office. It was located in what had been the library during the Bickerworth's occupancy. It was not what Deborah expected after experiencing the therapeutic setting of Dr. Reed's office. She looked to her mother as Nora wheeled Robert through the door.

"Are you kidding me?" she said in a whisper.

Deborah stopped and her eyes scanned the room. She examined the two stories of mahogany book shelves that lined the outside walls. The doctor's desk was in one corner of the room. On the opposite side was the therapeutic arena. It consisted of two leather couches, three leather chairs, and mahogany tables placed between the seats. On the tables were dimly lit lamps. To separate the space from the rest of the room, the seating arena was staged on a twenty-foot square Persian Tabriz. On an outside wall, which was visible from the niche, was a fieldstone fireplace with yellow flames that danced in the fire box.

Dr. Bruchel stood up from his desk and directed them to the couch. "Thank you for coming," he said. "Please, sit down."

Nora placed Robert's wheelchair in front of a side table and then proceeded to sit on the couch with Deborah. Dr. Bruchel sat in a leather chair facing them. He let them settle for a moment then he spoke.

"I understand, other than seeing your son in court, you have not had any interaction with John for the past ten years."

Nora looked confused and turned to Deborah.

"Answer Dr. Bruchel, Mom. Why do you think we're here?"

Nora took a breath and exhaled. She turned to Dr. Bruchel.

"That's not completely true. I..."

"Mom..."

"What?"

"Just tell the truth. In a few minutes you're going to see your son for the first time, face to face, in ten years, and you better prepare yourself. All your denial about John is about to come to a screeching halt."

Nora turned to Dr. Bruchel. "I guess that's true, but he's a very important man, Dr. Bruchel, and he's been very busy with work."

The doctor looked directly into Nora's eyes.

"Your son, Mrs. Williams, is a very disturbed man. The complexity of his scheme against your husband took a great deal of time to develop and coordinate. It was premeditated, and its purpose was to inflict tremendous suffering and anguish upon his family. Those are not the actions of a man troubled by work. Those are the actions of an excessively angry man who decided that rejecting his family for almost a decade was not punishment enough."

Nora turned to Robert and then back to Dr. Bruchel. "Why in heavens would our son want to punish us, Dr. Bruchel? Are you implying we were not good parents?"

"I'm going to bring John in now Mrs. Williams. I feel we are at a point in our session where it would be helpful for you to observe John's behavior and how he interacts with you, your husband, and your daughter."

Dr. Bruchel pulled a radio out of his right suit coat pocket. He put it to his mouth and pressed a button. "This is Dr. Bruchel. Bring John Williams to my office." He slipped the radio back into his pocket. He looked to Nora. "When John enters the room, feel free to try to interact with him."

His office door opened and Nora looked terrified. Two men escorted John into the room and walked him over to the couch. John looked away. Dr. Bruchel nodded and the two men let go of his arms and turned to leave the office. John raced to the furthest corner of the room and stood facing the wall. The two orderlies looked to Dr. Bruchel and the doctor nodded his head again. They left the room and closed the door. John was still facing the wall.

"There are pirates in the brambles, boys, get your swords!" he shouted.

Nora turned to Dr. Bruchel.

"Brimstone and gall, say that again and I'll cast anchor in you."

Nora got up and walked over to her son. "John," she said, "it's your mother. Talk to me, John. How are you? Are they treating you all right?"

John's voice went almost to a whisper as if talking to himself. "Discipline, that's what fathers believe in. We must spank the children immediately before they try to kill you again."

Nora stepped closer to John's back. "John, please..."

John turned and scurried to the other side of the room. "Wait, John, your father and sister are here too!"

He stopped at the bookshelves and turned his back to the room. Then in that same soft voice he said, "In fact, we should kill them."

Deborah was on the couch shaking her head. She watched for a few minutes more then put her head in her hands and looked down to the floor. After five minutes, Dr. Bruchel summoned the orderlies to escort John to his room. It took two white coats to round John up, and Nora's mouth hung open as she watched. The two men, one on each arm, dragged John through the door. His voice echoed down the hall. "Second from the right, straight on till morning."

Nora fell onto the couch and started sobbing as she tried to choke out the question. "What is wrong with John, Doctor, why is he saying those strange things?"

"Mrs. Williams, what John is speaking is not just random nonsense but rather belongs to something John has seen or read. It is very childish in tone. It has significance to John in that it has become his world, his reality where he is protected and he is safe."

"I don't understand Dr. Bruchel."

"Your son, who cracked deals with the most seasoned professionals, lived privately in a very different and delicate reality. When he was arrested, and his professional world collapsed, he retreated entirely into that alternate reality. Your son suffers from what we call dissociative identity disorder, more commonly known as multiple personalities. As to the contexts of the phrases, Mrs. Williams, if I can find the source perhaps I can begin to communicate and break through to John. Do any of those phrases sound familiar to you? Did you ever hear John speak like that as a child?"

Robert banged the letter opener on the frame of the chair. Nora looked up and turned her head toward Robert. He tapped it again.

"What's he trying to tell you, Mother?"

Nora shook her head as she looked to Robert.

"Nothing, Deborah, your father's just upset."

"Mrs. Williams?"

Oh Lord. "No, I've never heard that before!"

CHAPTER 44

Hans Janssen was not about to let it go. It was a compulsion left over from his time on the force. It was all about motive to a homicide cop and finding the why was like taking in air. It was instinctive, and Janssen's investigative drive had been kicked into high gear after John's arrest. What it centered on, though, had nothing to do with his high-profile insider trading, bribing government officials, or the conspiracy charges filed against him. The motive behind that was simple—greed.

This was much more complex than that, and it had taken the form of a nagging question that he couldn't get out of his head. Why had he wanted to torture his own flesh and blood in such a cold and calculated manner? Hans Janssen was determined to find that out.

Janssen worked two days and nights reconstructing John's entire scheme until he knew every detail by heart. He learned that on the force too: know your case inside out. It created the questions whose answers would give him the why. So he challenged the obvious first. What was John's reason for igniting his plan on a remote island days before Robert and Nora were scheduled to leave for the winter? He could've taped the note to the front door at Kruger Falls. Why take the risk when the only way on and off the island was a boat? Or was it? Did John Williams target the summer house, or was it just where it all came down? Janssen needed answers, so he booked the trip.

It was a cold November morning and white caps churned in the harbor. There were only two vehicles that waited in line for the 11:35. One was a delivery truck that waited near the chained up ramp, and the other was Hans Janssen's car parked behind it. As the boat appeared on the horizon cutting its way through the empty harbor, Janssen turned the blower one notch higher on the heater inside the car. He shifted his cast arm from the platform on the car door to his left thigh and watched the ferry make its turn. Mounds of water churned up dark silt from the inlet floor, and it spun around full circle, and then backed in toward the metal ramp.

The dock hands looped the thick ropes over the pylons. Janssen remained in his car huddled around a cup of coffee and thought about John Williams. How many years had it taken to hatch such a plan? He spent a great deal of time and money and for what? Williams had constructed a financial empire. He had everything he ever wanted at his fingertips, and the premise his lawyers put forth—that it was a planned operation intended as evidence of his mental state in case he was caught—Jansen thought absurd. He believed John's intentions were much more sinister than that. He had seen it before, and it had nothing to do with a criminal defense. And Janssen was out to prove he was right.

The deserted island had been left to the sea gulls and the drifting papers that shuffled over the parking lot. Jessup's Inn, just past the ferry landing on the left, looked empty and dark. Janssen parked in front of the wooden structure and eyed the long porch with its Victorian railing running the full length. The summer tables and chairs had been stored for the winter which created a cold and abandon look. Janssen climbed out of the car, walked up the two steps, and read the note that was taped to the front door.

"Went to Granger's Market," it said, "be back sometime."

He chuckled and stepped to the end of the porch and gazed left then right down the empty street. He returned to his car and drove past a closed up gift shop, past an empty parking lot covered in broken clam shells, and spotted an old weathered islander climbing out of his car. He drove into the post office parking lot and stopped near the man as he closed his car door.

"Excuse me," Janssen said. "I'm looking for Granger's Market."

"'Fraid you're goin' backward; you might try turnin' round. When you get to Jessup's Inn, take a left and you'll find it down on the left. Can't miss it."

"Is there a police station in town?"

"That'd be Sheriff Porter's office, just past Granger's on you're right. He doesn't do much sheriffing this time of year though; you might find him at home."

"Thanks," Janssen said.

"Happy to help ya," the man said.

Janssen drove past Jessup's and took a left. He passed Granger's and stopped and parked at a small building on the right. On the front of the cottage was a sign that said "Schaums Head Sheriff." Janssen parked in front, climbed out of his car, and tried the front door. It was unlocked. He went inside.

It was not much of a police station, one large room with a counter that separated the public from the constable. The sheriff sat at a desk behind the counter, sorting through something in a desk draw. He was a man in his forties. Janssen did his once over and calculated he was an islander who went to school on the mainland to become a cop. He had short dirty blond hair that was cut square at the top. He was dressed in blue jeans and a gray sweat shirt with a Carhartt sandstone bomber jacket hooked on the back of his chair. He must have heard the door open and close, but he didn't look up.

Janssen continued his visual inspection. He observed a badge attached to the outside of Porter's coat about heart high. He studied the gun attached to the sheriff's belt. Janssen recognized it: a 01070XSE Government-series colt, .45 caliber, four-inch barrel, eight plus one round capacity. An expensive piece for a lone island cop, he thought.

Without looking up, Porter asked, "Can I help you?"

"Maybe, not sure what I'm looking for though."

Sheriff Porter swiveled his chair around and stopped as he faced the counter. He squinted his eyes and examined Janssen for a moment, let his head drop toward the floor for a moment, then looked back up at Janssen.

"How you goin' to find it, if you don't know what you're looking for?" he asked.

"My name is Hans Janssen. I worked homicide out of New York City. I'm employed by Robert and Nora Williams."

"That'd be the Williamses out at Crab Point. You investigating a murder?"

"No, I'm going on a hunch something might have happened out there years ago."

"Real mess that Williams boy got himself into. This about that?"

"Maybe, like I said, I'm digging in the dark. I was hoping you could help."

"How's that?" Porter asked with his hands now clasped behind his head. He leaned back in his chair.

"I wanted to check the files from '70 to '78."

"Can't do that."

"Why not?"

"Cause they ain't here."

"Where are they?"

"In the basement at town hall."

"Where's that?"

"Next door."

"Well?"

"Hold onto your shorts, I have to lock up."

Town hall resembled the rest of the buildings in town in that it looked the same as it did when it was built. When Old Maid Abrams died, she deeded it to the town. The four rooms were used as offices and one had the door cut in half with a ledge that was used as the front counter. Only one person worked at town hall, and Janssen wasn't exactly sure what she did, but her name was Margaret. She said hi to Sheriff Porter but never asked why he was there.

Porter opened a door in the hall and proceeded to climb a flight of stairs. Janssen looked confused.

"I thought you said the basement?"

"The basement in Schaums Head is in the attic. Dig down below ground, up pops water. You don't build a basement unless you want a swimming pool."

One more flight and they landed in the attic. Porter opened another door. The attic was lined on opposite sides with wooden shelves holding up stacked boxes piled four high. Each one had a date marked on the front. The earliest date went back to 1950. Porter walked in front and read the markings.

"Now, which ones did you want?"

"I wanted '70 to '78."

"Right."

Porter slid out 1970 and opened it up. In three and half months of peak season only four incidents were recorded. The most serious was an argument at Jessup's Inn. A long-haired hippie, as it was written, refused to leave the restaurant when Tom Jessup refused to serve him lunch. It said he wouldn't serve a man with woman's hair. The long haired individual was escorted to the next departing ferry, and that was the end of the big summer brawl. The next three years, 1971, 1972, and 1973 were exactly the same (except without the long haired incident) and '74 was missing. Porter searched the rest of the boxes, up until '78, and then checked again for '74.

"I guess nothing happened in '74," Porter said.

"Maybe, maybe not," Janssen said.

"You think someone removed it from here?"

"Do you see any others missing?"

"You got a point there, Janssen."

"Who would have been around in '74?"

"Plenty of folk, but that don't mean they know anything. People don't talk about other people's business on Schaums Head. It ain't like the mainland out here."

"Who was the sheriff back then?"

"That'd be the one before me."

"Where can I find him?"

"Out at the cemetery."

"The cemetery?"

"Yep, Sheriff Taylor passed away last summer."

Janssen and Porter walked back down the stairs. Porter said good afternoon to Margaret, and Janssen thanked Porter for his time.

"I may call on you again," Janssen said.

"You know where to find me."

Janssen climbed into his car and drove to Jessup's Inn.

The door to the Inn was unlocked this time. Inside, Janssen stood in an old cozy sitting room with a fireplace. He walked over to the counter and rang the bell. Tom Jessup came out from a side door and said howdy. Jessup looked to be in his mid-seventies and wore an old rag sweater. He had silver hair and khaki pants that fell over his dock shoes.

"I'd like a room for the night," Janssen said.

"Guess you would unless you're plan on swimming back to the mainland. Next boat don't leave until 10:25 tomorrow morning."

"Is it possible to get a meal tonight?"

"If you don't mind eating with me and the misses, we're empty this time of year."

He gave Janssen a room key and told him it was the second on the right, first floor, just past the lobby. Janssen retrieved his overnight bag from the car, grabbed a magazine from the sitting room, and plopped down on the bed. He read for about twenty minutes and fell asleep.

CHAPTER 45

Dr. Bruchel scheduled the second meeting with the Williams family at a colleague's office twenty-five minutes from Kruger Falls. Robert—as was the case for some time now—climbed into the family car with assistance. The wheelchair was secured onto a handicap platform attached to the back of the vehicle. Deborah drove, and Nora sat in the back. Robert was in the front seat with a metal object clutched in his left hand. The letter opener, a heavy brass commemorative gift with the town insignia of Kruger Falls etched on its blade, had become Robert's voice. When he wanted his wife's attention, he banged on the metal frame of his wheelchair. Although primitive in nature, it had become Robert's communication with the rest of the world. It was all he had.

The residence, turned office, stood by itself on the edge of a small community on a quaint New England street. The columned porch in the front had a handicap ramp and Deborah pushed her father up and into the house. Dr. Bruchel greeted them in the foyer and led them to the living room that had been converted into an office. Deborah and Nora sat on the couch with Robert next to his wife in his chair. Dr. Bruchel sat in the leather chair opposite the three, flanked by a fireplace, a side table, and a lamp. Next to him, at his feet, lay a large satchel opened at the top. He reached inside and pulled out an eight by ten hard cover book and placed it on his lap.

"I am going to be asking you some difficult questions today, Mrs. Williams. The truthfulness of your answers will impact significantly the ability to deal with John's psychological disorders and the ultimate success of his therapy. I would like to know about John's childhood, Mrs. Williams, particularly from the ages of seven to ten."

"John had a very normal childhood, Dr. Bruchel. He was a very happy young man."

"Mom, cut the crap," Deborah said. "You shipped him off to schools. He spent summers at camp, and I hardly ever saw him. So cut the crap and tell Dr. Bruchel the truth. Tell me the truth!"

Robert banged his letter opener on the chair, a slow and constant sound of metal banged on metal. Nora grabbed his arm.

"It's ok, Robert, Deborah's a little upset. John's going to be just fine. He's just a little confused because—"

"Bullshit, Mom. He's been arrested by the FBI. John's screwed. God, I can't believe you. Why aren't you pissed off for what he did to you and Dad?"

"Mrs. Williams," Dr. Bruchel said, "I believe John has been living inside two distinct personalities for many years. He's managed to keep them separate, hidden behind a protective wall of wealth. His obsession to accumulate that wealth is controlled by his need to protect his alternate self, to insulate it from the outside world. His adult persona has no concept of right or wrong. Morality is defined by those actions necessary for the survival of his damaged and fragile real self. It is my professional opinion the development of his real self stopped maturing at the age of eight or nine."

Nora had become noticeably agitated. The expression on her face had become stiff and cold. "Dr. Bruchel," she said, "I've heard enough of this. John is not—"

"Jesus," Deborah said. "Take a look around you, Mom. I'm tired of living in some fantasy world that you want to protect. I'm a lying drunk. Your son's is an immoral—"

"I think we should go now," Nora said and she started to stand up.

"Sure, Mom, run away. Well, I'm not driving anyone anywhere. It's time this family faced the truth. I'm tired of not being able to live without a drink because I can't stand myself when I'm sober. I'm tired of asking you questions and getting excuses back. And I'm tired of not knowing why John disappeared from our lives. Your family is self-destructing around you and all you can say is everything is going to be all right. Your son's going to jail, Mom, prison! Either that, or he's going to spend the rest of his life in some mental institution because he's Dr. Jekyll and Mr. Hyde."

Nora fell back to the couch and patted Robert's hand.

"It's ok, Robert," she said. "It's ok."

Deborah dropped her head to her hands and rubbed her eyes.

Dr. Bruchel opened the book on his lap and turned to Nora.

"Mrs. Williams, do you recognize this saying: 'second from the right, straight on till morning'?"

Nora looked up dazed. She stared at the doctor.

"Mrs. Williams?"

"No," she answered in a whisper.

"What about this one: 'I'll teach you to jump on the winds back, and away we go'?"

"What is that, Dr. Bruchel?" Deborah asked.

"I've managed to locate the origins of John's ramblings, which by themselves are meaningless. However, attached to the context of its usage in this book, its meaning is both relevant and clear. These phrases correspond directly to his life's situation at any given time. It's really quite remarkable. John has memorized the entire book. In our meetings, when he speaks, he only responds with passages from the story. It is like a code. Once you decipher the translation by reading its context in the book, its meaning becomes clear."

"I don't understand," Deborah said.

"John is living his life as the main character of a book—this book. He has been doing so for years on a regulated basis. However, after his arrest, he totally assumed the identity and dialogue in full. I asked about John's childhood between the ages of seven and nine because this book is normally read too, or read by, seven to nine year olds. This book was chosen by John because its storyline had relevance to his life."

Dr. Bruchel turned his attention to Nora. "Mrs. Williams, if you wish to help your son, and your daughter, then we need you to participate fully in our therapy sessions. Your son is not all right, and I hear your daughter confirming she's suffering, indeed, too. There is no blame or shame assigned to opening up and facing the truth—only healing."

Nora stood up and walked to the back of Robert's chair and started to push it toward the front door. She turned.

"I'll be leaving now, Dr. Bruchel. We've had enough for today. Deborah, your father and I will be out at the car. Come, Robert, let's get some air, dear, shall we?"

Deborah sat shaking her head. She put her head in the palm of her left hand and pushed on her forehead, hard. Dr. Bruchel closed the book and placed it back into the satchel and observed Deborah's movements.

"Is there anything you can tell me, Deborah, anything about John or your past?"

"I don't remember anything," she said. "I'm working with Dr. Reed on that, but all I draw is a blank."

"You said John wasn't around much. What did your parents say was the reason?"

"They said John wanted to go to camp in the summer and private boarding school during the year. My mother never said any more than that."

"Is it accurate to say you're very angry at John?"

"I don't give a shit about John. I care about me. As far as I'm concerned he can rot in lock up the rest of his life. He's been nothing but a heartless asshole, and he makes me sick. I've got to go, Doctor. I need to take my parents home."

"I'd like to meet with you and your parents again. Will you agree to it?"

"It's a waste of my time."

"Deborah, this can help you move forward and find out the truth."

"I'll talk to them," she said and got up to leave the room. Dr. Bruchel escorted Deborah to the front door and put his hand on her shoulder. He smiled.

"You'd like to know, wouldn't you?"

"Know what?" she asked.

His lips came together into a sympathetic half smile, and she noticed a look in his eyes, like he already knew the answer to the question he asked. She took a couple of steps out of the door, onto the porch, and down to the walk which led to the street. As he started to close the door, she turned.

"Dr. Bruchel."

He stopped and looked to Deborah.

"Yes?"

"What is the name of that book?" she asked.

"*Peter Pan.*"

CHAPTER 46

Before dinner, Janssen located a map of the island and drove out to Crab Point. He maneuvered the single lane to the house, carved out of the rolling dunes like the trail of a plow after two feet of snow. The drifting sides were held together by low blueberry bushes, sheep laurel, black huckleberry, stagger bush, and wild rose. The sun had begun to descend in the western sky, and the ground cover looked dark and cold. As he approached the brown clapboard cape, a premonition overcame him, and a slight shiver sparked a shudder in his shoulders. The car rolled to a stop, and Janssen shut off the engine.

He exited the car and gazed at the vacant house as grains of sand slid over his Rockport shoes. The glass of the front door, where it all had started months ago, was still hidden behind a panel of protective plywood. He lifted the collar of his barn coat, pulled the sides of the jacket together, and walked around the side of the house.

When he arrived at the rear of the house, he stepped onto the back porch and stopped at the rail. He gazed out toward the marsh. An empty, cold sensation encircled him as the grasses bent with the breeze. He glanced north toward the wind-swept dunes and something bleak and dark rumbled inside of his gut. He froze. He had felt that same sensation once before, working homicide, and for a second it flashed through his body once again. It was a ghostly chill from the past, and like before, he couldn't ignore its presence. *Out there,* he thought, *something had gone terribly wrong—out there!*

Janssen didn't move as twilight consumed the mounds and the sun drifted lower. A strong gust swept through the shadows and its sound whispered like a voice from afar. He walked back to his car half dazed as he thought of the missing box from '74. He climbed back into the vehicle and drove down the sandy access road knowing exactly what he needed to do.

Janssen pulled into the vacant space in front of the Inn. Inside, Tom Jessup worked at the front desk in the lobby. His wife Sara set the dinner table in the dining room. Just off the lobby, Janssen stopped. He looked into the bar room that faced the harbor and the street. It housed eight wooden bar stools in front of a dark mahogany bar. Behind it hung a smoked glass mirror that was set into mahogany trim, and to each side were rows of glass shelves filled with bottles of liquor. Island memorabilia hung about the room, which included a picture of the Inn back in the early 20's. Janssen finished his examination of the bar room and approached Jessup standing at the front desk.

"Good evening," Janssen said.

"Evening."

He looked over to the bar.

"Is it open?"

"Sure, 'bout to have a cold one myself."

"Mind if I join you?"

"Nope, would enjoy the company."

Janssen sat, Jessup stood behind the bar, and soon two mugs of cold Bud had landed on the wooden top.

Janssen took a couple of swallows of the beer and studied Jessup as he lifted his mug. Janssen had questions, but he figured he'd let the Bud loosen up the answers first. Jessup nursed the beer and made conversation.

"Where on the mainland you from?" Jessup asked.

"White Plains, New York. You heard of it?"

"Can't say I have. Sheriff Porter tells me you were a cop."

"Manhattan, homicide."

Jessup shook his head. "Like another?" he asked as he nodded his head toward Janssen's mug.

"Thanks!"

As Jessup pulled the tap, he went exactly where Janssen figured he'd go. "So what's a homicide cop doing on Schaums Head?"

"I've been working for the Williamses," Janssen said.

"Shame about the boy."

"In fact that's why I'm out here."

Jessup thought about that for an instant. He slid the mug of beer to Janssen. "The boy, huh?"

"Yeah, the boy."

Jessup pulled the tap again and cocked the mug as it poured. He studied Janssen. Watched him turn his mug on the bar top, lift it up, take a swallow, then put it back on the bar. Then Janssen turned on his stool, put his elbows on the bar, and looked out to the harbor. He kept his silence even when Jessup came back with his beer. Jessup leaned on the bar about two feet away from Janssen.

"You investigating the boy?"

"Not the way you'd think," Janssen said and lifted his mug again.

"Which way's that?"

"Can't really say. It's confidential."

"Of course."

"Maybe you could help."

"How's that?"

"That thing back in '74 out at the Williams's place."

Jessup looked spooked. He picked up his beer, took a long swallow, and turned toward the mirror and picked up a glass. He started wiping the dust off. Janssen watched as Jessup studied his own reflection. Janssen waited. Jessup, so undone by the question, picked up another glass and started to wipe it with the bar towel. Janssen lifted his beer.

"You recall that?" Janssen asked.

"Don't know nothing about anything in '74 out at the Williams's place."

"I think you do."

"Well, you're wrong. Finish your beer. I'm goin' to check the misses to see how long before dinner's up."

He stomped off and left his beer next to the glasses he'd been cleaning. Janssen sat and pondered his next move. A few minutes later, Jessup showed up announcing dinner. Janssen picked up his beer went into the dining room and sat down.

Jessup poked at his dinner and Janssen decided to let him stew. He felt Jessup's eyes on him when he cut his potato and another time when he salted his fish. When they were just about finished dinner, Janssen finally got the setup he'd been waiting for.

"So what brings you to Schaums Head, Mr. Janssen?" Sara asked.

"That thing in '74 out at the Williams's place."

Jessup slammed his knife onto his plate. "I told you nobody knows nothing about—"

"Hush up, Thomas," Sara said. "If'n people hadn't kept their mouths shut and tried to help the boy back then, he might not be in the mess he is today."

"Sara, I'm warning you, it's nobody's business what happens on Schaums Head."

"Well it's high time somebody spoke up, even though it's too late now."

"Go ahead, Mrs. Jessup. It's never too late," Janssen said.

"Well—"

"Sara," her husband said, "for the last time I…"

"Shut up, you old sea dog! I listened to you back then; that was a mistake. It's been riding the back of my brain for over thirty years now, and it's about time to set it free."

She turned back to Janssen and took a sip of her wine. Tom Jessup sat with his arms folded, and his face as red as a cardinal sitting on a snow-covered branch. She took a deep breath and began.

"No one knows the whole truth except the Williamses, I suspect, and Sheriff Taylor and Doc Houge. If you're going to want to question them, both live out at

Schaums Head Cemetery, about two miles outside of town, and they ain't say'n much anymore. Word came down that night something awful happened out to Crab Point. It was a calm, warm night in late August, and a sense of terror hung over the island like an eerie fog. It was so thick I swear it felt like the Devil's breath. I ain't never experienced anything like it in the sixty years I've lived on Schaums Head, and I hope I never do again.

"Lance Patrone, who lives just north of Woodmans Cove, claimed he heard shots, but he couldn't say it as fact. Later that night, we were just closing down when Sheriff Taylor pulled up and came inside. He asked me for a coffee in a paper cup then told me to ring up Doc Houge. He told me to have doc meet him out at the Williams's place. I'd known Sheriff Taylor since he'd been a boy, and I can tell you by the look on his face, I didn't dare ask any questions.

"He took his coffee and left. The next day, I'd seen the boy sittin' in the car waiting for the ferry with his dad. He was as stiff as an ice cube just staring at nothing, his hair all messed up. He looked like his soul had been ripped from his body and left nothing but an empty shell. When he loaded onto the ferry that day, it was the last time we ever saw John Williams: He never set foot on Schaums Head again."

"What about the girl?"

"I didn't see her until she left with her mom the next day. Sheriff Taylor drove them to the dock. She looked a plum sight too. She came back with her parents, year after year, but never played with her friends like she used to. I swear, whatever happened out at Crab Point that night took both their souls and left them like a boat in the middle of the Atlantic without no way of getting about.

"Of course those of us that knew something had happened, well, we looked the other way. Never asked any questions and nothing was ever said. Their neighbors, the Halstons, sold shortly after that. They told me it felt like death hung out all over Crab Point and never went away. God help that little boy and girl, I used to say to myself. God help them."

Tom Jessup sat in his chair with his head hanging in his hands. When Sara finished, she drank the last sip of her wine and picked up the dishes and went off to the kitchen. Jansen walked to the bar and pulled another draft. Even though it was cold, he dragged a chair onto the porch. He drank his beer leaning on the rail staring at the lights across the harbor.

In the morning, he loaded onto the 10:25 ferry and headed to the mainland mesmerized by the wake of the boat. When he pulled his head up, Schaums Head was a dark line on the horizon behind a swath of sea foam and some sea gulls barely audible over the sound of the diesel powering the boat. As Schaums Head disappeared altogether, Janssen walked down to his car. He sat inside and stared through the windshield at the bow of the boat. As he pulled off the loading dock, and took a right onto the main road, he knew it wasn't over—not yet.

CHAPTER 47

Nora Williams agreed to meet with Dr. Bruchel one last time, at the insistence of her daughter. The meeting took place at the same office as the previous session, and Dr. Bruchel began by updating Nora on John's condition. Then he asked, as he had before, about John's childhood. Nora answered with the same evasive responses. Robert banged the letter opener on the frame of his chair and continued to do so as Nora spoke. Deborah listened briefly, and then interrupted her mother mid-sentence.

"The game's over, Mom. You can tap dance all you want, but it won't do any good."

"Whatever do you mean, dear?"

Robert banged with all his strength and startled Nora. She tried to calm his hand, but he looked into her eyes and banged defiantly twice.

"Everything is fine, Robert. Calm down."

Deborah stared at her mom with a look that drained the blood from Nora's cheeks. Deborah waited a moment then spoke. "I met with Hans Janssen for almost an hour yesterday."

"Did he find out who wrote that awful note?"

Deborah's head fell in disgust.

"Mrs. Williams I've seen the evidence," Dr. Bruchel said. "John did write those notes."

Nora turned her head defiantly.

The doctor continued. "Your son, Mrs. Williams, is stuck in the developmental age of an eight to nine year old. This psychosis is normally associated with severe trauma to the psyche, one that becomes too painful to face. The story of Peter Pan, a young boy who chose never to grow up because of this exact phenomenon, is the basis of John's fantasy world, which he perceives as safe." Dr. Bruchel pulled out a kid's Peter Pan hat. "This is an ex—"

"Where did you get that?" Nora asked.

"The officers found it in his home. He had an entire Peter Pan outfit made around this child's hat. What does this hat represent, Mrs. Williams?"

"I have no idea," Nora said.

"You're lying. I can see it on your face," Deborah said.

"No, I'm—"

"Damn it, Mother, tell the truth!"

"I'm afraid…"

"Mother."

"It was in a box in the attic out at Crab Point. It was his when he was a little boy."

"So John had the house broken into to retrieve his hat. Continue, Mother."

"That's all, really," Nora said.

"Nineteen seventy-four, Mother, you want to start or shall I?'

Robert banged against his wheelchair frame.

"I don't know what you mean, dear. Please, Robert, stop that banging. Robert, please, it's giving me a headache."

"Hans Janssen went to Schaums Head, Mother. He met with the Jessups."

"Oh?"

"So stop the charade. It was an August night in '74, Mother—talk!"

Nora's head went down and a tear rolled down her cheek. Robert continued to bang.

"Stop it, Robert," she said, "just stop it. We agreed. Deborah didn't remember and John seemed to get over it. After that first bad year at school, he changed. He became an 'A' student, Robert, and you made me promise never to discuss it again. Stop, I can't stand anymore of that banging."

He did stop. He looked up with his eyes at Nora, and with his first finger on his left hand, he waved it up and down.

"No, Robert, I can't. I won't. It never happened. It was just a bad dream. I wish you could talk Robert, you always took care of everything."

"Only four people knew, Mother, you, Dad, Sheriff Taylor, and Dr. Hogue. Mr. Janssen told me everything the Jessups said. I have a right to know what happened, for Christ's sake, my life has been a fucking mess."

Nora began to sob. Dr. Bruchel picked up a box of tissues and handed them to her. She pulled one out and blew her nose and then pulled another and wiped her eyes.

"Mother!"

"I can't."

"Yes, you can, Mother, you start from the beginning, and you tell me the whole story."

"Oh, Robert, please, please, I never wanted to think about that again, Dr. Bruchel?"

"Mrs. Williams, why don't you start with what you were doing that day?"

"Oh God!"

She started to weep uncontrollably.

"Oh God, I was just getting the huckleberry muffins ready in the kitchen. Robert was out on the pier tending to the crab traps. Those gosh darn crab traps. If it wasn't for those awful traps, none of this would have happened. He had promised the kids to go fishing in the inlet off the sand dunes when he was done on the pier."

Nora choked on a sob.

"Oh God! Why, good lord why?"

"What happened next, Mrs. Williams?"

"Oh sweet mother of God. Robert, help me, please help."

Robert dropped the letter opener, and it fell to the wooden floor with a thud. He wiggled his fingers, and Nora stared at his hand. He kept moving them until Nora picked up his hand and put it in hers. She could feel him squeeze.

"Please, Mrs. Williams, what happened next?"

She took a deep breath, and as she sucked in she made that gasping sound that comes with hard crying.

"Robert had lost track of the time with the traps. John and Deborah were so excited they took their fishing poles over the dunes to the inlet to wait for their father. I remember watching them walk, two little kids with fishing poles slung over their shoulders. They looked so cute and oh Lord, so innocent. They were only nine and seven."

Nora lifted her head from her hands and looked at her daughter huddled in a ball on the couch next to her. Deborah was looking down at the floor with her knees stuck under her chin. Nora wanted to reach out to her, but she was afraid. She felt a wall between them now.

"They disappeared over the dunes like they had many times before. I went back to pouring the muffins in the tin. When I finished, I put them in the oven to cook for eighteen minutes and went to the laundry room to finish ironing Robert's shirts. The next thing I know the bell went off for the muffins, and so I went to the kitchen and pulled them out. When I went to put the tin on the hot plate next to the sink, I saw Robert out on the pier still pulling traps.

"I went out the screen door, to the back porch, and called out to Robert. 'Robert,' I yelled, 'the kids are waiting for you.' They left twenty-five minutes ago. He looked up and waved and held up two fingers. That was his sign. He used to tell me how long he'd be when I called to him on the pier. After a couple of minutes, I saw him come walking toward the house, and then I heard him go into the back room where he stores the crabs in the old refrigerator. Then he says we'll be back in about an hour for dinner, and I watched him walk over the dune with his pole and tackle box. And I went to take the muffins out of the tin."

Nora took a deep breath and blew her nose and sobbed with her head in her hands. She picked up Robert's hand again and held it in hers. She looked at Deborah whose back now faced her, and her eyes faced the window on her side of the couch. She turned to Dr. Bruchel.

"Our lives would never be the same after Robert disappeared over that dune, and what happened under the eyes of God would never ever make sense. That's when it all came apart. Every day, since that day, I have stopped Deborah and John a thousand times from crossing over that dune, but the guilt never stops. It eats at me until I can no longer stand it, and then I pray, every day, I pray in my head. I haven't slept more than four hours a night in thirty-four years."

Nora stopped. Dr. Bruchel sat across from her and watched her struggle. He waited silently until Nora could continue. With Deborah's back still to her mother, she pulled out a smoke and lit it up. Dr. Bruchel didn't say a word. He quietly got up, went over to the window, and opened it half way. Before he could sit, Nora started to talk again.

"I heard the worst scream I ever heard in my life, and I ran to the front porch. Robert was standing at the top of the dune howling, as if his gut had been slit, and his insides ripped from his body. I ran as fast as I could to the top of the dune, and Robert was huddled around our daughter, and his cries of pain shot into my heart like a knife piercing my chest. As I ran closer, I could see my Deborah's bare legs hanging limp over Robert's arm, and his hand held her head to his chest. And then…and then…oh my poor child. I realized she was naked from the waist down. She was bleeding from her privates, and I fell to my knees and was sick. I kept vomiting until I had nothing left. Then I realized John was gone.

"I stood up and started running, screaming 'John' with all my breath. I got to the top of the second dune and looked back to Robert holding Deborah and I froze. I didn't know what to do. I started to run back toward Robert, but I wasn't aware I was moving. I wasn't aware of anything. We took Deborah to the house and I called Sheriff Taylor.

"That's when the image I'll never forget appeared out of the darkness of the hall closet. It was Robert, and the expression on his face and in his eyes looked that of a man possessed. His eyes were open wide, and he didn't say a word. In his hands was the shotgun he used for skeet shooting. He loaded it with a bunch of shells, and then he ran out the kitchen door. He was running as hard as his legs would take him. When Sheriff Taylor arrived, I didn't need to say much, and I pointed him in the direction Robert had gone. I saw him draw his pistol and check to see if it was loaded as he left the house. I have to stop for a minute, please."

"Take your time, Mrs. Williams. Whenever you're ready."

She looked at Dr. Bruchel, who nodded, and then she put her head in her hand and continued.

"I don't know how much time had passed. I was taking care of Deborah in the house, but I know it seemed a long time. When they came over the ridge, John was with them. He was being carried by his dad. Sheriff Taylor had Robert's shotgun. My husband kicked open the screen door with his foot so hard the door came off the hinges and landed on the foyer floor. He put John on the couch.

John's clothes were ripped. He had blood all over him, and he just stared straight ahead into nowhere. He had been violated too.

"It was starting to get dark when Sheriff Taylor took a shovel from the shed and walked back out over the dunes. I didn't ask any questions, but I knew exactly what happened. Robert and Sheriff Taylor had taken justice into their own hands. I was thankful for that. I wouldn't have been able to live knowing that monster was still alive.

"That day, I promised myself I would never admit what happened, otherwise, I was afraid I'd go insane. John went away to boarding schools. He wanted nothing to do with his family after that. He refused to ever return to Schaums head. Deborah couldn't remember; she had amnesia. Some doctor said it was a protective mechanism or something like that, so I figured it was best to leave it alone.

"I understand why John did what he did. He wanted to punish his father. He wanted his father to suffer as he had, because he blamed him for not coming when he said he would. The only thing he took from the island the day he left was the book he was reading—*Peter Pan*. I'm not a psychiatrist, but I figure that has something to do with how he's acting now. He just never wanted to grow up after that day. I know John's in a lot of trouble, and I wish there was something we could do to help."

Nora stood up and walked behind Robert's chair and froze looking at Deborah bound in a fetal position on the couch. Nora looked old, and worn, and tired as she placed her wrinkled hands on the handles. Before she started to push, she lifted her head.

"I've wanted to die a thousand deaths, just to make the memory go away. It never will. I hope, Deborah, you'll forgive your father and I and not be angry at your brother anymore. Maybe we can all be a family again. I pray for that every day."

CHAPTER 48

Time had passed since the meeting with Dr. Bruchel, and having learned the truth, Deborah's work with Dr. Reed had taken on new meaning. She started to remember parts of her past, but the molestation stayed far from her reach. Dr. Bruchel and Dr. Reed had both agreed that her recall of that tragic event might never come back. They also expressed to her that even though the trauma was blocked from her memory, she could learn how to deal with its fallout. On that issue, she had begun to make great strides, and she was now determined to finally live a constructive and healthy life.

Her anger toward her mother had tempered, and they were both trying to work through the years of denial, dishonesty, and distrust. She had also started to paint again—landscapes—and she had sold her first work at a gallery owned by a friend. She had been sober for almost nine months and found she had little interest in wasting anymore of her life to the bottle. With all of her progress, though, she had yet to visit John. That was to be next, she had said to Dr. Reed.

"I will visit John," she insisted, "but I will go out to the island, alone."

As for John Williams, he had plenty of money in the bank. His investment banking business, along with the Bombardier Challenger, and Bell-429 were all sold. After the sale of his business, he had 2.3 billion in the bank, less, of course, the seventy-five million that had to be put into escrow. He still owned the Rolling Hills Estate and the ranch out in Wyoming. And there were numerous numbered bank accounts they were still trying to uncover. A task that now seemed close to impossible.

The investigators had been challenged by the complex web he had woven in his attempt to cover his tracks. In giving their progress report to the court, they concluded his alternate personality had the IQ of a financial genius. They estimated it would take years to expose his massive trove of hidden wealth. The 2.3 billion was only the tip of the monetary iceberg, the report stated, and they estimated in the end that figure could quite possibly triple.

Of course there were still the legal issues and the law firm of Townsend, Bogart, and Stipple who was prepared to put forth a winning defense. The Brick was even more confident after learning the truth about John's past. John Williams, though, was still playing *Peter Pan* on Joanna's Island with the possibility of never setting foot in reality again. But if Dr. Bruchel had anything to do with it John Williams would function as a mentally competent individual someday. He had made it a professional challenge and quite coincidently the subject of his next book. But for now, John Williams lived in Neverland with Tink, Tootles, and the other boys.

Then there was Hans Janssen. He had written a book about the unsolved murder of Tristan McCobb. Knowing all the facts, it ended up on the New York Times Bestseller List. It took off like an F-14 from a carrier deck and with it came a movie deal. The book and movie package brought in a mound of cash, but Janssen continued to live as he had. He stayed in the same house, worked in his same home office, and drove the same six-year-old van. That was his life, Hans Janssen, private investigator, with his picklewursterwiser and Bud every Friday night.

One thing was different, though. Standing out at Crab Point, staring out to the dunes, what he saw in his mind's eye that afternoon changed him forever. It was the chill of pure evil, like nothing he had ever felt. He had seen plenty of horrific scenes as a homicide detective: murder, rape, mob hits, and suicide. But what happened to Deborah and John that August morning in '74...it cut through him so deep, he took most of the proceeds from the book and movie deals and built a home for abused children.

"It was the loss of innocence," he said to the crowd at its dedication. "You can't replace it, but perhaps you can heal it."

Janssen also visited Joanna's Island once a month to monitor John's progress. He also happened to be in the vicinity of the art gallery on the day when Deborah's work appeared. That first painting of hers that her friend had sold now hung on the wall in his office at home just above his computer screen, at his desk.

Robert Williams now walked on his own with the aid of the walker, but his handicap brought up an old dispute. The same issue that thirty-four years before had almost ended their marriage. What to do with Crab Point? The major difference this time was the circumstance, Robert's condition. After the horror in '74, Nora wanted to sell. She refused to go out the next year, but Robert insisted. He said they needed to move past what had happened and never discuss it again. Thus began the seeds of denial and thirty-four years of sleepless nights.

In the end, Robert, with his eyes and his letter opener, prevailed. Robert's insistence on keeping Crab Point, like before, was based on his determination that the evil that violated his family would not dictate the direction of their lives. He realized now, however, he had done exactly that. He had refused to acknowledge the truth, and that became tantamount to an invisible cancer, and it grew, unchecked, until it commanded the souls of both his children. It was a frightful and sobering epiphany for a man of seventy-two, particularly a man unable to speak.

Now, as he sat in his wheel chair and stared out over the dunes, that day was as clear in his mind as if it happened yesterday. He watched as the thirty-eight-year-old man walked up the dune with his fishing pole and tackle box. He looked so young and full of life. As he neared the top, the image began to fade. He felt a tingling in his head and then a pain on the side of his temple. He struggled to focus on the man at the top of the dunes. Everything went blurry, he tried to blink. An instant later he was there, and he walked down the other side. John and Deborah came running up to their father. John was so proud of the fish he had caught he waved it in front of his

dad. Robert rubbed John's head, smiled, and they ran off together toward the glimmering lagoon, excited to finally fish with their father.

The day before her father died, Deborah had planned to take the boat to Joanna's Island. She cooked an early breakfast that she enjoyed with Ramone. By four forty-five in the morning, Deborah was on the road, nervous, and wondering what to say when she first saw John. She arrived at the boat dock just before nine. It was already being loaded with the supplies and the staff. She boarded and found an isolated place to stand on the deck. She neither spoke nor engaged visually with any of the staff on the way to the island. When they finally tied off at the dock, she felt her stomach flutter and her heart start to race. She climbed out of the boat and made her way to the mansion.

Dr. Bruchel met Deborah in the lobby and escorted her to his office. Deborah sat on the couch and slid to one side. Dr. Bruchel sat in his chair and looked over to Deborah. "How are you doing, Deborah?" he asked. "It's been quite some time since your last visit."

"I've come a long ways, Dr. Bruchel. Dr. Reed has been very helpful. How is John?"

"He's making progress. He still depends on the book and his character in our therapy sessions. He talks to me, albeit through Peter, but that direct address shows a willingness to reach out and connect. I am hoping your presence will encourage John to begin to take the risk of climbing out of the safety of his character. Are you nervous, Deborah?"

"Yes, in fact I'm frightened to death."

"That's understandable, what would you like to say to John?"

She looked out the window for a minute thinking about what Dr. Bruchel had asked. "What should I say?"

"There are no rules. You can say anything you'd like."

Deborah went silent. It lasted minutes as the many thoughts rumbled through her head. She had so much to say it was hard to choose. Then she went blank, nothing but wide open eyes, and she became aware that the silence had gone on for quite a time. Her eyes slowly rolled to Dr. Bruchel.

"Are you ready?" he asked.

"I think so."

"Would you like some more time?"

Deborah shook her head. "I'm ready."

"Ok," he said and stood up. "Follow me."

The doctor led Deborah up the main stair case to a large hall. At the second door on the right, Dr. Bruchel took out a key and slid it in the lock. He opened the door, and Deborah spotted John sitting on a window seat staring out to the water. Dr. Bruchel put out his hand, and when she stepped inside, he pulled the door and it quietly shut. She stood there in the large open space looking at her brother's back. She took two steps toward him, and he turned his head.

"Wendy, is that you?"

"It's me, John, your sister Deborah."

He looked perplexed for a moment and turned his head to one side. "Hello, Wendy."

She took a step closer.

"What is it?" he asked. Then he took a long look at his sister as she stood frozen in the middle of the room. "You promised," he said. "You promised to never grow up."

"I am a woman now, John, and I'm trying to get well."

John fell back onto the window seat and pulled one leg up onto the cushion and laid his arm over one knee.

"I don't know," he said, "but I am quite young. Wendy, I ran away the day I was born."

"No, John, you grew up with me, Mom, and Dad. In the summers we would go to Crab Point. You and I would play together in the sand. I remember that now. Do you remember John, the squirt guns on the back porch, helping Dad with the crab traps, the bucket and shovels? Do you remember now, John?"

"It was because I heard Father and Mother talking about what I was to be when I became a man. I don't want to ever to be a man. I want always to be a little boy and have fun."

Deborah's head fell toward the floor. She thought of how much she had hated John, hated the awful person he'd become. She raised her head and looked at the little boy in a grown man's body, and she felt a tear fall from her cheek. She wiped the trail with her finger.

"John, I know everything now. I know what happened to you...what happened to me that awful day out at Crab Point. I want you to come back now. I want you to be my brother again, John. Please, come back!"

John jumped to his feet, pushed his chest out, and propped his hands on his hips.

"Why do you have to spoil everything?" he asked. "We have fun, don't we? I taught you to fly and to fight. What more could there be?" He turned his head and then snapped it back toward his sister. "What? What else is there?"